Emily raised her eyes and looked about the room for that tall, well-remembered figure.

She didn't immediately perceive him standing amidst a group of gentlemen in the far corner of the room.

It was only when he turned his head and she received the full impact of an unwavering gaze from all-too-perceptive gray eyes that she realized that the gentleman immaculately attired in a long-tailed black coat, which emphasized the breadth of superb masculine shoulders, and tight-fitting trousers, which did little to hide the muscular shapeliness of long legs, was none other than the being who continued to plague her dreams all too frequently even after all these years.

"Oh, dear God! He's coming over," she muttered. "Why couldn't the wretched creature have allowed me at least a few minutes in order to compose myself?"

"Hello, Em," he responded in a deep, throaty tone that was no less appealing than the smile he bestowed upon her....

* * *

Lord Hawkridge's Secret
Harlequin® Historical #238—June 2008

Author Note

My story is set in what many of you consider to be the most romantic period in our history—the Regency. First and foremost, *Lord Hawkridge's Secret* is a love story. However, for those of you who enjoy a mystery to solve, this book also contains a strong intrigue element. Its endearing heroine is spirited, its hero is charming and its sinister villain is utterly loathsome—in other words the story contains something that will, hopefully, appeal to a wide range of tastes.

I hope you enjoy it!

LORD HAWKRIDGE'S SECRET

ANNE ASHLEY

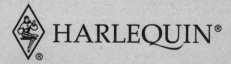

HARLEQUIN®

TORONTO • NEW YORK • LONDON
AMSTERDAM • PARIS • SYDNEY • HAMBURG
STOCKHOLM • ATHENS • TOKYO • MILAN • MADRID
PRAGUE • WARSAW • BUDAPEST • AUCKLAND

ISBN-13: 978-0-373-30547-6
ISBN-10:   0-373-30547-8

LORD HAWKRIDGE'S SECRET

Copyright © 2004 by Anne Ashley

First North American Publication 2008

This edition published by arrangement with Harlequin Books S.A.

® and TM are trademarks of the publisher. Trademarks indicated with
® are registered in the United States Patent and Trademark Office, the
Canadian Trade Marks Office and in other countries.

www.eHarlequin.com

Printed in U.S.A.

ANNE ASHLEY

was born and educated in Leicester. She lived for a long time in Scotland, but now lives in the West Country with two cats, her two sons and her husband, who has a wonderful and very necessary sense of humor. When not pounding away at the keys of her word processor, she likes to relax in her garden, which she has opened to the public on more than one occasion in aid of the village church funds.

Chapter One

Miss Emily Stapleton cast a glance at her silent companion, seated beside her in the curricle, before fixing what one languishing dolt in Brighton the previous summer had been overheard to describe as deep pools of sheer enchantment on the road ahead.

Tooling herself about the countryside had swiftly become one of her favourite pastimes, especially since the long and dreary winter months had given way to what was betraying every sign of becoming a very fine spring. All in all, she decided, experiencing a feeling of smug satisfaction, life at the moment was exceedingly pleasant, free from cares.

Her decision to remove to Dorsetshire and live with her paternal grandfather had undoubtedly been a heart-rending one to make, and one, moreover, of which her beloved late mother would have staunchly disapproved, but even so Emily had never regretted the choice she had made. After all, the alternative had been unthinkable, and a subject upon which, even after almost half a decade, she still found it distressing to dwell.

By dint of long practice, she once again succeeded in thrusting the painful memory to the back of her mind as she cast a further glance, brimful of mischief this time, at her companion. 'You're very quiet, Sarah. Not nervous, I trust, at being driven about by a female? Even my watchdog,' she added, deliberately raising her voice for the benefit of the small, stocky individual perched on the back, 'is secretly impressed with my ability, although he stubbornly refuses to admit to it of course.'

Jonas Finn's deep grunt in response made Sarah chuckle, something which she tended to do far more frequently whenever in the company of her closest friend. 'I'm not in the least nervous,' she assured her, 'and I'm enjoying the experience very much. I would have come out with you long before now if I hadn't been so busy with all the arrangements for the party next week.'

Exercising masterly self-control, Emily managed to refrain from comment, even though there was much she would dearly have liked to say, and possibly would if there wasn't a noticeable improvement in her companion's day-to-day existence in the very near future.

One of the things that had very much increased her enjoyment of residing in Dorsetshire during the past years had been the swift friendship which had sprung up between her and Sarah Nichols, who had been invited by her godmother, Lady Deverel, to make her home at Deverel Hall a matter of a few months before Emily herself had come to live with her grandfather.

Undoubtedly their orphaned status was the common bond from which a solid friendship and a deep, almost sisterly affection had rapidly emerged. Many in the locale had expressed genuine sympathy for them both. Which, Emily considered, in her case at least was totally unmerited. The Honourable Mr John Stapleton might not have been the ideal person to take charge of his orphaned granddaughter. Undeniably he was selfishly set in his ways, and considerably vague on occasions, but for all his woolliness of mind, which Emily privately thought was a sham for the most part, they rubbed along together remarkably well.

He had from the first made her very welcome, and had permitted her to do more or less as she pleased; whereas poor Sarah had been invited to live in a household where its occupants were not above taking full advantage of her presence to such an extent that her status was little above that of a housekeeper-cum-companion. And an unpaid one at that! It made Emily fume to think that her sweet-natured friend was so put upon by those who were happy enough to call her Cousin, even though the connection was remote. To be fair, though, Emily was forced to own that Sarah herself was much to blame for her present lifestyle.

'And I suppose you have seen to all the arrangements in your usual efficient way.'

Grey eyes were swiftly lowered. 'I—I haven't been responsible for them all. Godmama has been of immeasurable help.'

'A likely story!' Emily scoffed. 'Your godmother couldn't organise the lighting of candles in a front parlour! And as for that pampered daughter of hers… I do not doubt that you will be so much at Drusilla's beck and call from now until her birthday party takes place, ensuring everything is perfect, that you'll be given precious little time to organise your own toilette.' Once again she risked taking her eyes off the road ahead to cast her friend a suspicious glance. 'I'll wager you've not even begun to make up that length of pink silk you purchased the other week.'

The sheepish expression was answer enough. 'No, I thought not,' Emily muttered. 'If you give it to me I'll make a start on the gown. I might not be your equal with a needle, but at least I can cut it out for you.'

Sarah betrayed her mortification in a very becoming blush. 'Oh, no! I wouldn't dream of taking advantage of our friendship by asking such a thing.'

'You won't be, because I offered,' Emily pointed out, determined to have her way in this.

A flicker of gratitude sprang into Sarah's eyes. 'Well, if

you're certain you don't mind, I would be most grateful. I did wonder when I'd find time to make a start on the dress. I understand that Cousin Charles has invited several of his friends to the party whilst he has been staying away in London. In fact, there will be so many guests putting up at the house that I've offered to give up my room so that we can accommodate all Drusilla's friends too.'

This intelligence induced Emily to take her eyes off the road once more in order to subject her friend to a prolonged, considering stare. 'And where do you propose to sleep? In one of the attic rooms, I suppose, with the rest of the servants?' She had meant it in jest, but it swiftly became clear, when Sarah appeared reluctant to meet her gaze, that she had hit upon the truth. 'You don't mean to tell me that that is where the Deverels are expecting you to sleep?'

'Well, yes. But—but I did suggest it in the first place… And it's only for a few days.'

'I don't believe I'm hearing this!' Emily announced, hard put to conceal her disgust. She had never been afraid to speak her mind, most especially when in the company of people with whom she was well acquainted, and so did not think twice about adding, 'Well, you're not! You can stay with Grandpapa and me. And I won't take no for an answer!'

The invitation, though forcefully delivered, was kindly meant, and Sarah, gazing ahead at the stretch of road which traversed Kempton Wood, was very tempted to accept. 'Well, if you're certain your grandfather wouldn't object to having a— Look out!'

Sarah's unexpected warning coincided with a considerably gruffer one delivered from the rear of the carriage. With lightning reflexes, Emily quickly had her horses veering to the left in an attempt to avoid a collision with the staggering figure that had unexpectedly emerged from the edge of the wood.

Hurriedly bringing her team to a halt, Emily glanced back

over her shoulder to discover to her intense dismay the man now lying sprawled on the ground. 'Oh, dear Lord!' she cried. 'I must have hit him, after all!'

Without a second thought she tossed the reins to Sarah, before jumping down from the curricle and racing back along the road, her faithful and ever vigilant groom at her heels.

'Be careful, miss,' Jonas warned, drawing out the pistol which he invariably carried whenever accompanying his young mistress about the countryside. 'It might be a trap. There could be others lurking. I don't reckon you did run him down.'

Although occasionally described as stubborn and head-strong, Emily was not so wilful as to ignore sound advice. 'No, I didn't think I had,' she agreed, approaching the recumbent figure with caution and swiftly detecting the dark stain seeping through a charred portion of his coat. 'No, it isn't a trap, Finn. He's hurt. He's been shot!'

Dropping to her knees, Emily carefully turned the man over on to his back before gently resting his head in her lap. He wasn't very old, no more than twenty-five or six, she judged, but she very much feared from the position of the wound in his chest that he was destined not to celebrate a further birthday.

Lids, badly swollen, flickered as she brushed the blond hair back from his grazed forehead, and a moment later she was subjected to a puzzled, faraway look from eyes of a similar hue to her own.

'Lie still,' she urged gently, as he made a feeble attempt to raise an arm. 'We'll get help to you soon.' She glanced up at her groom, who remained avidly scanning the wood, and was about to instruct him to go back to the house to get help when the stranger began to speak, thereby instantly regaining her attention.

'No…time.' His voice was so faint that Emily only just managed to catch the words. 'Must…must get word to The Kestrel to be in—in…Raven…m-midnight…six…six-teenth.'

'What's that he said, miss?'

'I'm not certain, Jonas. Sounded utter gibberish to me,' she admitted.

'He's probably lost his wits, miss.'

'No, Jonas. I'm afraid he's just lost his life,' she enlightened him, as the stranger's head lolled to one side, and his last breath passed between the cut and swollen lips.

It took Emily a moment or two to recover from the very unpleasant experience of having someone die virtually in her arms, then, with the admirable self-control which she always displayed in times of stress, she rose to her feet, mistress of herself once again. 'There's nothing more we can do for the poor fellow now, except drag him off the road. We'll go directly back to the house. You and the stable-lad can come back here to collect the body in the cart, and then go straight over to see Sir George Maynard and apprise him of what's happened, whilst I, in the meantime, see Miss Nichols safely returned to Deverel Hall.

'Now, for the love of heaven don't argue, Finn!' she ordered, when he was about to do just that. 'I'm quite capable of driving the two miles to the Hall without your escort.'

A little over an hour later Emily was back in the pleasant house which had been her home for the past few years, and was endeavouring, without much success, to explain to her somewhat eccentric grandsire precisely what had taken place during the eventful journey back from the local town.

Appearing faintly bewildered, he regarded her in silence for a moment over the rim of his half-moon spectacles. 'Shot?'

'Yes, Grandfather, shot.'

'But I thought you just said that you'd run him down.'

'No, I didn't say that,' she corrected, striving to be patient with the old gentleman, who could be something of a trial on occasions. 'Do try to pay attention, sir. I said I thought I must have run him down, but I hadn't. He'd been shot.'

He bent a look of mild reproach upon her. 'But you cannot go about the county shooting people, my dear. I dare swear a great many folk deserve it. But it simply won't do. Will not do at all! Besides, Sir George won't be best pleased when he hears about it.'

'Oh, for heaven's sake!' Emily exclaimed, just as the door opened and her grandfather's housekeeper showed none other than the local magistrate himself into the parlour.

Sir George Maynard, a large, grey-haired gentleman with a big barrel chest, which his waistcoats strained to cover, and deceptively merry blue eyes, which little escaped, was a much respected figure in the community. He was an old acquaintance of John Stapleton's, and had a fondness for his friend's granddaughter, which he betrayed now by casting her a sympathetic smile, whilst giving her slender hands a brief, reassuring squeeze.

'A very distressing experience for you, my dear. Wouldn't have had it happen for the world.'

'Glad to hear you've taken it in such good part, George!' Mr Stapleton announced, instantly gaining his friend's attention. 'Least said soonest mended, eh? I've already given her a scold, so it's best we forget about the whole business.' He glanced about in a vague manner. 'Now, what brought me in here in the first place, Emily?'

'Your book, Grandfather. It's here on the table.' She picked it up and handed it to him. 'Why don't you return to your library, and leave me to talk to Sir George. I'm certain he'll be happy to join you for a glass of port later.'

Never needing much encouragement to repair to the room where he spent much of his time, Mr Stapleton was happy to leave, and Emily was even happier to close the door behind him, before turning to her visitor whose round face was wreathed in an understanding smile.

'A bit vague this morning, eh?'

Emily raised one fine brow in a sceptical arch. 'He's only

vague, as I suspect you must realise, Sir George, when he doesn't choose to be troubled by something.'

She invited her visitor to take a seat and then, without asking, as he had never been known to refuse, automatically poured him a glass of wine. 'You've spoken to Jonas Finn, I do not doubt, and have seen the body?'

'Yes, m'dear,' he acknowledged, after sampling the contents of his glass and watching her gracefully lowering her slender frame, which was a delight for a man of even his advanced years to behold, into the chair opposite. 'I don't suppose for a moment there's much more you can add, so I've no intention of plaguing you with a barrage of questions. I've arranged for the body to be removed to the undertaker's in Kempton.' The Baronet regarded her in silence for a moment. 'You didn't recognise the fellow, I suppose?'

'No, sir. Never set eyes on him before today.'

'Er…Finn did just happen to mention the man said something to you before he died.'

Emily nodded. 'But nothing that made any sense. He spoke so faintly I could hardly catch what he was saying.'

'Pity. It might have given us a clue as to his identity.' The local Justice of the Peace paused to sample a drop more of the excellent claret whilst all the time studying his companion's delicate features above the rim of his glass. 'What—er—did he say precisely, m'dear?'

All at once Emily suspected that much more lay behind the stranger's death, that he had not merely been set upon, badly beaten and shot, and that Sir George was definitely keeping something to himself. She was very tempted to do likewise, but then thought better of it. 'I gained the distinct impression he was keen on ornithology. His last words, if I remember correctly, were about birds—kestrels, I think. But, as he had just stumbled out of Kempton Wood, perhaps seeing birds was the last thing he remembered.' She shrugged. 'Who can say?'

Just for a second or two there was an added sparkle in the

Baronet's merry blue eyes. 'Well, if you should recall precisely what it was he did say, perhaps you'll let me know.'

'I dare swear it would all come back to me if I took time to think about it,' she didn't hesitate to assure him. 'Though I must be honest and admit that it's an incident I would far rather forget.'

'Very understandable, m'dear.' Tossing the remaining contents of his glass down his throat, he rose to his feet. 'Well, I'll be on my way. I've an urgent appointment to keep and must set out for London this afternoon. Perhaps you'd be good enough to inform your grandfather that I'm forced to cancel our Friday evening's chess session. But you can tell him I remember the exact state of play, and that we'll resume the game after my return.'

Sebastian Hawkridge, seated behind the desk in his library, was gazing through his morning's correspondence. His intelligent forehead was furrowed by lines of deep concentration as he scanned the missive in his hand. His mien clearly betrayed the keen perception of an extremely astute gentleman, but it was a countenance that few in the polite world had ever been privileged to see.

To have played the part of a fashionable fribble would have been a role too hard to maintain. Yet he had certainly done his utmost in recent years to give the impression that he cared for nothing so much as the pursuit of pleasure. On occasions even this portrayal had been difficult to preserve, but it had been vital to keep up the pretence in order to enable him to undertake a very personal crusade, without arousing the least suspicion among his fellow peers.

Always alert, he clearly heard the sound of the doorknocker filtering through from the hall. He had issued strict instructions that he did not wish to be disturbed, and so knew the moment his butler entered the room that the caller's business must indeed be urgent for his trusted servant to disobey an order.

'I'm sorry to disturb you, my lord, but a Sir George Maynard is here to see you on a matter, he assures me, of the utmost importance.'

It took Sebastian a moment only to recall the gentleman to mind and appreciate the precise nature of the business which must have brought him to the house. 'Yes, show him in, Clegg,' he instructed, and then rose from his desk in readiness to receive his unexpected visitor.

Once he had furnished him with a glass of wine and had him comfortably established in a chair by the hearth, his lordship swiftly dispensed with pleasantries. 'Your visit, sir, is unexpected. But I doubt you have journeyed to the capital merely to make a social call. Bad news, I assume.'

'Afraid so, Hawkridge. Sir Giles Osborne informed me that in the event that I was unable to get hold of him, I could safely pass on any information I attained to you. Sir Giles, so I've been informed, is out of town, but he ought to know as soon as possible that the man he sent into Dorset has been murdered.' Sir George wasn't slow to detect the flicker of sadness in the younger man's penetrating grey eyes. 'Was he by any chance a friend of yours?'

'We were acquaintances only. I know that Sir Giles thought highly of him. Anderson was a good man.'

Leaning back in his chair, Sebastian stretched out his muscular legs, displayed to advantage in a pair of tight-fitting breeches and shining Hessian boots. 'I think it's safe to assume that he was killed because he had discovered something. Osborne, as you probably know, suspected that stretch of coastline was being used by smugglers, and those he's keen to apprehend. He'll be back in London early next week, but I doubt he'll be in a position to replace Anderson speedily. His people are stretched pretty thinly on the ground, so I understand. Nevertheless, I'll have a word with him when he does return.'

Sir George regarded the younger man in silence for a

moment. 'I'm aware that your interests are somewhat different from Osborne's, but that you do exchange information
from time to time. I haven't read of any robberies in the newspapers recently, so I can only assume that whatever Anderson
had discovered would have been of more interest to our
mutual friend.'

'More than likely,' Sebastian agreed. 'Who discovered the
body, by the way?'

'The granddaughter of a near neighbour of mine.'

The shapely hand raising the glass to Lord Hawkridge's
lips checked for a moment, and his gaze was suddenly dis-
concertingly direct. 'You wouldn't, by any chance, be referring to Emily Stapleton?'

'Why, yes!' The Baronet was clearly astonished. 'Are you
acquainted with her?'

His lordship's ruggedly masculine features were all at once
softened by a surprisingly tender smile. 'Oh, yes. I know
little Emily Stapleton, right enough. I've been acquainted
with the family all my life. She and her mother were my
nearest neighbours when I resided in Hampshire. In fact,
Emily's mother was my godmother.'

Once again Sir George didn't attempt to hide his surprise.
'Great heavens! I never knew that. I remember her mother and
father very well. Laura was a lovely woman. It was so very sad
that her marriage to Philip Stapleton was so tragically short.
He died at the Battle of the Nile.' He shrugged. 'Still, I suppose
you knew that. Emily doesn't remember her father too well, of
course. But her mother's death hit her pretty hard, poor child.'

'I know that too, sir. I was with her at the time.' Sebastian
released his breath in a long sigh. 'She's still happy enough
living with her grandfather, I understand?'

· 'Oh, yes, my boy.' Sir George's portly frame shook as he
gave vent to a chuckle. 'Damnable intrepid little thing! Jaunts
about the countryside tooling her own carriage now, would
you believe?'

There was no semblance of a smile on the younger man's face. 'I'm well aware of it!' Disapproval was clearly evident in the clipped tone. 'I was given little choice in the matter. The little minx forced my hand!'

Sir George's bushy brows rose sharply. 'I'm sorry, my boy. I don't perfectly understand. Why should Miss Stapleton's behaviour concern you?'

'Because, Sir George, I am her legal guardian and not John Stapleton, as most people believe. And I would be very much obliged to you if you would keep that information to yourself.'

Although not perfectly understanding the need for secrecy, Sir George didn't hesitate to give his word, before his thoughts returned to the reason for his visit. 'Anderson said something to young Emily before he died. I didn't like to question her too closely. That young lady has a head on her shoulders, and I didn't wish to arouse her suspicions. Didn't want her involved in all this cloak-and-dagger stuff.'

'And she didn't tell you what he said?'

Sir George shook his head. 'Said something about Anderson being keen on bird-watching, would you believe? But I can't imagine that that can be right.'

His expression once again keenly alert, Sebastian rose to his feet and stood before the hearth to stare intently down at the burning coals. 'I was wrong, sir. Unless I'm gravely mistaken that message might well have been for me. It's vital I find out exactly what he said.'

'I'll go and visit Emily the instant I get back.'

'No, don't do that. It would be better if I questioned her. I'd learn a great deal more than you would. As mentioned, I've been acquainted with her all her life, and know how to handle her. Damnation!' he cursed softly. 'I would have preferred to have waited, but Fate it seems is forcing my hand.'

Understandably, he turned to discover a puzzled expression on the Baronet's plump features, but chose not to elaborate. Instead he said, 'Would I be right in thinking that the Deverels are close neighbours of yours, and that there's to be a party held at their home in the not too distant future?'

'Why, yes! Have you been invited?'

'I was, but turned it down. Charles Deverel and I were up at Oxford together. Unless I'm much mistaken he's still in town.' Placing his half-finished glass of wine on the mantel shelf, Sebastian went striding over to the door. 'I don't wish to appear rude, sir, but I must go out and run Deverel to earth without delay, and somehow get myself re-invited to that damnable country party without, I hope, arousing suspicion.'

Chapter Two

Raising her eyes from the book which she had obtained from the lending library on the very day she had come upon the stranger at Kempton Wood, Emily gazed across at the sofa, where Sarah sat busily hemming the last few inches of her new gown, and frowned as something odd occurred to her.

'Sarah, did Sir George Maynard ever question you about that unfortunate incident last week?'

'No. Why do you ask?'

'Because it seems to me he's taken the murder of that stranger very lightly. Which is most unlike him. He's usually so conscientious. He returned from London four days ago, but hasn't made the least attempt to question me again.'

Sarah shrugged. 'Perhaps he doesn't think there's anything further you can tell him.'

'Ah, but there is!' Emily enlightened her, closing her book and tossing it aside. 'You see I've been thinking about the incident a good deal, and I now recall precisely what the stranger said to me before he died.'

'In that case why don't you inform Sir George?' Sarah suggested, exhibiting her usual sound good sense. 'He'll be at the party tomorrow night. And so too shall I now that my new gown is finished!' she added, her mind swiftly turning to far more important matters as far as she was concerned. She held the garment at arm's length the better to survey the finished result. 'I cannot thank you enough for all the work you did on this. If it hadn't been for you I'd never have finished it in time.'

'If you must thank someone, then thank Budd,' Emily responded, refusing to take the credit. 'She did most of the work on it, not I.'

'In that case I shall make a point of doing so. Your housekeeper's an absolute treasure!'

'I'm very well aware of it,' Emily assured her. 'If it hadn't been for dear old Budd I'd have been saddled with a duenna, would you believe?'

Sarah frankly laughed. 'For someone who enjoyed a deal of freedom throughout her childhood, far more than most girls are privileged to experience, I cannot imagine you would have taken too kindly to having your treasured independence drastically curtailed by a chaperon.'

'How well you know me, my dear. No, I should not!' Emily admitted. 'Fortunately Budd stepped into the breach by suggesting that she keep an eye on me until a suitable duenna was found. Whether grandfather then forgot the idiotic notion, or was happy to leave matters as they were, I'm not certain.

'Oh, yes, I'm very well aware that Lady Deverel, among several others hereabouts, thinks it highly improper for a young woman of my age not to be suitably chaperoned,' Emily went on when she detected her friend's wry grin. 'But it's nonsensical, Sarah. I live with my grandfather, a venerable, elderly gentleman of sober habits. All right, I'll admit that a cook-housekeeper might not be considered by most as an ideal chaperon, but no one could suggest that dear Mrs Budd isn't respectable.'

'That's true enough,' Sarah was forced to agree.

'And since my arrival, of course, we've added to the household staff by employing Amy, the parlourmaid, and one of the village girls who comes in every day to help with the cleaning, so Budd isn't precisely overworked, and is able to spend time with me when the need arises. And as I somehow acquired the running of the household, the servants usually come directly to me for instructions, so things go along pretty smoothly, and everyone is happy.'

Once again Sarah was unable to suppress a smile. 'In other words you ruled the roost not long after taking up residence here, and have not called upon Budd's services too often, I suspect.'

'There's been absolutely no need for me to do so,' Emily wasn't slow to point out. 'But she's always on hand on those rare occasions when younger gentlemen call at the house and the proprieties need to be observed. And then, of course, the instant I step outside Jonas Finn appears. He's worse than six duennas!'

She frowned suddenly as a thought occurred to her. 'It wasn't by any chance Lady Deverel who suggested to Grandfather that I ought to have my own personal groom, was it?'

'I cannot recall her ever mentioning it, no. What makes you ask?'

Puzzled, Emily shook her head. 'I don't know, but I've always thought it most odd that Grandfather should have thought of employing a personal groom for me. It isn't the sort of thing that would cross his mind. Come to that, I'm rather surprised he ever considered employing a duenna. I wonder which interfering busybody was responsible for putting such an idiotic notion into his head in the first place?'

As no immediate candidate sprang to mind, Emily didn't dwell on the conundrum over long, and turned her head to gaze briefly through the French windows at the very pleasing sight of the garden beyond the terrace bathed in bright April sunshine. 'I do hope the weather remains fair. We can go out riding again tomorrow if it does.'

She turned back in time to catch a faint frown puckering

her friend's brow. 'What is it, Sarah? You said how much you enjoyed our ride this morning.'

'Yes, I did,' she readily confirmed. 'I haven't ridden in such a long time. And I should dearly like to join you again, except…except tomorrow I promised Godmama that I would return to the Hall and help with the flower arrangements.'

Emily managed to suppress a snort of derision, but could not resist saying, 'Oh, Sarah, I despair of you sometimes.'

Grey eyes clearly betrayed puzzlement. 'But why? There will be plenty of opportunities to go riding while I remain here. I really did enjoy this morning's exercise, and it was so kind of you to loan me one of your habits.'

'I'd let you keep the wretched thing if I thought there was the remotest possibility of your making use of it after you return to the Hall.'

Striving to maintain a firm grasp on a temper which sadly could on occasions erupt with quite surprising force, Emily rose to her feet and went to stand before the window. 'Are you honestly trying to tell me that Lady Deverel and the divine Drusilla, with the help of an army of servants, are incapable of arranging a few vases of flowers?'

'Of course not. But Godmama considers that I have a flair for such things and particularly requested me to do the flowers for Drusilla's birthday party.'

'You are at that confounded family's beck and call from dawn till dusk!' Emily exclaimed, not so successful this time in putting a guard on her tongue, and Sarah was clearly surprised by the depth of contempt.

'But—but I thought you liked the Deverels?'

Emily swung round, determined now to speak her mind. 'Lady Deverel is undeniably a charming woman, and I do like her, yes. But even you cannot deny she's dreadfully indolent. I always rubbed along very well with her late husband. But Drusilla's nothing more than a spoilt beauty, too accustomed to having her own way. And getting it too! And Charles is an utter clodpole for not exerting more authority over his household since coming into the title.'

'emily, how can you say so?' Sarah retorted, betraying a surprising show of annoyance for someone whose disposition was in general very placid. 'Charles is a most thoughtful, charming gentleman. He never fails to offer his thanks for the small tasks I perform. And he isn't a clodpole!'

Not unduly surprised by this display of staunch loyalty on Sarah's part, Emily turned to stare out of the window once more, thereby concealing a wickedly knowing smile.

She had long since been made aware of the fact that both she and Sarah were considered immensely pretty young ladies by the majority of those living in the locale. Undeniably, when seen together, they made a pleasing contrast: she with her shining, dusky locks; Sarah with her blonde curls. Although neither of them might be considered conventionally beautiful, both had been blessed with regular features and excellent figures, and were handsome enough to win a second glance from the vast majority of masculine eyes. Consequently it was little wonder that their continued single state had given rise to a deal of gossip and speculation in recent years.

For her part, Emily experienced no desire to find herself a husband, and had made no secret of this fact in an attempt to dissuade any would-be suitors foolishly offering for her hand. Four visits to Brighton in as many years had produced several proposals of marriage, all of which she had kindly but firmly refused. Her disinclination to wed, she supposed, might have been easier to understand if she had revealed a dislike of masculine company, but in fact the opposite was true.

She rubbed along remarkably well with her grandfather who, it had to be said, was not the most scintillating company for much of the time, preferring the peace and quiet of his large and well-stocked library, where he could pursue his many and varied hobbies. She was unfailingly gracious to her grandfather's male friends who visited the house, and was upon friendly terms with them all. Younger men, however, with the possible exception of Sir Charles Deverel, whom she had always regarded as a perfect gentleman, she tended to keep at a distance.

Emily considered that her friend's continued single state was a little easier for the local gossips to comprehend. Although Sarah came from an old and well-respected family, her parents had not been wealthy and her dowry by all accounts was woefully small. Any discerning gentleman, however, wouldn't take account of this, for Sarah's sweet nature and charming manners, coupled with her undeniable ability to run a large household efficiently, certainly went a long way to make up for any lack of fortune.

It was generally felt that it was a great pity that Lady Deverel, having suffered the loss of her husband the previous year, had been obliged to postpone launching her only daughter into Society. It had been Lady Deverel's intention to include Sarah in the proposed visit to the capital, and many had voiced the belief that both young ladies would have found themselves engaged before the Season was over. Emily, on the other hand, knew better. Although she felt sure that Drusilla, undeniably a beauty, would have had no difficulty in securing herself a suitable husband, she felt equally certain that any proposals which might have come Sarah's way would have been politely but firmly refused.

Perhaps, she mused, some might consider that Sarah had set her sights too high, and that it would be far more sensible to be practical and encourage the attentions of the local vicar who had been showing a marked interest in her of late, but Emily thought differently. Why should Sarah agree to marry a man she did not love, when there was every chance she might attain her heart's desire?

Emily turned her attention away from the view beyond the

window to discover the angry spots of colour still lingering in her friend's delicate cheeks. 'I knew you would be unable to resist coming to your darling Charles's defence.' She smiled as the becoming flush deepened. 'You might have succeeded in concealing your long-standing attachment from the world at large. But you've never fooled me.'

All at once Sarah appeared unable to meet that knowing, blue-eyed gaze. 'I cannot imagine what you mean,' she announced, delightfully flustered.

Emily's glance was openly sceptical. 'Oh, I think you know perfectly well what I mean. You've been in love with Charles almost from the moment you went to live at Deverel Hall. Don't attempt to deny it,' she added, when Sarah looked about to do just that. 'I have little difficulty in interpreting the signs, simply because I've experienced the emotion myself.

'Surprised, Sarah?' Emily's shout of laughter contained precious little mirth. 'Yes, I can see you are. Clearly I'm far more adept at concealment than you.'

Sarah gazed across at her dearest friend in dawning wonder. 'You—you've been in love, Em? You've never said anything before.'

'It isn't something I care to think about too often, let alone talk about,' she admitted. 'Even after several years I still find it painful.'

Sarah frowned. 'You must have been very young.'

'I was. But then I'd loved Sebastian Hawkridge all my life. I simply adored him when I was a child, used to follow him about everywhere. He was our nearest neighbour, and my mother's godson.'

'What happened?' Sarah asked gently, and for a moment thought she was destined to learn nothing further.

But then Emily said, 'As you know, when I was fifteen my mother insisted that I spend a year at that seminary in Bath. At the time, I assumed she did so because I was something of a tomboy, behaving in a less than commendable fashion on occasions. I realise now of course that the real reason was because she knew she was dying. During my visits home, she succeeded in concealing her illness remarkably well, but when I returned permanently, after the year at school, I realised just how ill she was. She didn't wish me to come and live here. She had always been very fond of her father-in-law, but considered him totally unsuitable to look after a sixteen-year-old girl. But she judged Sebastian, almost nine years my senior, more than capable. What she didn't know, and I discovered quite by chance, only a matter of a few months before she died, was that Seb was in love with someone else. Even so, he willingly agreed to marry me. The engagement was strictly private, and known to very few, and the wedding had been arranged for late August. But my mother's death, quite naturally, changed everything.'

Although she had spoken without betraying any of the searing hurt which even now could well up at a moment's notice, Emily was unable to suppress a heartfelt sigh. 'I went to see my betrothed, a week after my mother's funeral, and told him I couldn't go through with the wedding, that I had only agreed to marry him because my mother had been so set on the idea. I said that I thought I was too young to know my own mind, and that I would much prefer to live with my grandfather than marry.'

'And the gentleman in question believed you?'

'Oh, yes—he believed me. And I haven't set eyes on him since the day he came to see me off in my grandfather's carriage, although he continues to write to me from time to time.'

'Oh, Em. I'm so sorry.' No one could have doubted Sarah's sympathy. 'I had no idea. And did your former fiancé marry the woman he loved?'

'Sadly, no. And I have often speculated on why not. Perhaps he considered, as she was engaged by that time, that it was too late to offer himself as a candidate for her hand, and things were better left as they were. She married a certain Baronet a few weeks after I came to live with Grand-father. I had thought that Sebastian might meet another young woman who would capture his interest, but seemingly he has not. In fact since coming into his title he appears, if what the gossip columns contain is true, to have acquired rather rakish habits.' She gave a shout of laughter. 'What a lucky escape I had!'

Sarah frowned. 'But if he hasn't met anyone else, Emily, perhaps he still retains a sincere regard for you.'

'Oh, I'm sure he does. If we had married, I'm certain too we'd have rubbed along together quite wonderfully well. Un-fortunately I was, and still am for that matter, far too proud to figure as second-best in any man's life, merely a substitute for what he really wanted.'

Emily waved a hand in a dismissive gesture. 'I have yet to meet anyone who could take Sebastian's place in my heart and I doubt I ever shall. My case is hopeless, I fear. But yours isn't.' Eyes which had been dimmed by sadness and bitter regrets were unexpectedly brightened by a hint of mischief. 'Charles, I honestly suspect, cares more deeply for you than he realises. All you need to do is be patient and wait. I'm certain eventually he will come to appreciate the depths of his own feelings.'

'I'm afraid my case too is hopeless. I know Charles is very fond of me, but I have little to offer him.'

'You underrate yourself,' Emily countered. 'What's more, you and Charles are perfectly suited. You are both easygoing souls, happy to live a quiet country life. All Charles really wants is a comfortable home which is run efficiently. And who better to fill his needs than you? After all, you've been doing precisely that since you went to live at Deverel Hall.'

Sarah smiled wanly. 'I know I could make him happy, if only…'

'Don't abandon hope,' Emily warned gently. 'It will create a void that nothing can fill. Believe me, I know.'

* * *

Although Emily and Sarah were blissfully unaware of the fact, the subjects under discussion were only a few miles from Deverel Hall. The journey from the capital had been made in record time, and in immense comfort, owing to the fact that they had travelled in the well-sprung travelling carriage belonging to Lord Hawkridge.

'I must say, Seb,' Charles Deverel remarked, drawing his gaze away from the pleasing sight of very familiar landscape flashing past the window, 'I'm glad we consigned our valets and baggage to my carriage and made the trip in yours. This is a superb turnout you have here. Never had such a comfortable journey in my life!'

'It is merely one of the benefits of becoming the head of the family, dear boy, as you very well know,' was the languid response.

Charles regarded his friend in silence. Like most of Lord Hawkridge's close friends, he knew that Sebastian had been entirely contented living the comfortable life of a wealthy country gentleman in the fine property his father had left him in Hampshire, where he had been happy to indulge his passion for outdoor pursuits. Which made his drastically altered lifestyle in recent years somewhat hard to comprehend.

From what Charles understood, his friend now seemed to spend most of his time in the capital, accepting invitations to a seemingly endless round of parties, balls and soirées, and indulging in various dalliances with a number of society beauties, as well as enjoying more intimate relationships with several notorious Cyprians. On the surface it appeared that he had changed out of all recognition, but Charles couldn't help thinking that deep down he was still the same solid, reliable and trustworthy fellow he had known during those years at Oxford.

'I must say, Seb, I was rather surprised that you changed your mind and decided to honour our little affair down here with your presence. It won't be one of those spectacularly lavish and fashionable parties you've grown accustomed to attending in recent years—just a small, informal do with a few close friends and neighbours.'

Lord Hawkridge held his friend's slightly troubled gaze levelly. 'Do you imagine I've grown so high in the instep that I think myself above attending a country party?'

'Not a bit of it!' Charles hurriedly assured him. 'Fact of the matter is I'm surprised that you seem to spend most of your time in the capital these days.'

'And that is precisely why I decided it was time for a change.'

Once again Charles regarded his companion in silence, before saying, 'You never wished for the title did you, old fellow? In my case it was different, of course. I was raised for the express purpose of stepping into my sire's boots when the time came.'

Lord Hawkridge reached into the pocket of his immaculate jacket, which clearly betrayed the hand of a master tailor, and drew out a snuffbox. 'No,' he admitted, after sampling its contents. 'Both of my cousins losing their lives in that boating accident came as a shock. But as I was next in line I was given little choice in the matter. During the past few years I've grown accustomed to losing those whom I hold most dear. That is why I now live life to the full. One never knows just when the Grim Reaper might come knocking on one's door. He can be quite indiscriminate and appears to choose those who are most undeserving to have their lives cut short.'

Charles wasn't slow to understand. 'You're thinking of dear old Simon, aren't you?'

'Among others, yes,' his lordship admitted.

'The authorities never discovered who held up the coach, stole the necklace and killed poor Elizabeth, did they?'

'No.'

Charles shook his head sadly. 'Poor Simon, he never recovered from his wife's death.'

'No, he never did,' Lord Hawkridge confirmed. 'Had I known what he intended to do that night, I would have taken steps to prevent him. The loss of the necklace meant nothing to him; Elizabeth meant everything. But he might have recovered in time.'

The bitter regret in the deep, attractive voice was not hard to detect. 'Surely you don't hold yourself in any way to blame?' Charles enquired. 'How could you possibly have guessed that poor Simon meant to put a bullet through his brain?'

There was a bitter set now to his lordship's generous mouth. 'One is always left wondering if one could have done more.'

'Put it from your mind,' Charles urged him, as the carriage slowed to turn into Deverel Hall's impressive gateway. 'Ah, we're here! Let us hope the ladies have everything organised. At least I know I can always rely on Sarah.'

As Lord Hawkridge had no idea to whom his friend was referring he refrained from comment, and merely accompanied Charles into the well-proportioned Restoration mansion which put him in mind of the ancestral home he had inherited in Kent, both buildings having been designed and constructed by the same architect.

Although he had known Charles for more than a decade, Sebastian had never visited the Deverels' country estate before. Nor, apart from the late Sir Augustus Deverel who, unlike his son, had enjoyed paying regular visits to the capital, had he met any other member of the family.

His lordship's address was excellent, and in recent years had been polished to such a degree that he had little difficulty in flattering the most formidable matrons. Consequently it was a simple matter to bring a tinge of colour to the plump cheeks of the Dowager Lady Deverel whose faint claim to beauty had long since faded.

He had no need to flatter the golden-haired girl seated

beside her mother, for she was undoubtedly a diamond of the first water and, unless he much mistook the matter, Miss Drusilla Deverel knew this very well.

'I apologise, ma'am, if my unexpected arrival has inconvenienced you in any way,' he remarked, returning his attention to the Dowager, before lowering his tall frame into the chair positioned directly opposite the sofa on which the ladies were seated.

'Not at all, sir. Two of Drusilla's friends can easily share a room. Most of our guests are not arriving until tomorrow. But we are expecting several to turn up later today, so I can safely promise some jolly company at dinner.'

'You sound as if everything is well in hand for the party, Mama,' Charles remarked, drawing her attention away from the gentleman whose name she had mentally added to the list of those whom she would be very happy to call son-in-law.

'Oh, yes, dear. Everything is arranged.'

'And no thanks to Sarah,' Drusilla put in petulantly, the result of which, her mother noticed, not only brought a swift look of disapproval to her son's handsome face, but unfortunately drew a slight frown to the very eligible Baron's intelligent brow.

'That is hardly fair, dear,' she countered swiftly. 'You've Sarah to thank for arranging almost everything. And she was even kind enough to give up her room so that you could invite more people than was originally planned.'

'What's this?' her son demanded, suddenly alert. 'I thought we'd agreed that in the circumstances it was to be only a small affair?'

'Well, yes, Charles, we did. But you must remember that poor Drusilla has had to forgo the pleasures of a Season. And when we began to make a list of those we knew we simply must invite, the numbers just seemed to swell.'

'How many have you invited?' he demanded, frowning suspiciously.

'One hundred and fifty,' Drusilla enlightened him, looking very well pleased. 'It will be a splendid party, not the shabby little affair you had planned, Charles.'

Sebastian, quietly sipping the wine which the butler had kindly handed him, couldn't resist smiling to himself. Somewhere at the back of his mind he seemed to remember Charles mentioning once that his mother had suffered several miscarriages after having given birth to him, and more than a decade had passed before she had been successfully delivered of another healthy child. Little wonder, then, he mused, that the long awaited second offspring had been cosseted and indulged from birth. It was clear that even now the beauty of the house was all too frequently allowed to have her way; a sorry state of affairs which her brother, if his expression was any indication, would very much like to rectify.

'Let me remind you, Drusilla, that our father has been dead for less than a year. I consider it in extremely bad taste to hold such a large party, although I suppose it's far too late to do anything about it now.'

'Much too late,' his mother agreed. 'And you mustn't concern yourself, Charles. The event might be grander than first planned, but Drusilla knows that she must behave with propriety and not dance.'

Although Sebastian noted the beauty's resentful expression, her brother evidently did not, for he changed the subject by asking, 'Where is Sarah, by the way?'

If anything Drusilla appeared even more resentful. 'She's staying with the Stapletons. And just when we need her here the most!'

'Well, you can hardly blame her, my love,' Lady Deverel soothed. 'I myself did not quite like the notion of the dear girl sleeping in one of the attic rooms.'

'What's this?' Charles fixed a reproachful look in his mother's direction. 'Surely you didn't expect Sarah to sleep with the servants?'

'Of course not, dear,' Lady Deverel swiftly assured him. 'Sarah herself very obligingly offered to give up her bedchamber, and I was more than happy for her to stay with her friend for a few days, rather than move to one of the attic rooms.'

Sebastian noticed the look of disapproval lingering in his friend's eyes. As he himself had been an only child, he had never been plagued by troublesome siblings or family squabbles. The closest he had ever come to having a sister was his cousin Caroline, who had been a frequent visitor to his Hampshire home in her childhood.

He had accepted this invitation to stay at the Hall with the gravest misgivings, for he had made a point, since coming into the title, of never accepting invitations to houses where a daughter of marriageable age resided, for the simple reason that seeking a suitable bride had never once entered his thoughts, and he had tried his utmost to avoid raising false hopes in any fond mama's breast. All the same, he was beginning to think that, apart from the serious aspect of this visit, it might well prove to be an amusing diversion putting up with the Deverels.

Whether or not he would derive the same amount of pleasure out of coming into contact with a certain other young lady again, only time would tell.

Chapter Three

The following day, as she was crossing the hall, Emily noticed the letters collected from the receiving office that morning lying on the table. There was one for herself from a friend whom she had made while attending that seminary for a year, and with whom she corresponded on a regular basis, and there were two for her grandfather.

Slipping her own missive into the pocket of her gown to read later, she carried her grandfather's letters into the library, where she discovered him, as expected, seated behind his desk, metal-rimmed spectacles perched on the tip of his thin nose, avidly studying a musty old tome. As he made no attempt to raise his head to discover who had invaded the privacy of his sanctum, Emily availed herself of the opportunity to study him for a moment, unobserved.

Silver-grey hair swept back from a high forehead that clearly betrayed the intelligence of a man who throughout his life had made many sound investments which had enabled him to live very comfortably indeed, and pursue his many and varied hobbies. His vagueness, as she well knew, was merely a ruse, a means by which he could acquire the solitude he valued so highly. He was essentially a very private gentleman who preferred his own company, but he also enjoyed the companionship of his particular friends from time to time, and was not averse, on the odd occasion, to attending some large social event.

Which was perhaps just as well, Emily reflected, as she moved further into the room, because he was going to be obliged to mix with a large crowd this evening, if what Sarah had divulged was true. 'Finn called at the receiving office after he had taken Sarah over to the Hall in the carriage, Grandfather, and there are two letters here for you,' she informed him, placing the missives on the edge of a desk littered with papers, and numerous objects of no practical use whatsoever.

Lined with musty-smelling books, and various stuffed birds glaring down from the glass cases positioned on the various shelves, the whole room, not just the desk, was an absolute shambles. It was only ever dusted two or three times a year, and then only in the Honourable John Stapleton's presence, so that he could be certain nothing was moved. It had to be said, however, that in general he knew precisely where to lay his hands on any particular book or document. It was acknowledged too that he was a fount of wisdom, knowing a great deal about numerous subjects.

As he didn't attempt to speak, Emily cast her eyes along one row of thick, leather-bound books, before her gaze strayed to a particularly fearsome-looking specimen in one of the glass cases on the shelf above. 'Grandfather, you know a deal about birds.' This succeeded in winning her a brief glance. 'Are there any ravens in Kempton Wood?'

'Never seen any myself. Plenty of rooks there. Why do you ask?'

She shrugged. 'Oh, no reason really. I just recall someone mentioning that he'd seen a raven there, that was all.'

'Might have done.' Surprisingly she had succeeded in winning his full attention. 'Seem to remember that at one time it was known as Ravens Wood. Here, pass me that map in the box over there—the longest one, this end.'

Thus adjured, Emily collected the map, and then handed it to her grandfather to unroll and spread out on top of the papers on his desk. 'There, what did I tell you,' he announced, prodding a spot on the map with one bony finger. 'Now, let me see… Ah, yes! This map was printed in 1715. So it was known as Ravens Wood less than a century ago.'

'I wonder what made them change the name?' Emily asked, perching herself on the edge of the desk, the better to check the detail for herself.

'Names of places sometimes change, child. And Kempton itself has grown considerably in size during the past one hundred years. Perhaps the inhabitants thought the wood ought to be called after their town.'

'Yes, possibly,' she agreed, before her eyes strayed once again to the fearsome creature peering down at her from its glass cage. 'Do you happen to know anything about kestrels, grandfather? Is that one up there?'

He followed the direction of her gaze. 'No, that's a sparrow hawk. That's a kestrel, up there in the cabinet on the end. They're both birds of prey. Why do you ask? And why all this interest in birds all of a sudden?'

'Oh, no reason really.'

'In that case, if there's no purpose to your incessant questions, you can go away and leave me to continue with my studying. And get off my desk, child! You'll make a mess of my papers!'

'Ha!' was all the response he attained from his undutiful granddaughter, though she did as bidden and went over to the door. 'By the by, you haven't forgotten that it's the party tonight? I've instructed Budd to lay out your evening attire.'

'No, of course I haven't forgotten!' he responded testily. 'Now go away, child, and talk to that pretty friend of yours, and leave me in peace.'

'I would willingly do so if she had returned from the Hall. All the same, Grandfather, consider me gone.'

* * *

As Sarah was kept busy at Deverel Hall for much of the day, Emily was not destined to see her again until that evening, shortly before they were due to set off for the party, when Sarah, having managed to get herself ready remarkably swiftly, and appearing as if she had spent hours over the task, entered Emily's bedchamber.

For a few moments Emily studied her through the dressing-table mirror, where she sat adding the finishing touches to her own toilette. She had never seen her friend so charmingly attired. The pink silk enhanced her fair prettiness, and the few fashionable touches added by Sarah herself were so skilfully incorporated into the ensemble that anyone might be forgiven for supposing that the gown had come directly from some famous Bond Street modiste.

'You look lovely, Sarah,' she announced, wondering what Charles himself would think when he saw his staunch supporter so fashionably dressed. 'Where did you acquire the silk shawl?'

'Lady Deverel presented it to me just before I left the house, and this new pair of evening gloves. She said they were a little something for all the hard work I'd done. I felt so guilty taking them. After all, she did very kindly purchase the material for my new dress.'

It would have afforded Emily the utmost pleasure to voice her opinion of that lady's so-called benevolence. However, given the fact that if Sarah attained her heart's desire, Lady Deverel would become her mother-in-law, she refrained, and merely remarked that Drusilla's attire undoubtedly cost a great deal more.

After donning the pearl necklace and matching earrings that had once belonged to her mother, Emily rose from the chair, revealing that her own appearance left nothing to be desired. From the arrangement of her dusky locks, which young Amy, although by no stretch of the imagination a competent lady's maid, had managed to arrange in a simple yet pleasing style, to her satin slippers, she looked every inch the fashionable young lady.

'That blue silk certainly emphasises the colour of your eyes,' Sarah remarked. 'You look stunning.'

Emily flashed her a rather mischievous smile. 'Well, we must do our poor best to offer Drusilla a little competition, mustn't we? We cannot have her monopolising all the beaux.' She took a moment to study her overall appearance in the full-length mirror. 'I amaze myself sometimes,' she admitted. 'Six years ago, I didn't give a hoot how I looked, but now I wouldn't dream of leaving the house less than perfectly groomed. I doubt any of my old Hampshire neighbours would recognise me now.'

'I think perhaps one of them would,' was the soft rejoinder.

Emily was not slow to detect the change in her friend's demeanour. 'Why, you're looking very serious all of a sudden! Whatever's the matter?'

For a second or two Sarah appeared to find the toes of her soft pink slippers of immense interest, then she said quietly, 'When I was over at the Hall today, I discovered that Charles had returned the previous afternoon with a friend of his from London…Lord Hawkridge.'

Only for an instant did Emily check before sliding her fingers into her long evening gloves. 'I have been acquainted with the Deverels for almost five years, and yet I never realised that Charles knew Hawk. Dear me. Life is full of surprises! Grandfather, I do not doubt, will be delighted to see him.'

'And you?' Sarah prompted gently.

Emily's shrug of indifference was not wholly convincing. 'I suppose our paths were bound to cross again sooner or later. The aunt I visit in Brighton each summer is planning to take her eldest daughter to London next spring, and was hoping I would join them. I felt that, if I did go, I would be certain to bump into Sebastian at some point. The meeting has come a little earlier than expected, that is all. Come, let us repair downstairs. We don't want to leave Grandfather waiting.'

Throughout the short journey to the Hall, Emily was acutely aware of Sarah's keen regard. And how clever of her not to be fooled! she mused, desperately striving to maintain at least the appearance of the self-possession that she was far from experiencing.

She could quite easily, she supposed, have feigned a sore head and declined to attend the party at the last moment. But that was a coward's way out, and it simply wasn't in her nature to behave like a frightened child and run away from unpleasant situations. Added to which it stood to reason that, as he was in the area, Sebastian would pay a visit to the house sooner or later, if not to see her then at least to pay his respects to her grandfather. Surely it was better to come face-to face with him this first time, after so many years, in a crowded room, where she would be obliged to exchange a few brief words, and could easily escape by mixing with the other guests, than go through the agony of seeing him alone, where the strain of attempting to hide her continuing regard for him might prove just too much even for her? She wasn't so foolish as to suppose that it would be easy to keep those more tender feelings well hidden, especially from someone who had never evinced the least difficulty in reading her moods, but she knew she must endeavour to make the attempt.

Their arrival at the Hall coincided with that of several other neighbours, and they had perforce to await their turn before alighting at the impressive front entrance. The Restoration mansion looked as fine as it had on those occasions years before when Sir Augustus and Lady Deverel had entertained lavishly. Emily could fully appreciate now why her friend had been absent for much of the day, for there seemed to be a vase of flowers, beautifully arranged, and exuding the most delightful fragrance, on every available table in the spacious hall; and many, many more, she swiftly discovered, were decorating the large salon where the party was being held.

For a few brief moments she was able to set aside her own concerns as she stood in line to greet the host and hostess, and noticed Charles's eyes widen a fraction when they fell upon Sarah. The Dowager Lady Deverel, standing beside her handsome son, greeted each member of the party graciously, and even Drusilla, looking positively radiant in a dazzling creation of white gauze over satin, was prompted to remark upon the elegance of both Sarah's and Emily's gowns.

'Would I be correct in supposing that Drusilla has been warned to be on her best behaviour this evening?' Emily remarked in an undertone, as they quickly moved away from the entrance in order to allow the next party of guests to greet their host and hostess, and her grandfather had made directly for the masculine company to be found in the room set out for cards.

Sarah couldn't forbear a smile. 'I could not say with certainty. But I do know that Charles was not best pleased to discover that the affair was to be far grander than first planned. Furthermore, you must give Drusilla her due. She might be terribly spoilt, but she's definitely no fool. It is her ambition to make a truly splendid match, and showing a sulky face to the polite world isn't likely to attract many contenders for her hand. I believe she has set her sights quite high—a countess, no less, although Godmama mentioned earlier, when I was here, that her daughter is rather taken with your Lord Hawkridge.'

'He isn't *my* Lord Hawkridge,' Emily countered, hoping that she hadn't sounded waspish, but fearing from her friend's suddenly guilt-ridden expression that she had. 'I'm sorry, Sarah. As you might have guessed already I am a trifle on edge this evening.'

The fingers of her left hand received a brief, reassuring squeeze as Emily raised her eyes and looked about the room for that tall, well-remembered figure. She didn't immediately perceive him standing amidst a group of gentlemen in the far corner of the room. It was only when he turned his head and she received the full impact of an unwavering gaze from all too perceptive grey eyes that she realised that the gentleman immaculately attired in a long-tailed black coat, which emphasised the breadth of superb masculine shoulders, and tight-fitting trousers, which did little to hide the muscular shapeliness of long legs, was none other than the being who continued to plague her dreams all too frequently even after all these years.

'Oh, dear God! He's coming over,' she muttered, striving to control the sudden pounding of that erratic organ beneath her ribcage. 'Why couldn't the wretched creature have allowed me at least a few minutes in order to compose myself?'

Although Emily had finally revealed her true state of mind, Sarah wouldn't have supposed for a moment that the young woman beside her was suffering the least distress, for on the surface she appeared remarkably composed, extending a steady hand, which was immediately captured and retained in shapely fingers, and greeting the man whom she had never ceased to love without so much as a tremor in her pleasantly mellow voice.

'Hello, Em,' he responded in a deep, throaty tone that was no less appealing than the smile he bestowed upon her, before glancing briefly in Sarah's direction.

Emily, quite beautifully maintaining her control, was not slow to perform the introductions. 'I do not believe you are acquainted with my friend Miss Nichols, Lord Hawkridge.'

'No, I have not had the pleasure,' he admitted, releasing Emily's fingers in order to clasp Sarah's small hand briefly in his own.

'You were out when I arrived at the house, sir,' she hurriedly remarked in an attempt to hold his attention and allow Emily time to take a few steadying breaths. 'You had driven over to see Sir George Maynard, I believe.'

'I didn't realise that you were acquainted with our local magistrate, Hawk,' Emily commented, easily regaining his full attention.

'Oh, we've bumped into each other on a few occasions at our club, don't you know.'

Sarah detected her friend's slight frown at the drawled response, but was unable to remain to offer further support, for Lady Deverel was attempting to catch her eye, and she was obliged to slip away.

'Pretty girl,' his lordship remarked, taking out his snuffbox, and receiving a second frowning glance. 'What's wrong, Em?' he asked as deep blue eyes looked him over from the carefully dishevelled arrangement of his mid-brown locks down to his fashionably clad feet. 'Don't I pass muster?'

To her amazement Emily found herself experiencing an acute stab of disappointment at the needless affectations he appeared to have acquired during their long separation. 'I strongly suspect that those tales I've been reading about you in the newspapers in recent years are all too true. Be careful, Hawk, that you do not turn yourself into a complete man-milliner.'

Only for a second did his eyes narrow fractionally, before he returned the small silver box, its contents untouched, to his pocket. 'You too have changed, m'dear.' His gaze lingered for a moment on the square-cut neckline of her dress and what it temptingly revealed. 'You have blossomed into a woman.'

Emily was powerless to prevent the tell-tale colour rising in her cheeks. She did not like this Sebastian Hawkridge. No, not a whit! The man she well remembered had been no tailor's dummy, nor had he possessed the knowing gaze of the hardened rake. She had always felt so safe, so secure whenever he had been with her. She felt anything but safe now in the company of a man who might easily have been a complete stranger.

'Yes, Lord Hawkridge, I fear we have both changed.'

'In your case, m'dear, the changes are most definitely for the better. You have become a most elegant young lady.'

'And you, sir, have become an accomplished flirt,' she parried lightly in an attempt to conceal her rapidly mounting disappointment. 'You'll be telling me next that I'm the most beautiful girl in the room.'

The crooked half-smile which she remembered so well was suddenly tugging at one corner of his shapely mouth. 'Oh, no, my dear. You may have altered during our years apart, but not, I strongly suspect, to the extent that you are susceptible to insincere flattery. Miss Drusilla Deverel has the edge in the looks department, as you well know,' he returned, with that admirable candour which she had always admired.

'That's better,' he announced, with a further easy smile, when she found it impossible to suppress a chuckle. 'Now, before that young man who is purposefully heading in our direction whisks you away, would you grant me the pleasure of calling upon you tomorrow? I've been hearing some wonderful tales about you startling the populace by tooling yourself about the countryside in a curricle. Perhaps you might even be gracious enough to take me up beside you?'

'Of course,' she responded without considering the wisdom of her answer. But it was already too late to change her mind. The son of a near neighbour was standing before her requesting her as a partner in the next set of country dances, and Lord Hawkridge, after executing a graceful bow, chose not to linger.

Although far more successful in concealing the fact, Sebastian had been equally disturbed by this their first meeting in a very long time. The years he had spent in London perfecting the role of a wealthy, pleasure-seeking care-for-nobody had certainly stood him in good stead for just such an occasion as this. But it had not been easy to maintain the impersonation where Emily was concerned, even for those few short minutes.

When last he had seen her she had been scarcely more than a girl, coltish and slightly awkward, but the intervening years had wrought many changes. 'Blossomed' was the word which best described it, he decided, relieving a footman of a glass of champagne, and positioning himself beside the wall, where a huge vase of flowers partially concealed him from those taking part in the dance. Yes, Mother Nature had certainly performed her task well where Miss Emily Stapleton was concerned, bestowing upon her delightful feminine curves, and finely honing the delicate features into perfect symmetry.

But had all the changes been purely superficial? he could not help wondering, as he keenly followed her graceful progress down the set. Or had she matured mentally too? First impressions would suggest strongly that she had. Was the time now right for him to honour the pledge that he had made to the late Laura Stapleton? Should he attempt to woo her daughter in earnest? More importantly, could he afford to wait any longer? It would be madness to assume that, just because Emily had betrayed no interest in any gentleman during their years apart, she would continue to remain content with her single state. Another Season in Brighton with her late mother's sister was looming large on the horizon. Then afterwards perhaps London might beckon, where numerous gentlemen bent on making the leap into matrimony would look very favourably upon such a sweetly packaged piece of merchandise. Time, clearly, was no longer on his side. She was the only female to whom he had ever proposed marriage, and against all the odds she had rescinded. Was he really prepared to risk the possibility of experiencing the humiliation and pain of rejection a second time? His mind might advocate the use of caution, and yet…

Smiling to himself, Sebastian carried his wine across to the room set out for cards. For tonight his head would continue to rule his heart. But for how much longer acumen could persist in winning the battle over desires if he remained in this locale was anybody's guess!

Chapter Four

Understandably enough, Sarah's conversation at the break-fast table the following morning was all of the party, and how enjoyable it had been. Even John Stapleton surprisingly expressed his pleasure in the evening, before he sought the quiet confines of his library. Only Emily, it seemed, had been less than favourably impressed. She had arrived at Deverel Hall experiencing the gravest misgivings at the prospect of coming face to face with Lord Hawkridge. Yet a few hours later, when she had left in the carriage, she had felt nothing so much as acute resentment over his behaviour towards her.

Not once, throughout the entire evening, had he taken the trouble to ask her to dance. What was worse, he hadn't attempted to seek her company a second time. Yet on several occasions throughout the evening she had seen him moving gracefully about the dance floor, while entertaining his various partners with his light-hearted banter. Moreover, he had been among those besotted fops who had languished at Drusilla Deverel's pretty feet.

But why should she care? Emily wondered, desperately striving to convince herself that she was not suffering from that most unpleasant emotion—jealousy. It stood to reason that, now he had come into the title, Sebastian would one day be obliged to take the matrimonial plunge if only to beget an heir. When he had proposed to her he had been just plain Mr Hawkridge, and she had much preferred that man. The person she remembered, sincere and reliable, bore little resemblance to the male mannequin whose concerns undoubtedly didn't rise above the set of his neck-cloth or the arrangement of his locks. Yet just once, when they had spoken together, she had believed she had glimpsed the Sebastian Hawkridge of old.

Perhaps she had imagined it, though, she decided, automatically rising from the table to help Sarah and Mrs Budd clear away the breakfast dishes. The man of whom she had thought so highly had been far too discerning, far too astute to be beguiled by a lovely face. He would have had little difficulty in recognising the selfish conceit lurking beneath Drusilla Deverel's beautiful façade. She shook her head, at a complete loss to understand what had happened to him. Was it possible for someone's nature to change so much in the space of a few short years? Yes, perhaps it was, she decided, after a moment's consideration. All the same, she could not rid herself of the niggling suspicion that the manner he had adopted at the party had been something of an act.

'Are you going out this morning, Miss Emily?'

Startled out of her reverie by the housekeeper's enquiry, Emily recalled the foolish promise she had made and was now obliged to keep.

'Unfortunately, yes, Budd,' she responded testily, which induced Sarah and the housekeeper to exchange startled glances, for they both knew how much she enjoyed being out in the fresh air. 'Would you be kind enough to ask Amy to go across to the stables and inform Finn that I require the curricle in half an hour.'

Silently cursing herself for taking the trouble to entertain someone who appeared to have had little difficulty in ignoring her very existence, not just last night, but for the past five years, while conveniently forgetting that his lordship had never once failed to send her a present on her birthday, Emily begrudgingly took herself back upstairs to change her attire, and was in the process of tying the strings of her bonnet, when Amy entered the bedchamber to inform her that both Lord Hawkridge and Sir Charles Deverel had arrived at the house.

Although still consumed by biting resentment, Emily did not delay in making her way down to the parlour to discover Sarah there too, dressed in her outdoor clothes. The faint hope that Lord Hawkridge might have called to cancel the planned outing was quickly dashed, but her spirits revived when Sir Charles announced his intention of joining the outing and taking Sarah up beside him.

'You look remarkably well pleased about something,' his lordship commented, attaching himself to Emily the instant they stepped out of doors.

She was, but she had no intention of admitting to it, especially not to the man whose conduct she found increasingly puzzling, for today he had dropped that annoyingly affected drawl, and was more casually attired, seeming far more like the Sebastian Hawkridge of old.

'I feel that there's more than just a touch of spring in the air today,' she responded lightly. 'Why shouldn't I be pleased?'

'Yes, I must agree. Spring, it appears, is nipping at a few people this year.'

Emily looked up at him sharply, noting the glint in his eyes before he turned to watch Charles assisting Sarah into the phaeton, and wondered for a moment what he had meant, before deciding that he, like herself, must have observed the attention Charles had paid his cousin at the party. It was without doubt the only satisfying aspect of the entire evening, especially when Charles had made a point of dancing with Sarah. Which was more than the man beside her had requested her to do! Resentment reared its ugly head again, and it was as much as Emily could do to stop herself from slapping his hand away when he politely assisted her into the carriage.

'There's no need for you to come along, Finn,' Lord Hawkridge announced, clambering up into the seat beside her. 'I'm capable of taking care of your young mistress.'

Emily could hardly believe her ears, and almost found herself gaping in astonishment. What a crass nerve to be giving instructions to her servants! she inwardly fumed, and was not reluctant to give voice to her annoyance.

Sebastian regarded her for a moment in silence, noting the angry set of the determined little chin, as she gave the bays the office to start. 'I'm sorry, Em,' he apologised softly. 'I took it for granted that you wouldn't require your groom's presence. I didn't take into account that you might have become nervous in my company.'

'Of course I'm not nervous!' she snapped, before something struck her as odd. 'And how came you to know my groom's name, may I ask?'

A moment's silence then, 'I was speaking with your grandfather last night. I suppose he must have mentioned it then. He spoke highly of Finn, as I remember. Said that he went everywhere with you.'

Having by this time regained control over her temper, Emily could only wonder at herself for losing it so easily in the first place. It simply wasn't like her to take a pet over mere trifles, and behave like some overindulged child who had been thwarted. Unfortunately she had never experienced the least reluctance in giving full rein to her feelings when in Sebastian's company, and old habits, it seemed, were hard to break.

'Yes, he does,' she confirmed, striving to concentrate on her horses, and ignore the warmth exuding from that powerful frame too closely positioned beside her in the seat. 'Grandfather engaged him shortly after I came to live in his house.

I must confess I resented it at first, not being allowed to go out on my own, but I've grown accustomed,' she admitted. 'Not that I think his presence is necessary. Nothing ever happens down here.'

'That isn't what I've heard,' he countered, swift as a flash. 'I understood you came upon a body, lying in the road, not so very long ago.'

Emily didn't attempt to hide her surprise. 'How on earth did you discover that? I don't believe Grandfather told you. I doubt he even recalls the incident.'

'No, it was Sir George Maynard, as it happens. I believe I mentioned I called to see him yesterday. When he discovered I was acquainted with you, it—er—came up in the conversation.' Sebastian paused to study the delicate profile once more. 'It must have been very distressing for you, Em.'

'It certainly wasn't a pleasant experience,' she admitted. 'He came stumbling out of Kempton Wood, just a little further along this road. I thought I'd hit him at first, but then I discovered he'd been shot.'

'He wasn't dead, then, when you found him?'

'No, but he died shortly afterwards. At first Finn thought it might be a trap, but we didn't see anyone else about. The man appeared to have sustained a beating before he was shot. The attack must have occurred sometime before we came along. None of us heard a firearm being discharged.' Emily drew the curricle to a halt as they arrived at the spot where the incident occurred. 'Somehow, though, the poor devil managed to summon up sufficient strength to get himself as far as the road. It was just about here.'

His lordship took a moment to gaze about him, before asking, 'And he didn't give a clue as to his own identity, or the identity of his assailants?'

It was at that moment, as she watched those shrewd grey eyes continue to scan the woodland off to the left, that it occurred to Emily that he was betraying an uncommon interest, and that perhaps far more lay behind the seemingly innocent questions than mere idle curiosity. 'No, he didn't. Why do you ask?'

When finally he returned his attention to her, there was something oddly disturbing in his gaze. 'Would it surprise you to know that I still concern myself about you? If there is a lawless gang in the area, preying on the occasional hapless traveller, I shouldn't wish for you to become the next victim. You are still very…precious to me, Em.'

She swallowed in an attempt to rid herself of the painful ache which had suddenly attacked her throat, and hurriedly turned her head to stare at the road ahead, lest her expression betray the depth of feeling she still retained for him. 'I thank you for your concern, sir,' she said at length, relieved to discover that her voice at least remained steady, 'but I think in this case your anxiety is misplaced. I have not heard of any other such incidents in the locale in recent months. Besides which, I do not personally believe that he was set upon by scoundrels, bent on relieving him of any valuables he might have been carrying. I strongly suspect that he was killed for a completely different reason.'

Suddenly aware that Charles's phaeton was some distance ahead, Emily instructed her bays to move off, and they were soon bowling along at a smart pace, proving to Sebastian that she could handle the team well, her hands light but in full control.

'What makes you suppose that?' he enquired, when she had successfully caught up with their friends and could concentrate once more on something other than her horses.

'Oh, because of something he said to me before he died,' she answered, having little difficulty in picking up the threads of their former conversation. 'It didn't make much sense at the time, but I'm beginning to think that it was some sort of code.'

'Sounds mysterious,' he declared, as they reached the outskirts of the thriving market town.

'Yes, it is rather. He uttered three things before he died—kestrel, raven, 16th at midnight. Ravens Wood just happens to be the old name for Kempton Wood. It's my belief he wanted "The Kestrel" to be in the wood tonight at midnight. But as I've no idea who this "Kestrel" might be, he's destined, I fear, to miss the assignation.'

'Yes, so it would seem,' he agreed, sounding faintly bored with the subject now. 'Ahh! It would appear that Charles has decided to stop for refreshments at the inn. Shall we be hospitable and join them? Then perhaps you'd allow me to take the ribbons on the return journey?'

'Nervous, Hawk?' she teased, easily relapsing into that wonderful camaraderie which had existed between them.

'I have never been less so,' he assured her, smiling in a way which made her foolish heart lurch painfully. 'Finn has taught you well. However, at the risk of sounding pompous, I believe there are one or two small pointers I can teach you that you might find of value.'

It was some time later, after she had arrived back at her grandfather's house, and Charles and Sebastian had taken their leave, that Emily began to dwell upon what had been a surprisingly enjoyable impromptu visit to Kempton, and once again began to feel a little suspicious about Sebastian's interest in what had taken place by the wood two weeks before. It might, of course, have been nothing more than idle curiosity, and she didn't doubt that he had been genuinely sincere when he had voiced concerns for her safety, but even so she couldn't rid herself of the niggling suspicion that there had been more to his interrogation than mere inquisitiveness.

Leaving Sarah to pore over the latest fashion journals in the front parlour, Emily invaded the privacy of her grandfather's sanctum. She had never made a habit of doing so during the years she had resided in his house, but it was not totally unknown for her to sit with him from time to time, quietly reading a book. When she made no attempt to select something of interest, and merely seated herself in the chair beside his desk, her somewhat taciturn grandsire did elect to abandon the paper he was perusing long enough to enquire what she wanted.

'You haven't come here to ask me more questions about rooks and ravens, kestrels and hawks, have you, by any chance?'

'No, Grandpapa, I just… What did you say?' An amazing possibility having suddenly occurred to her, Emily raised her eyes to the feathered specimens in their glass cases. 'Kestrels and hawks…hawks and kestrels,' she repeated, rising so abruptly to her feet that the chair she had been sitting on almost toppled over. 'Oh, what a fool I've been! I should have realised at once. Of course, that's it!'

Leaving her grandfather to stare after her in some astonishment, Emily whisked herself out of the room and returned to the parlour, where Sarah betrayed no less surprise when informed that her help was urgently required.

'Heavens, Emily! Whatever is the matter?'

'I've been a fool, that's what the matter is! I should have guessed…I should have realised at once!' She began to pace up and down, cursing herself under her breath for being such a simpleton. 'I should have known that he didn't come down here just to attend Drusilla's birthday party. She isn't his type, unless his tastes have changed drastically. And I do not believe now that they have! No, he came here for an entirely different reason. And I'm determined to prove that I'm right!'

Sarah placed the fashion journal to one side. 'What on earth are you talking about?'

'I haven't time to explain now. I've too much to think about, and it will take careful planning. Finn mustn't discover what I'm up to.' Blue eyes narrowed suspiciously. 'Yes, and that's another thing I'm determined to sort out, because unless I much mistake the matter, there's more to his being here too!'

Sarah was all at sea and it plainly showed, but Emily refused to satisfy her curiosity for the present. 'Listen, Sarah,' she interrupted, 'there's something I must do, and I need your help. I seem to remember your saying not so long ago that you came upon a trunk or two of old clothes belonging to Charles in one of the attic rooms. I want you to go over to the Hall and search among them to see if you can discover anything that will fit me—trousers, shirt, jacket… Oh, and a hat, if there is one.'

If possible Sarah looked more bewildered than before. 'Why, whatever are you planning to do?'

'I'm planning to sneak out of the house tonight for a couple of hours or so,' Emily willingly divulged, much to her companion's further astonishment. 'I need you to lock the door after I've gone and let me back in when you hear my signal. I'll throw some gravel up at your window, something like that. We can plan all that later. The important thing now is to get you over to the Hall, so I'll go round to the stables and order the carriage made ready.'

'Are you not coming too?'

Emily shook her head vigorously. 'It doesn't require two of us to search through a couple of trunks. Besides, I dare not risk coming face to face with Hawk. He'd know I was up to something. He always knew when I was planning anything when I was a child, confound him! Don't be fooled by that lazy manner of his, as I'm ashamed to admit I was briefly,' she warned. 'He's as astute as ever he was. Believe me, little escapes his notice. So be on your guard, and avoid him if you can.'

'I'll be careful,' Sarah assured her. 'But what are you planning to do in the meantime?'

'I intend to bask in the sunshine of my grandfather's approval by offering to clean his silver-handled duelling pistols. He won't be suspicious. I've done it before. Then I'll load one of them and take it with me tonight. Only as a precaution, you understand?'

Sarah was secretly impressed. 'Good gracious! Who taught you to do that?'

'Hawk did. He taught me many things, including never to accept people at face value.' Her smile was distinctly tender. 'That is a lesson I shall try never to forget again.'

'Why the house seems positively deserted!' Charles announced, entering his library to discover just Lord Hawkridge, comfortably established in a chair by the hearth and perusing the most recent edition of the *Morning Post*. 'Most guests have already left, and the few remaining intend to leave tomorrow. I'm glad you've decided to stay on for a few days.'

'I'm enjoying the country air,' Sebastian assured him, without bothering to raise his head from between the printed sheets.

After settling himself in the chair opposite, Charles regarded his friend in silence for a moment. 'As I mentioned before, I'm rather surprised you spend so much time in the capital. Since you came into the title, you've rarely left the place.'

'One must be seen, m'dear,' was the languid response.

'Cut line, old chap!' Charles ordered, as unimpressed by the affected drawl as Emily had been. 'You don't fool me. You care as much for grand social occasions as I do myself. Although I must admit I did enjoy our party.'

'Yes, I could see that you did,' Sebastian responded, the folds of the newspaper hiding his amused grin. 'Your cousin Sarah is a charming young woman.'

'She's an absolute treasure! Don't know how we ever managed before she came to live with us. Mama has never been what one might call efficient at running a household. I've known for quite some time that Sarah has dealt with most aspects of the day-to-day running of this place. And damnably competent she is too!'

'A pearl beyond price, then, wouldn't you say?' his

lordship responded, before an item of news caught his attention. 'And speaking of pearls, Lady Westbury's famous necklace was found—er—missing several weeks ago, and has not turned up. There's a reward being offered for its safe return. How interesting! It would appear that the Season has started earlier this year.'

Sir Charles wasn't granted the opportunity to enquire precisely what his friend had meant, for the door opened and his sister came tripping lightly into the room, complaining as she did so that Lord Hawkridge had been neglecting her that day, and reminding him in the next breath of his promise to accompany her for a stroll in the garden.

'Good heavens, Drusilla!' her brother exclaimed testily. 'How many beaux do you want languishing after you at any one time? Cedric Granger and Percy Lemmington have been dancing attendance upon you all day.'

Sebastian had little difficulty in recognising when a spoilt beauty's feathers had been slightly ruffled. Miss Drusilla Deverel was a young lady accustomed to having her own way and not having her actions criticised by other members of her family. Charles, it seemed, irritated by something, had no intention on this occasion of pandering to her whims. It would have afforded Sebastian the utmost pleasure to do likewise, for pampered young women had never figured high on the list of those with whom he desired to spend much time. Notwithstanding, in this instance he was quite prepared to bear Miss Drusilla company for twenty minutes or so, most especially as it would grant him the opportunity afterwards of slipping unobtrusively away in order to put certain measures into effect.

Consequently he didn't hesitate to place the newspaper down on the table beside his chair and rise to his feet. 'No, no, Charles, a promise is a promise. Never let it be said that Sebastian Hawkridge was not a man of his word.'

'No one would ever accuse you of that,' Charles assured

him, before the sound of wheels on gravel reached his ears. 'Now who is that paying us a call, do you suppose?'

'It is someone leaving,' Sebastian enlightened him, after glancing out of the window in time to see the equipage moving away from the house.

'I didn't realise we'd had a visitor.'

'Oh, it was only Sarah, Charles,' his sister enlightened him. 'No one of consequence. She was here only a short while. Came to collect something, I believe.'

His fair brows snapping together, Charles went striding over to the door. 'I consider Sarah a very valuable member of this household. When she does decide to remove back here I expect you in particular to treat her with a deal more respect than you have been wont to display in the past, otherwise you might find yourself packed off to Bath to spend a prolonged visit with Great-aunt Henrietta!'

By the look of mingled resentment and fear which flitted over exquisite features, Sebastian felt sure that the matron in question was somewhat formidable and not a firm favourite with the beauty of the house.

'What on earth do you suppose has come over him?' Drusilla asked, appearing genuinely bewildered, as Charles swept out of the room without uttering anything further. 'I cannot imagine why he's so out-of-all-reason cross.'

'Ahh, I expect it is spring nipping at him, my dear,' Sebastian enlightened her with a crooked half-smile, as he slipped her arm through his and patted her fingers reassuringly. 'But do not be alarmed, child. It is unlikely that you shall ever succumb to the affliction.'

Chapter Five

Emily was swiftly forced to accept that she was nowhere near as intrepid now as she had been as a child. Years before, she would never have taken the least account of the chill night air, wouldn't have nearly jumped out of her skin at the mere hooting of an owl, or imagined that every sound and every shadow was something sinister, just lying in wait to entrap her. Moreover, after twenty minutes of scouting the fringes of the wood, made infinitely more eerie by brief glimpses of moonlight filtering through the thick canopy of foliage high above her head, she was forced to acknowledge that this was not perhaps the most sensible course of action she had ever taken in her life.

Even if she was right, and Lord Hawkridge was here somewhere, concealed in the undergrowth, finding him would be a virtually impossible task. She could hardly call out his name, thereby alerting anyone else who might be lurking to her presence. Furthermore the wood covered a wide area, so there was no guarantee that Sebastian would have positioned himself in this particular section.

Yes, it had been unutterable madness for her to attempt to confirm her suspicions in this way by coming here tonight, she silently told herself, pausing beside the trunk of a sturdy elm. She glanced back over her shoulder in the general direction from which she had come, and had almost decided to abandon her efforts, and return to where she had left her mount tethered at the edge of the wood, when she detected the snapping of a twig directly behind her. The next moment something solid struck the backs of her legs just below the knees, felling her in a trice. All at once a large hand clamped over her mouth instantly smothering her cry of mingled fright and pain, while a substantial amount of bone and muscle effortlessly pinned her to the ground, confining her arms and making it impossible to reach the weapon concealed in the pocket of her borrowed jacket.

Eyes, glinting ominously, peered down at her from above the woollen muffler successfully concealing most of her captor's face. Then just for a moment they widened fractionally, as he unexpectedly pulled off her floppy hat, allowing the long hair to tumble about face and shoulders, clearly revealing her sex.

'I'll wring your dratted neck, my girl!' an unmistakable voice growled, and Emily, totally unmoved by the threat, almost cried out in relief as he removed his hand from over her mouth and pulled down the muffler to reveal an expression which betrayed more clearly than words ever could his annoyance at discovering her here.

'What the blazes do you imagine you're playing at, Emily?' the man she had been searching for demanded, easing himself away so that she could remove the pistol, which had been digging painfully into a certain part of her anatomy, and sit up. 'And what the devil are you doing with this?' he added, removing the firearm none too gently from her fingers.

Given his present mood, she decided it might be wise to answer, even though she considered the question totally unnecessary. 'Surely you didn't imagine that I'd ever be stupid enough to venture out unarmed?'

He appeared not one iota appeased. 'Where the deuce did you get it from?'

'It's Grandpapa's.'

He regarded her now with acute suspicion. 'Do you mean to tell me you're here with his full knowledge and approval?'

'Of course not,' she answered, truthful to the last. 'Although it was he who inadvertently confirmed what I had begun to suspect. And I simply had to come and try to discover if my suspicions were correct and you were the mysterious "Kestrel".' Excitement brightened her eyes. 'What on earth are you about, Hawk?'

If anything he looked angrier than before, and certainly in no mood to satisfy her curiosity, as his next words proved. 'You've come very close on several occasions in the past to receiving your just deserts, Emily Stapleton, but never more so than now.'

Indignation held her mute, but only for a moment. 'You wouldn't dare!' she hissed, in no doubt as to precisely what he was threatening. 'Besides, I'd squeal my head off, and scare away whoever it is you're hoping to see.'

His distinctly unpleasant smile was a threat in itself. 'I'm a patient man. I can wait.'

She didn't doubt that he was in earnest, and so decided it might be in her own best interests not to annoy him further, and merely regarded him uncertainly for a moment, as she positioned her back against the tree trunk beside him. 'May I have my pistol back?'

'No, you mayn't!' he snapped, slipping it into his own pocket. 'You can sit still and be quiet.'

She dutifully obeyed the hissed command, until sometime later when the church clock at Kempton began to chime the midnight hour. 'I can't hear anything, can you, Hawk?' There was no response, so she remained quietly scanning the woodland surrounding them for a further lengthy period. 'Of course, whoever it is who is meant to be coming might be in quite a different part of the wood,' she suggested as the clock solemnly tolled the passing of the hour.

This won her a brief, considering glance from attractive, almond shaped eyes which were noticeably less angry now. 'There are others positioned about the area.'

She didn't attempt to conceal her amazement. 'You brought others from London with you?'

'Only my servants. My groom is somewhere about.'

She relapsed into silence again, considering what he had told her, and, more importantly, what he was keeping to himself. 'Then you must have attained help from Sir George Maynard,' she finally announced, after deciding the local Justice of the Peace must have been the one in whom he had confided. 'I hope Sir George's people don't stumble upon some hapless poacher,' she added, after failing to elicit a response.

She was more successful this time. 'If they see anyone, then I suspect it will be someone thus engaged. I expressed my doubts to Sir George when I saw him yesterday evening.' He sounded quite matter-of-fact, as though he wasn't expecting a successful outcome to the night's escapade. 'It's such a deuced odd location. Why arrange an assignation in a wood when you can hold a meeting in the comfort of a house, or inn? It just doesn't make sense.'

'But that's what the man told me, Hawk,' she assured him, at last feeling the effects of sitting too long on the cold, damp ground.

His response to the shiver was to reach out and place an arm about her, drawing her closer to share the warmth of his voluminous cloak. Only for an instant did she stiffen, then he felt her relax against him, as she had done on scores of occasions in the past. He smiled to himself, remarking as he did so, 'Anderson was near dead when you found him. He could not have been too coherent.'

She raised her eyes to the rugged profile that had remained etched in her memory during their years apart. 'Anderson? Was that his name? What was he doing down here?'

'He was an agent, Emily. And a damned good one.'

She frowned at this. 'A spy, you mean?'

'If you choose to describe it so, then yes. But he was working on behalf of this country. He was obtaining information for a man who is determined to uncover a network of spies.'

Again she studied the strong contours of his face, her eyes coming to rest on the shadow of stubble covering the cleft in his chin. He seemed inclined to confide in her now, so she felt no compunction in asking, 'Is that what you do?'

'Only in as much as whenever I discover information which I think might prove valuable I pass it on. My objective is somewhat different. I am determined to uncover the identity of the man who was responsible for the late Lord Sutherland's demise, and who has been the brains behind several successful jewel robberies.'

Emily had read reports in various newspapers during recent years of the theft of certain well known and highly valuable items of jewellery which, as far as she was aware, had never been recovered. She had also known the late Viscount Sutherland, and remembered well those occasions when he had stayed in Hampshire with Sebastian. They had been very close friends since boyhood, more like brothers, and she didn't doubt that Simon's death must have been a bitter blow to the man beside her.

'I did read an account of his death in the newspaper, Seb,' she admitted softly. 'But I understood that it was an accident.' All at once she knew that this wasn't the case. 'What really happened?'

He gazed down at her, and even in the gloom she couldn't fail to see the sadness in his eyes. 'He committed suicide, Emily. For the sake of the family, Simon's young brother and I did our best to make it appear an accident. I had been with Simon that evening. About an hour after I had returned home, his brother Michael came to fetch me in the carriage. He had been staying with Simon for several weeks, and had been out with friends that night. When he arrived back at the house, he discovered Simon in the library, slumped over the desk, the note he had left splattered with his blood.

'We destroyed the note, and Michael and I informed the authorities that Simon was recovering well from the death of his wife. I told them that he had planned to spend some time with me in Kent, that we intended, among other things, to hold a competition at my ancestral home to see who was the best shot, and that I had left him earlier in the evening cleaning his pistols. The truth of course was very different.'

His sigh seemed to hang in the night air for a long time. 'Two months before, his wife had been journeying to her parents' home in Surrey when her coach was attacked. She had been carrying several items of jewellery with her, including the famous diamond necklace Simon had bestowed upon her shortly after their marriage. The report in the newspapers stated that she had suffered a miscarriage shortly after the attack and had died as a result. This was not true. She was violated, Emily, and then strangled. The female companion travelling with her suffered a similar fate, and the coachman and groom were murdered also.

'Poor Simon never recovered from the death of his wife and his unborn child. Had I known what he intended to do that night I would never have left him. But I vowed, when I saw him laid to rest beside his wife, that I would avenge their deaths, no matter how long it took me.'

For several minutes Emily didn't trust herself to speak. She may have been gently nurtured, shielded from birth from the more unsavoury aspects of life, but she knew well enough what had happened to Lady Elizabeth Sutherland.

'Dear God!' she muttered at length. 'How dreadful... And how totally unnecessary. Those responsible for the attack on Lady Sutherland didn't need to resort to such lengths. Why didn't they simply steal the jewels and go?'

'Because they're unspeakable fiends, that's why,' he spat between gritted teeth. 'Lady Sutherland and her servants are by no means the only ones to have fallen foul of those devils over the years. When Lady Melcham's diamond necklace was stolen from her home, her butler became a further casualty. Although the authorities have no idea as to the identities of the perpetrators of these horrendous crimes, it is generally believed that the brains behind them is someone of my own class, someone who moves freely in Society and discovers by various means the whereabouts of these highly prized items of jewellery at times when they are most easily purloined—when they are being carried about the country, for instance, or when they are left in a house while the master and mistress are away, with fewer servants to guard them.'

As Emily sat quietly digesting what she had learned, something occurred to her as rather odd. 'You mentioned that all the pieces stolen are well known. That being the case, how on earth do the thieves dispose of them? Surely no one in this country wealthy enough to purchase such highly prized items would be foolish enough to do so, and risk prosecution?'

'We believe they are being sold abroad. In fact we are reasonably certain that Lady Melcham's necklace and the one which belonged to the Sutherland family are now in the hands of an Italian nobleman who possesses another in the set. They are being taken out of the country by the same means by which secret information is passed on.'

'Smugglers?'

'Yes, Emily. And unless I'm very much mistaken Anderson got wind of a shipment of goods being landed hereabouts. I expect too that he learned that a valuable pearl necklace, which was recently reported stolen, would be taken out of the country on the same vessel landing the contraband.'

'Yes, that's possible,' she agreed. 'We're only a matter of three or four miles from the coast here.'

'Which makes me wonder why the meeting, possibly for the exchange of the necklace, would take place here?' Sebastian looked about him assessingly, much as he had done when they had driven out in the curricle. 'It would have made more sense for it to have happened somewhere along the coast. Freetraders don't hang around for long. They run the risk of being spotted by our patrolling vessels, or Preventive Officers scouting the coastline.'

'So you think the handing over of this pearl necklace was the message Anderson was trying to get to you?'

'Almost certainly. I'm not involved in the hunting down of spies. That is quite another gentleman's department. And Anderson's message was definitely for me—"The Kestrel". However,' he added, rising to his feet and helping Emily to do likewise, just as the Kempton church clock confirmed that a further hour had passed, 'I think we must accept the fact that we're not going to get our hands on the miscreants this time.'

Experiencing a mixture of disappointment because their vigil had proved fruitless, and relief that it was over at last and she could seek the warmth and comfort of her bed, Emily automatically followed Sebastian out of the wood. It didn't occur to her that he was heading in an entirely different direction from the one by which she had arrived, until she discovered herself in a field where two horses were tethered to a fence and a very familiar, stocky individual stood guarding them.

'What in the world are you doing here, Finn?' she demanded to know, as they drew closer and she could see, even in the dim light, that his astonishment was no less marked than her own, though she managed to conceal hers rather better. Then she recalled the suspicion that had filtered through her mind the day before when Sebastian had addressed her groom by name. 'Evidently you're acquainted with his lordship, Finn. Just how well acquainted are you?'

He appeared unable to meet her gaze. 'Well, I—er—I—'

'Why don't you go and collect your mistress's horse, Finn,' his lordship suggested before the groom's tongue became too entangled in knots. He transferred his attention to Emily who was looking anything but pleased now. 'I assume you did ride here and not walk?'

'I left my mare over there.' She gestured behind her. 'In the next field.'

Finn needed no further prompting and swiftly mounted, leaving his lordship to soothe the ruffled feathers of a female who it had to be said was not always easily pacified.

'You can stop glowering at me, you little termagant!' his lordship ordered without preamble. Unfortunately the command lacked any real conviction owing to the fact that he was singularly unsuccessful in keeping his voice steady, and was quite unable to suppress a smile. 'You didn't honestly suppose that after watching you leave Hampshire in your grandfather's carriage I would conveniently forget your very existence, not to mention break the promise I had made to your mother to take care of you?'

Emily turned away lest her expression betray the heartache this simple admission engendered. Even now, after almost five years, the pain never lessened whenever she began to dwell on the fact that the only reason he had been prepared to marry her was to fulfil the promise he had made to her mother. Oh, he was fond of her, right enough—anyone with a ha'p'orth of intelligence couldn't fail to perceive that. But affection was no substitute for that most tender of emotions.

'Be reasonable, Em,' he coaxed, quite failing to appreciate that the tense set of slender shoulders might have stemmed from something other than pique. 'I couldn't just leave you in your grandfather's care. He would never have maintained a proper guard over you.'

'So you employed Finn to do the job, to spy on me!' she snapped, sounding genuinely miffed, and to a certain extent she was. 'Exactly whose servant is he—yours or my grandfather's?'

'He's yours, Emily,' Sebastian corrected. 'And he's devoted to you. You know that.' Grasping her shoulders, he gave her no choice but to turn and face him squarely. 'Yes, it was I who acquired his services initially, and sent him down here. But he has your best interests at heart, not mine. He merely agreed to help to keep a lookout in this section of woodland tonight.'

She might have been generous enough to acknowledge the truth of this if something else hadn't suddenly occurred to her which added substantially to her annoyance and which enabled her to ignore the continued touch of those shapely hands on her upper arms. 'And I suppose it is you I have to thank for putting that ridiculous notion into Grandpapa's head about engaging the services of a duenna?''

He had the grace to look a little shamefaced. 'Yes,' he admitted. 'I thought you might like some feminine companionship, although I did not press the issue when your grandfather wrote and told me you were set against the idea. I could understand that you'd not take too kindly to being chaperoned, after years of relative freedom. But as I'd made that pledge to your mother, I was determined to do all I could to keep my word.'

Torn between respect and resentment, Emily regarded him in silence for a moment. 'Very well, I can appreciate the reasons behind your actions in the past. But you will oblige me, Lord Hawkridge, by not interfering in my affairs in the future. And as for you,' she added rounding on her groom, who at that moment arrived back, leading her horse, 'your continued employment as my servant is far from certain, *Judas* Finn. You and I shall be having a long talk tomorrow.'

Removing his hat to scratch his grizzled hair, Finn watched his young mistress mount without assistance and ride away. 'Don't much like the sound of that m'lord. How much ought I to tell her?'

'As little as possible, Jonas,' Sebastian replied, casting the groom a meaningful look. 'When I feel the time is right I'll inform her that I have every right to interfere in her affairs. In the meantime—' he delved into his pocket for John Stapleton's pistol, and handed it up to the groom "—give her this. It might go some way in restoring you in her good books.'

Not appearing wholly convinced, Finn did what he had been entrusted to do, and set off at a gallop to ensure that his lordship's ward came to no harm.

Although Emily attained very little sleep that night, she surprisingly arose little later than usual the following morning, and was more than willing to acquiesce to Sarah's request to make a trip to the local town.

They spent a pleasant hour visiting the shops, where Sarah purchased various bits and pieces, and then returned to the inn where the carriage awaited them, only to be informed by Finn that he'd learned that the road home had become blocked by a hay cart which had shed its load.

'Oh, not to worry,' Emily responded cheerfully, quite forgetting that her faithful groom was not precisely basking in the sunshine of her approval at the moment. 'We'll return by way of the coast road. It's a pleasant morning, and it's a pretty run.'

'I've lived in Dorsetshire for as long as you have, Em, and I've never travelled this way before,' Sarah disclosed as the carriage turned off the main road and they bowled along a narrow country lane with many twists and turns.

'I've ridden along here only once, shortly after I came to live with my grandfather. The road passes through Gremlock. It's a small fishing village and quite quaint,' Emily informed her, and then smiled to herself as her companion appeared content to stare out of the window at what for her was unfamiliar landscape.

True to her word Sarah had remained awake to unlock the door during the early hours. Agog with curiosity she had accompanied Emily back upstairs, but the instant Emily had said, 'As I told you, I went out to discover if something I suspected was true. My suspicions turned out to be correct. But more than this I cannot reveal, lest I betray the trust of—of a friend,' Sarah had not attempted to discover more and had returned quietly to her own room.

Emily could not help but admire Sarah's placid nature and self-control. Had their roles been reversed, and she had been the one to remain awake to unlock the door, she felt sure she would have persevered until she'd discovered much more.

'Now, what's to do?' Emily muttered, abandoning her reverie, as the carriage came to an unexpected halt in the middle of Gremlock's main street.

Pulling down the window, she poked her head out, and was informed by Finn that it was only a drayman unloading, and they wouldn't be delayed for very long. Leaning out a little further, Emily caught sight of a barrel being rolled down into the tavern's cellar, then raised her eyes to see the inn's weathered sign swinging to and fro on its rusty hinges.

'Oh, dear God,' she murmured, her face losing every vestige of colour. 'Whatever have I done?'

Chapter Six

One might reasonably have supposed that any gentleman of wealth and rank, and therefore in a position to command most any luxury, could not be other than highly satisfied with his lot; and to a certain extent Lord Hawkridge had enjoyed the privileged life he had been leading in recent years. Yet he could not deny that there had been occasions, sadly too numerous to count, when he had been afflicted by rank boredom. And never more so than now!

Maintaining the mask of polite interest, which effectively concealed his rapidly increasing ennui, he glanced across at the corner of the room where the beauty of the Deverel family was attempting to entertain him and her relatives with a selection of popular tunes on the pianoforte.

Like so many of those who had been paraded before him in recent years by their ambitious mamas, Drusilla Deverel had little to commend her except her looks. Although he was not averse to feminine company, and had enjoyed several highly satisfying liaisons since residing in the capital, he had only ever wished to take one female to wife. His love for her had remained constant, and he felt certain, especially after having spent these past days in Dorsetshire, that the situation was unlikely ever to change.

The rendition finally came to an end, and Sebastian was blessedly spared the necessity of having to suffer a further example of Miss Deverel's mediocre talents by the entrance of the butler who announced the arrival of Miss Stapleton. Only Sebastian, who had become quite adept at concealing his feelings in recent years, did not betray surprise at the un-expected visit, and rose at once to his feet as Emily, looking stunning in a stylish dark-blue riding habit, the cut of which emphasised the slender shapeliness of her figure, whilst its colour enhanced the stunning hue of those unforgettable eyes, swept into the room.

Charles, who had risen also, appeared very pleased to see her. 'What a delightful surprise, Miss Stapleton!' His hopeful gaze slid past her to the open doorway. 'Has Sarah accom-panied you?'

'No, sir. I left her back at the house happily assisting Budd in cutting out material for another new gown,' she answered, noting with pleasure the look of disappointment he quite failed to conceal, before Drusilla captured her attention by remarking,

'Great heavens! It isn't like Sarah to take such an interest in her appearance. She never seems to care what she wears.'

Sebastian was not slow to observe his ward's look of contempt which followed Miss Deverel's tactless observation, and seemingly Lady Deverel noticed it too, for she hurriedly intervened by announcing that it was high time that her god-daughter had a few new gowns.

'I must confess, Miss Stapleton, I have missed her company greatly during these past days. I don't suppose she mentioned when she would be returning to us? Apart from Lord Hawkridge, who has delighted us all by agreeing to stay on for a few days, all our guests have left us. I have given instructions for Sarah's belongings to be returned to her room, so there is no necessity for her to avail herself of your kind hospitality further, unless she chooses to do so, of course.'

'I shall ensure that she is made aware of your eagerness

for her return, ma'am. I'm in no doubt that she has very much enjoyed her short stay with us. But I also know that she is not one to be idle for long. She's unaccustomed to inactivity, as you are very well aware.'

Little baggage! Sebastian thought, hard put to it to suppress a smile. Although she seemed far less forthright than she had been years before, evidently Emily was still not reticent to express her opinions on occasions. At least Charles, who was suddenly looking very thoughtful, was under no illusions as to what she had meant.

Sebastian, watching that candid blue gaze focus in his direction, quickly detected a flicker of entreaty before her expression became a reproachful mask. 'You are quite in my black books, Lord Hawkridge,' she proclaimed, sounding genuinely miffed. 'You have delivered a crushing blow to my ego this day by quite forgetting my existence, and your promise, I do not doubt. Indeed, yes, ma'am,' she reiterated, when Lady Deverel betrayed mild surprise. 'What think you of a gentleman who pledges to escort a lady out for a ride, for old time's sake as it were, and then quite fails to turn up at the appointed hour?'

After the previous night's escapade Sebastian was under no illusions whatsoever that Emily had lost none of that indomitable spirit. The little madcap was just as adventurous as she had been in her childhood. But one thing she was not, and had never been, and that was an unmitigated liar. She would never fabricate such a story unless there was a very good reason for doing so. Clearly she had discovered something and wished to impart her news in private. Consequently he didn't hesitate to support her tale.

'My dear Miss Stapleton, I cannot apologise enough.' He clapped a hand momentarily over his eyes. 'Oh, my lamentable memory! My only excuse is that the prospect of having Miss Deverel entertain us on the pianoforte this afternoon thrust everything else from my mind,' he announced, the result of which sent Drusilla quite pink with pleasure, brought a satisfied expression to her doting mother's plump face, and a muttered warning from Emily that he was in grave danger of overplaying his role.

Maintaining his countenance with an effort, Sebastian lingered only for the time it took to beg the use of a mount, and then departed with all haste to change his attire, leaving Charles to escort Emily round to the stables.

'I would happily accompany you, but unfortunately I have arranged to spend an hour this afternoon with my steward, so must deny myself the pleasure,' he informed her, the instant they had stepped outside.

Although Charles was very much the gentleman, Emily sensed that there was more to this display of gallantry than merely a wish to offer his escort. Consequently she was not unduly surprised when, after issuing instructions to his groom to saddle his own mount for Lord Hawkridge, he enquired in the next breath if Sarah had mentioned when she would be returning to the Hall.

'She has said nothing to me, sir,' she admitted, suppressing a smile of satisfaction. Clearly he was missing his cousin. 'I must admit that I shan't be happy to see her go,' an imp of mischief prompted her to add. 'She's such wonderful company.'

'Indeed, yes,' he responded, his brows drawing together in a worried frown, as though he feared Sarah just might be persuaded to stay away for longer.

Emily was sorely tempted to imply that her friend might do just that, but managed to resist the prompting of her baser self this time. She had never made any secret of the fact that she liked Charles Deverel. She might wish that he would assert himself a little more on occasions, at least in his dealings with certain members of his immediate family. It was hardly her place to interfere, however. Besides which, Sarah appeared to like him just as he was, and that was what really mattered.

'As I mentioned to your mother, I cannot imagine Sarah will remain with us for very much longer, sir. But I do think it would betray a sad want of tact on my part to ask her when she intends to return to you. She might easily misconstrue my motives and believe we are now tired of her company. And nothing could be further from the truth!' She cast him a fleeting, sideways glance, before suggesting, 'There is nothing to stop you from riding over, however, and asking her yourself.'

He appeared much struck by this. 'I shall do so tomorrow, Miss Stapleton, if that is convenient?'

'I can safely promise you, sir, that your visit will be most welcome.'

A door opening behind them caught Emily's attention, and she cast a glance over her shoulder to see Lord Hawkridge striding with all the natural grace of a born athlete across the stable-yard. The smart yet far less formal riding attire brought vividly to mind the Sebastian Hawkridge she remembered so well; that kind-hearted young man who, like some indulgent elder brother, had been happy for the most part to have his godmother's daughter bearing him company when out riding or fishing, or trailing at his heels whenever he fancied a spot of shooting in the wood which formed part of the boundary between his and his godmother's property. Emily had simply adored him then. How she wished that her youthful idolatry had not deepened!

She turned away to mount her horse lest he detect something in her expression to betray the love which had not diminished one iota during their years apart. Seemingly she was successful in her endeavours, for the first thing he did, as they rode out of the yard, was to take her roundly to task for her behaviour at the Hall.

'You very nearly sent me into whoops, you little baggage, when you advised me not to overact. Not to mention your remarks to Lady Deverel concerning Miss Nichols.'

Not in the least chastened, Emily cast him a mocking

glance. 'You forget, Hawk. I've been unfortunate enough to hear Drusilla play. I've no musical bent myself to speak of, but at least when I play a tune it's recognisable. And as for Sarah…' there was a distinct hint of stubbornness about the set of her chin now '…it's high time the family appreciated just what she does in that house!'

'From things Charles has let slip during the past few days, I do not believe he is labouring under any illusions,' he didn't hesitate to assure her, before he turned to cast a suspicious glance at her delightful profile. 'But I sincerely trust you are not attempting a spot of matchmaking, Emily. If you take my advice you'll not interfere. One might act with the best intentions, and end by doing far more harm than good.'

Especially to oneself! she thought bitterly, staring resolutely ahead. If only he knew what it had cost her not to interfere in his life by not holding him to his promise to marry her. She might have been only sixteen, but there had been nothing wanting in her feelings for him. She had willingly forfeited her own future happiness in the hope that he might one day attain his. Although he might never be in a position to offer for the woman he really loved, her unselfish gesture had allowed him to do so if the opportunity should one day arise. She had granted him the freedom to follow his own inclinations. If that wasn't a prime example of not interfering in someone's life, then she didn't know what was!

'I have no intention, my lord, of attempting to change the course of anyone's life.'

The assurance earned her one of those intensely penetrating grey-eyed looks which he had not infrequently bestowed upon her in the dim and distant past whenever he had suspected her of attempting to conceal something from him, but she had no intention of satisfying his curiosity this time. Digging her heel into her mare's flank, she proceeded to take a short cut across part of the land belonging to Sir George

Maynard, and didn't attempt to slacken her pace until the outskirts of Kempton came into view.

'I'd forgotten what a bruising little rider you are, Em,' he remarked, drawing alongside once more. 'It's high time you had another mount, something with a touch more spirit.'

Relieved that he was evidently disinclined to resume their former conversation, Emily found a smile coming effortlessly to her lips. 'I've frequently considered approaching Grandpapa, but I could not easily part with this gracious lady,' she went on, leaning forward to stroke the mare's neck. 'She was the last gift Mama ever bestowed upon me.'

'I know,' he acknowledged softly. 'But if I could ensure that she was sold to a good home, would you then consider my looking for a new mount?'

Undoubtedly the offer had been kindly meant. Yet Emily was immediately on her guard and favoured him with a long, considering look which was no less penetrating than his own could be on occasions. 'Why should you wish to concern yourself, my lord? What possible interest can it be to you whether I choose to acquire a new mount?'

There had been no hint of resentment in her voice, merely suspicion, which he evidently didn't fail to note, for his expression became just for one fraction of a second distinctly guarded before he raised one broad shoulder in a shrug. 'I quite naturally concern myself about you still. Good Lord, Em! Have you forgotten just how close we used to be?'

If only that were possible! She would give much to be able to forget that the happiest times in her life had been spent in the company of the being now riding alongside her. 'Of course I haven't forgotten,' she admitted in a voice which sounded falsely cheerful even to her own ears. 'I only hope your continued fondness for me can withstand what I'm about to reveal,' she added in the same light-hearted tone, before once again digging her heels into her mare's flank.

Unfortunately her attempt to ride just a little way ahead

again was unsuccessful this time. He had soon caught her up and she was conscious of those grey eyes scrutinising her profile. Fortunately the ordeal of attempting to appear as though she hadn't a care in the world did not last for too long. Travelling down the narrow twisting lanes was far swifter on horseback than it had been in the carriage earlier in the day. The fishing village was blessedly soon reached and she didn't waste any time in revealing what she had discovered that morning.

'Ahh, yes,' he murmured, staring up at the painting of the black bird on the rough, wooden sign. 'The Raven Inn… Yes, my dear, that is much more likely to have been the meeting place,' he added, turning his mount and moving on before they drew too much attention to themselves.

'I'm so sorry, Seb,' she apologised softly, real perturbation in her voice. 'It's all my wretched fault. You cannot imagine how often I've cursed myself since I glimpsed that sign this morning, and remembered what you'd said.'

'You weren't to know of the inn's existence,' he responded, showing that he held her in no way culpable, but she could not so easily absolve herself from blame.

'If I hadn't attempted to be so clever, you wouldn't have been misled. I was so certain that the Raven must refer to Ravens Wood. And because of my crass stupidity you have missed the opportunity, if not of capturing those indirectly responsible for your friend's death, at least of attaining some kind of lead.'

'There'll be another time,' he assured her.

She couldn't suppress a crooked half-smile at the attitude he was adopting. It was so typical of him, and one of the things that she most admired in his character. He was capable of great anger on occasions, but for the most part he retained a commendable control over his emotions, and was not one to brood unnecessarily over things that could not be changed.

'It's just like you to adopt that attitude,' she said, not reticent to share her thoughts this time. 'But it doesn't make me feel any better. You have come all the way to Dorset for absolutely no purpose. Needless to say, if there is anything I can do to help in the future, you know you've only to ask.'

Half expecting a rebuff, or at the very least a repeat of the warning issued earlier not to interfere, Emily was surprised to discover him regarding her intently once more. Only there was something strangely calculating about his gaze this time.

'I might just hold you to that promise, Miss Emily Stapleton,' he utterly confounded her by responding.

A good night's sleep did precious little to lessen Emily's feelings of guilt, and her mood wasn't improved when she went down to the breakfast parlour to be informed that Sarah had every intention of returning to the Hall the following day. She was tempted to try to persuade her friend to stay at least until the end of the week, but refrained. Sebastian was so right: it didn't do to interfere in others' concerns. Even with the best will in the world she could, indeed, quite easily end by doing more harm than good. Moreover, if what Sebastian suspected was true, and Charles had come to appreciate Sarah's worth, it did not necessarily follow that he would ever come to feel more than a deep affection for her. And didn't she know just how heartbreaking that could be! At least, though, she was in a far better position than Sarah. She wasn't obliged to live in the same house as the man she loved. Which was perhaps just as well, for unless she much mistook the matter, Sebastian, after their ride to the coast yesterday, was under no illusions that something was troubling her deeply.

She gave herself an inward shake. Really she ought to take a leaf out of Sarah's book and display more self-control. After all, almost five years had elapsed since she had broken off their engagement, ample time for the wounds to have healed. They hadn't, though, and she must resign herself to the very real possibility that they never would.

With a reasonable amount of success she managed to shake

off her mood of depression, but as soon as breakfast was over she declined to join Sarah and Budd in the front parlour, where she knew they had every intention of poring over the latest fashions in the *Ladies Journal* to choose a style for Sarah's proposed new gown, and instead took herself back upstairs to her bedchamber in order to don a wide-brimmed straw bonnet and collect her book.

As she descended into the hall once more, she encountered the maid who informed her that the Reverend Mr William Pettigrew had called, and had been shown into the parlour. Although it was by no means unusual for the well-respected clergyman to pay the occasional impromptu visit, Emily strongly suspected that Sarah's presence under the roof was the lure which had brought him here this time, for it was strongly rumoured that Mr Pettigrew, a widower of two years standing, was in search of a helpmeet, and stepmother for his five young children, and he had been paying Sarah marked attention after the Sunday services in recent weeks.

Deciding that, with Budd present, Sarah was suitably chaperoned, and experiencing no desire whatsoever to spend half an hour in the company of that worthy, if faintly lugubrious, gentleman whose conversation was as tedious as his sermons could be on occasions, Emily slipped quietly out of the house. She had only just made herself comfortable in one of the wicker chairs on the terrace, when she detected the sound of hoof beats, and saw two riders, both of whom were instantly recognisable, entering the stable-yard.

Although delighted to see Sir Charles Deverel, she could have wished that he had made the visit unaccompanied. She could have wished too that his eagle-eyed companion had not immediately perceived her, but did her level best to conceal the adverse effect the mere sight of her former fiancé was having on her equilibrium, as he mounted the steps to join her on the terrace.

'You are out and about bright and early today,' she greeted them cheerfully.

'Never keep town hours when in the country,' Sebastian enlightened her, slipping into the chair next to her own without being invited.

Charles, far more formal, remained standing, glancing towards the house. 'Is Sarah about?'

'Yes, she's in the parlour, helping to entertain Mr Pettigrew, no less,' Emily didn't hesitate to enlighten him.

Charles appeared mildly surprised. 'No one in the household is ill, I trust?'

'No, we're all in fine fettle. Mr Pettigrew favours us with the occasional visit. No one could ever accuse him of neglecting his parishioners. And of course he's quite partial to Sarah's company, as you've possibly observed yourself. Or perhaps you haven't,' she went on, desperately striving to suppress a mischievous smile. 'I keep forgetting that you've been away in London recently.'

The look of astonishment on the young Baronet's handsome face wasn't nearly so amusing as the low growl of disapproval emanating from the gentleman seated beside her. Sebastian, at least, was under no illusions as to what she was about.

'Are you suggesting, Miss Stapleton, that he has designs upon Sarah?' Sir Charles asked, appearing decidedly troubled now.

'Who can say?' She shrugged. 'If he has, though, I'm sure they're entirely honourable. He's been a widower for over two years, and it's common knowledge that he's on the lookout for a wife.'

If possible Sir Charles appeared both astounded and appalled now. 'But—but he's an old man, old enough to be her father.'

'Oh, come, sir,' Emily countered, somehow managing to maintain her composure. 'He'd be no more than seven or eight years older than yourself. I'm not suggesting that Sarah has any inclination to marry. But she could do a lot worse than accept Mr Pettigrew if he did ask her. After all, he has a comfortable living, and is well respected.'

This, not surprisingly, only succeeded in intensifying Charles's disturbed look. 'But surely she wouldn't seriously consider accepting him?'

'We've never discussed the matter,' Emily admitted with total honesty. 'All I do know is that Mr Pettigrew holds her in high regard. But I doubt very much that he came here this morning with the intention of proposing marriage, so why do you not join them in the parlour? It was, after all, Sarah who you came to see, was it not?'

He seemed to hesitate for a moment and then, much to Emily's intense amusement, went striding round to the front of the house.

'I shall take leave to inform you, young woman, that you are an unprincipled little baggage,' Sebastian did not hesitate to tell her the instant his friend was out of earshot. 'I thought I told you yesterday not to interfere in matters that were none of your concern.'

Although she quite failed to suppress a gurgle of laughter, Emily was about to refute the suggestion that she was meddling, before something occurred to her that instantly wiped the smile from her face. 'How I conduct myself, Lord Hawkridge, has absolutely nothing whatsoever to do with you.'

He regarded her in silence for a moment, before surprising her by rising to his feet. 'We'll leave that for the present. Come, there is something more important I must discuss with you, and I do not wish to be overheard by anyone in the house.'

Emily found herself automatically complying with the request, and accompanying him to the seclusion of the rose garden, where he reseated himself on the wooden bench placed amidst what in a few short weeks would be a mass of fragrant blooms, before drawing her gently down beside him.

'After I had escorted you home yesterday, I began to consider seriously your willingness to aid me in my endeavours to unmask the fiend who induced my good friend Simon to take his own life,' he began, after staring fixedly at a superb specimen of a rambling rose cascading over the wooden archway. 'And eventually a way you could be of invaluable help occurred to me.'

Emily experienced a frisson of excitement, which went some way to lessen her acute awareness at being in such a romantic setting with the being whom she loved above all others. 'You know I'd do anything to help, though apart from keeping a close watch on that inn, I do not see that there's much I can do.'

Shapely masculine brows snapped together. 'Don't even think of doing such a foolish thing, my girl, otherwise I shall be extremely angry!'

Although bridling at the dictatorial attitude, Emily couldn't forbear a smile. That was precisely the tone which he had always adopted whenever she had contemplated doing something that he considered outrageous. The more she was in his company the more she realised he hadn't changed one iota, and to a great extent she was glad of it. Even so she wished he wouldn't continue to treat her as though she were still some unruly child, and see her for what she now was—a young woman quite capable of making her own decisions.

'I wish you wouldn't glower at me in that odious fashion, Hawk. You put me in mind of that huge stuffed owl Grandpapa keeps in a glass case on the landing.' She was forced silently to own that it was hardly the most flattering comparison she could have made, and yet surprisingly it vanquished the frown and had him ineffectually attempting to suppress a smile. 'How can I be of help?'

He was all at once serious. 'I need a reason…a valid reason to return to this area from time to time. I'm certain in my own mind that the rendezvous will be used again, perhaps not in the immediate future, but certainly at some point. I could, of course, continue to visit Deverel Hall, but to do so at frequent intervals might give rise to—er—speculation, especially where Miss Deverel is concerned, and that is something I wish to avoid at all costs. Yet, at the same time, it cannot be denied that paying frequent visits to one's affianced bride would be the perfect cover.'

Emily was appalled, and didn't attempt to hide the fact. She might not hold Drusilla in the highest regard, but she would never stand by and see her served such a bad turn. 'You are not suggesting, I trust, that you intend to become betrothed to Miss Deverel just so that you can visit Dorsetshire whenever you choose?'

'Oh no,' he assured her, before he dropped his bombshell. 'It is my engagement to you that I wish to announce to the polite world.'

Emily would have been certain that she had misheard, had misunderstood, if his expression had not remained so sincere. A surge of wounded pride sent her almost stiff with rage. That he would even think of asking her to enact such a charade beggared belief. The grounds for their first engagement had been hard enough to withstand. But to suggest a second betrothal, and for such a reason, was the ultimate insult!

'I trust you are not in earnest,' she managed to squeeze through tightly compressed lips, while valiantly suppressing the desire to leave him where he sat, and storm back into the house.

'I assure you, my dear,' he responded in a voice that was as unwavering as his gaze, 'that I have never been more serious about anything in my life. You are…perfect for what I have in mind.'

Reaching out, his lordship clasped one slender hand, and held it securely in his own, thereby denying her the opportunity now to leave without an undignified struggle. 'I trust you, Emily. I know that when…if you agree to my proposal you will see it through to the end.'

If he expected this to appease her, he was swiftly destined to discover his mistake, when she darted him a look of mingled indignation and contempt. 'How can you ask such a thing of me? It is the most outrageous reason for an engagement that I've ever—'

'Please allow me to explain, my dear,' his lordship interrupted gently. 'Then, when you've heard me out, you can give me your decision.' He paused for a moment to study the slender tapering fingers, and felt them trembling slightly, but made no attempt to release his hold. 'Do you remember the other night, when we were in the wood, I mentioned certain diamond necklaces which had been stolen?' He received a curt nod in response. 'They belonged to a set designed by an Italian artist who visited this country during the early years of the last century. The necklaces were supposed to represent the four seasons. The necklace depicting spring was purchased a few years ago by an Italian Count who, it is strongly rumoured, is a descendant of the artist. Two others belonging to the set, as I mentioned before, have been stolen in recent years, and it is believed have found their way into the hands of the aforementioned Count. I suspect he would pay a small fortune to possess the one remaining necklace, depicting winter, to complete the collection.'

Against all the odds Emily found her interest mounting and studied his lordship's intense expression in silence for a moment, before asking, 'And who owns that particular necklace?'

'I do. It has formed part of the family's jewels since it was purchased by my great-grandfather. He presented it to my great-grandmother on the occasion of their wedding. In more recent years, my grandmother and my aunt Augusta never wore the stones, both finding the necklace too constricting about the throat. It has been safely kept in the bank's vault for more than three decades.' His smile was a fraction crooked. 'So, as I am sure you can appreciate, my dear, becoming engaged would grant me the opportunity to display the magnificent adornment to the world at large again.'

'And, more importantly, offer someone the opportunity to attempt to steal it. The proverbial carrot before the donkey… Yes, I do see,' Emily readily conceded, her resolve not to lend herself to such an outrageous escapade being slowly eroded by her innate thirst for adventure, and a resurgence of the desire to help if she could.

His lordship's smile turned strangely secretive. 'I'm so glad that you do,' he murmured, at last raising his eyes, and holding hers captive as easily as he retained the hold on her hand. 'Believe me when I tell you that I do not ask this of you lightly. Naturally I shall ensure you are not put at risk. But it is important you understand, Emily, that the engagement cannot be like our last one, private and known to very few. This time it must be announced to the world. You must come to London, mix with the cream of the *ton,* and be seen wearing the jewels. The person I'm intent on unmasking might be a callous, murdering swine, but he's no fool. The merest suggestion that the engagement is not genuine would, I feel sure, put him on his guard and persuade him not to take the bait.'

Once again he paused to study delicate features now frozen in an expression of deep thought. 'Be under no illusions, my dear, that should you agree to my proposal you will be my affianced bride… So, what is your answer?'

Almost at once he received the response he most desired. 'Yes, of course I'll do it.'

But a moment later Emily did not know what stunned her more—the fact that the fateful words had passed her lips, or the brief, feather-light kiss his lordship pressed against the corner of them before she could avoid the fleeting contact.

'I promise you, you'll not regret it,' Sebastian announced, little realising that she already was.

Rising, he drew her to her feet, and entwined her arm through his, offering her little choice but to accompany him back towards the house. 'I must not tarry. I've much to do during the next few days to prepare for your stay in town. As I'm sure you'll appreciate, you must be suitably chaperoned. I'll leave Dorset tomorrow and pay a visit to Bath. My aunt Hester would make the ideal duenna. As soon as she's settled in town, I'll send my carriage back here. I want Finn to accompany you, and you must travel with a female companion. That young maid of yours should serve the purpose, don't you agree?'

Feeling as if she were being swept away on the tide of his lordship's determination, Emily found herself dumbly agreeing to the dictates of the man who had played such a significant part in her life years ago. It seemed he had every intention of resuming the role, which he proved beyond doubt in the very next breath when he announced his intention of making their betrothal known immediately.

All at once Emily was receiving the heartfelt congratulations of both Sir Charles Deverel and her grandfather, swiftly followed by the Reverend William Pettigrew's assurance that he would consider it an honour to conduct the ceremony if they chose to be married in Dorsetshire. Only Sarah's response seemed slightly muted, the reason for which became clear a short while later, when all the guests had departed and she persuaded Emily to take a further turn about the garden.

'This is all very sudden, is it not?' she suggested gently. 'You broke off your engagement to Lord Hawkridge years ago because you believed he was in love with someone else. What has made you change your mind and agree to marry him now?'

'Simply seeing him again, I suppose. My love for Sebastian has never wavered,' Emily answered, the knowledge that she had spoken no less than the truth salving her conscience.

The swift response won Sarah's immediate approval. 'I can only assume that his lordship's feelings for his cousin must have undergone something of a change in recent years, because he certainly doesn't bear the appearance of a man suffering from unrequited love. Quite the opposite, in fact! And there is that in his eyes when they rest upon you….'

But it isn't love that you imagine you see, only the deep affection of a surrogate brother, Emily longed to retort, but the promise she had made not to reveal the true state of affairs to a living soul forced her to keep her own counsel.

Raising her eyes, Emily gazed across at the wooden bench, where she and Sebastian had sat just a short time before. It really was hard to believe that there could be a more perfect setting to receive a proposal of marriage. At least it would have been perfect, she silently amended, if the proposal had been prompted by love. It was hard to believe, too, that only that morning she had considered herself very fortunate not to be in Sarah's position in as much as she was not forced to reside under the same roof as the man she loved. Yet, very soon her situation would be considerably worse than her friend's. Not only would she be living in the same house as Sebastian, but she would also be living a lie by acting the part of a happily engaged young woman for the benefit of the polite world. Dear Lord! What madness had possessed her to agree to such a thing?

Chapter Seven

Although his lordship had gained the reputation of being a social animal in recent years, few females had been privileged to cross the threshold of his town house in Berkeley Square. Consequently Lady Hester Dawlish, after her arrival in London at the beginning of May, felt singularly honoured to be residing in what was commonly held to be one of the most elegantly appointed bachelor residences in London.

The large drawing-room, decorated in subtle shades of green and cream, was perhaps her favourite room in the house, and she took a moment to cast an appreciative eye over her surroundings before fixing her gaze on the person responsible for selecting the tasteful furnishings.

'emily, I feel sure, will adore staying in this lovely house, Sebastian.'

This pronouncement put an end to his lordship's idle contemplation of the hearth, and brought a crooked, half-smile to his shapely mouth. 'You think so, Aunt? I wish to heaven I were so certain!'

Her astonishment was evident, even before she said, 'Why, my dear, whatever can you mean? Any woman would feel honoured to be mistress here!'

'Ahh, but you forget, Emily is something out of the

common way. Although she might have enjoyed several Seasons in Brighton in recent years, she remains a country girl at heart, and one who, moreover, doesn't take kindly to petty restrictions. That, in part, was the reason why I requested your help,' he admitted, rising to his feet and moving across to the table on which several sparkling decanters stood. 'I was certain, you see, that you would not be forever reminding her of how she should comport herself, but would be there to offer the wisdom of your vast experience if she felt the need of a little guidance. Believe me, the last thing in the world I desire is to see her change into one of those colourless, simpering misses who invade the capital each Season.'

'Do you think there is any likelihood of that?' Lady Hester smiled reminiscently, as her nephew handed her a glass of Madeira and resumed his seat opposite. 'As I recall she was something of an intrepid little thing, forever into mischief, although if my memory serves me correctly she had changed somewhat the last time I saw her. It was the year her mother died, when Caroline and I stayed with you that last time in Hampshire, a few months before your cousin's wedding to Farrington,' she reminded him, and watched as his expression changed dramatically and his mouth set in a hard, uncompromising line.

'Oh, Sebastian! Do you bear me any ill will?' she cried, giving voice to something that had troubled her increasingly over the years.

One shapely brow rose in a quizzical arch. 'Ill will…? Whatever for?'

'For not making the least attempt to dissuade Caroline from marrying that wretched creature.'

'Rid yourself of the notion. It was entirely Caroline's decision to marry him. She was two-and-twenty, hardly a child.' He sighed. 'And I did my best to dissuade her, but to no avail.'

Lady Hester's sigh was equally heartfelt. 'Oh, if only she had waited! Things might have turned out so vastly differently for her.'

'I'm certain they would have done,' his lordship agreed sombrely. 'But we cannot alter the past, and to be truthful it is the future which concerns me now.'

'Yes, yes of course,' she agreed, valiantly attempting to shake off her melancholy. 'I must confess I was rather surprised when you unexpectedly arrived in Bath and informed me of your engagement. But I shouldn't have been. You were always so very fond of Emily, although I'd be less than truthful if I didn't own that there was a time when I foolishly imagined that you might make a match of it with…'

Her words faded as she detected the gleam of wry amusement in her nephew's eyes. 'Yes, well…that is all in the past, and I'm very much looking forward to seeing little Emily again. Has she changed very much?'

'You may decide for yourself,' he said, rising at once to his feet as he detected the sounds of an arrival filtering through from the hall, 'for unless I much mistake the matter she is here at last.'

Sebastian had almost reached the door when it was opened by his butler, Clegg, and Emily appeared in the aperture. Had he been expecting a bright smile and cheerful greeting, then he would have been heartily disappointed, and the slight flinch he clearly detected when he clasped her hand and brushed his lips lightly across her cheek was enough to make him suspect that all was far from well with the young lady who would soon be introduced to the polite world as his future bride.

'I trust you had a comfortable journey?' Retaining his grasp on slender fingers, he led the way across to the sofa where his aunt sat. 'You remember Lady Hester Dawlish, I'm sure.'

'Of course,' she answered promptly. 'Though it has been a while since last I saw you, ma'am.'

Secretly impressed by the very refined manner of the young woman who in her formative years had been something of a mischievous scamp, Lady Hester drew Emily down beside her. 'I was asking Sebastian just before you arrived whether you had altered to any degree, and I can see for myself that you have. You are quite the young lady now!'

'When she chooses to be,' his lordship murmured, thereby earning himself a darkling look from a pair of stunningly lovely violet-blue eyes which only moments before had betrayed a marked degree of unease.

'You are not to tease her, Sebastian, otherwise you will run the risk of her breaking off the engagement before the *ton* has been granted the opportunity to make her delightful acquaintance,' his aunt warned, suppressing a chuckle.

His smile was distinctly tender as he transferred his gaze to the younger woman who, it had to be said, was still looking uncomfortable in her fashionable surroundings. 'Oh, no, she would never do that,' he announced, supremely confident. 'If she were to experience second thoughts she would discuss them with me in private first, not run away like a frightened child and leave me to face the ridicule of the polite world. However, in the event that she is suffering from any premarital nerves,' he added, when Emily appeared unwilling or unable to meet his gaze, 'she must wait until tomorrow to confide in me.'

This drew her head up, as he knew it would, and he couldn't fail to recognise the look of disappointment. 'You are going out, Hawk?'

'Yes, the wretched creature is leaving us to our own devices on your first evening here, my dear,' Lady Hester answered before her nephew could do so. 'He tells me he has an urgent appointment which he simply must keep. But I'm certain we'll go along famously without him. It will grant me the opportunity of showing you about this lovely house, and introducing you to your new abigail.'

'Abigail?' Emily queried, surprise swiftly replacing disappointment, as she gazed across at Sebastian for confirmation. 'I know I insisted that you were accompanied here by your housemaid, Em, but I was assured by Lady Hester that you'd require the attentions of a skilled abigail whilst you remain in town. Don't concern yourself. I'll see that the parlourmaid is returned safely to Dorset in a day or two. And be certain also that I would not desert you so soon after your arrival if I had any other choice.'

'You are not to concern yourself about me. As your aunt remarked, I'm sure we'll go along famously in your absence,' she responded, sounding all at once remarkably cheerful, but Sebastian was not fooled by the feigned display of buoyancy. She was troubled about something, and would not leave it too long before confiding in him, he felt sure.

When she awoke the following morning to the unusual sounds of carriage wheels on cobblestones and street hawkers' shrill cries, Emily was more than ever determined to discuss her grave misgivings which had increased dramatically throughout the previous evening, even though she had enjoyed Lady Hester's pleasant company very much.

After quickly making use of the bell pull, she padded across the room to gaze frowningly down at the street below her window. Although accustomed to living in the country and waking to the sweet sound of birdsong, she had some experience of living in towns and cities, but the streets in neither Bath nor Brighton were as busy or as noisy as those here in the capital. Throughout the night her sleep had been disturbed by the rumble of carriages passing below her window and by the raucous shouts from revellers, out enjoying the many pleasures London had to offer. No doubt she would grow accustomed in time to a city that never slept, if she remained here long enough.

The click of the doorhandle caught her attention and she turned to see Skinner, the female who had been engaged as her personal maid, entering the room. In stark contrast to the soft, feminine surroundings, Skinner was a tall, angular woman, with a thin, harsh-featured face. Yet, as Emily had discovered the evening before, when Skinner had appeared in the bedchamber in order to help her dress for dinner, looks were deceptive, for although the maid wasn't given to smiling much, there was nothing morose in her nature, and she was undeniably skilful in her work.

If she was surprised by the early summons, she certainly betrayed no sign of it, and merely enquired whether she should arrange breakfast to be brought up on a tray.

'Good heavens, no!' Emily responded, appalled at the mere thought. 'I'm not ill. I never eat breakfast in bed, or rarely so.'

There was just a suspicion of twitch at one corner of the maid's thin-lipped mouth. 'In that case, miss, I'll ring for one of the housemaids to fetch you hot water. I trust you slept well?' she added, after giving the bell pull two sharp tugs.

'As well as I'm ever likely to while I remain under this roof, Skinner,' Emily responded drily. 'I'm afraid I'm accustomed to country hours and always rise early, though how anyone can manage to sleep in the mornings here in the capital defeats me.'

'Yes, miss, it is noisy. I'm not quite used to it myself yet.'

Emily didn't attempt to hide her surprise. 'Are you not from London, then, Skinner?'

'I was born here, miss, but left many years ago. I've been living in Bath for the past twenty odd years.'

That explained a great deal, for Emily had wondered, when he had informed her that she was to have her own personal maid, just how Sebastian had gone about acquiring the services of an abigail. She didn't doubt for a moment that he was capable of doing most things, but even he was unlikely to know what skills were essential in a good lady's maid.

'Would I be right in thinking that it was Lady Hester who engaged you, Skinner?'

'That's right, miss. She and my late mistress were good friends. She didn't require my services herself, but after my mistress passed away, she very kindly offered to help me obtain a new position. I was that relieved when she told me she'd found me a new post.'

Emily hadn't the heart to tell her that the position wasn't likely to be of long duration. Although she would attain her majority in the not too distant future, she was very well aware that she wouldn't come into her inheritance until she attained the age of five-and-twenty. She could of course ask her grand-father to pay Skinner's wages, and she didn't doubt for a moment that he would do so. But did she really require the services of a skilled abigail, living as she did for the most part a quiet life in the country? Moreover, would Skinner be content to remain all year round buried in rural Dorsetshire?

Undoubtedly she would discover the answers to these questions in the fullness of time. What concerned her at present was preparing herself for the day ahead, which she set about doing the instant a pitcher of hot water arrived in her room.

'I must say, Skinner, I do like the way you arrange my hair,' Emily remarked, quick to offer praise where it was due.

'Ahh, bless you, miss. It isn't hard to dress hair like yours. You're an abigail's dream, so you are! I could see that the instant I first set eyes on you.'

Touched by the compliment, Emily cast the maid a shy smile through the dressing-table mirror, before rising to her feet. The more she chatted away to Skinner the more she liked her. But it would not do to become too attached, she reminded herself, at least not until she knew precisely what lay ahead in her immediate future, and there was only one way she was destined to discover that.

'Do you happen to know if either Lady Hester or his lordship has risen yet?'

'As a rule, Lady Hester doesn't leave her room until well after midday, miss, and always takes breakfast in bed. His lordship too keeps town hours.'

Successfully concealing her annoyance, Emily slipped a

light shawl about her shoulders. 'In that case it looks as if I'll be eating the first meal of the day alone for the duration of my stay in town.'

This prediction, however, turned out to be grossly inaccurate, as Emily discovered for herself when she entered the breakfast parlour a few minutes later to discover his lordship, surprisingly, already seated at the table, working his way through a substantial pile of ham and eggs.

'Great heavens! I didn't expect to see you here, Hawk!' Emily said by way of a greeting, as she slipped into the chair beside his own, and immediately helped herself to the contents of the coffee-pot. 'I was led to believe that you were something of a slug-a-bed these days.'

With the merest nod of his head, his lordship dismissed the footman before his irrepressible companion had an opportunity to utter any further outrageous remarks within his servant's hearing.

'I shall take leave to inform you, young woman, that you betray a sad want of respect for your future husband. Most gentlemen wouldn't hesitate to beat some manners into you.'

Sebastian regarded her keenly, certain in his own mind that it was not the idle threat which had wiped away that delightful smile. 'What's wrong, Em? Are you having second thoughts? I knew there was something troubling you the moment you arrived yesterday.'

Not surprised by this admission, Emily reached across the table for a freshly baked roll, before favouring his lordship with an earnest look. She had never been wholly successful in concealing her troubles from him. Certainly nothing could be gained by attempting to do so now, even though just his presence seemed to have eased much of her former disquiet— most of it, yes, but not quite all.

'I'm not comfortable with the pretence, Hawk,' she began softly. 'Deception has never come easily to me. As you very well know, I make a poor liar. So as you must appreciate I find this spurious engagement faintly distasteful. I have found it no easy task to maintain the pretence thus far, especially not after the announcement appeared in the newspapers, and the house was invaded by an endless stream of well-wishers, and Grandpapa took to addressing me in front of all and sundry as Lady Hawk.'

The rumble of laughter was not precisely the reaction she had expected from the man who had always shown a deal of understanding for the feelings of others. 'You might find it amusing, but I most certainly do not!' she snapped, applying her knife to the breakfast-roll with unnecessary force and sending showers of crumbs in various directions across the table.

'I'm sorry, sweetheart. But the sobriquet does suit you, you know.'

'And how am I supposed to take that?' she demanded, torn between amusement and indignation, whilst casting a measured glance at the faintly aquiline feature on his ruggedly attractive face. 'You're not suggesting, I trust, that I too have a great beak of a nose?'

'I'll have you know, young lady, that the aristocratic line of the Hawkridge proboscis is much envied by all discerning members of the *ton*.'

He could see at once that she was not to be humoured, or sidetracked from the matter which concerned her most, and temporarily abandoned his breakfast to reach for her hand. 'If you honestly feel you cannot continue with the engagement, you only have to say so, Em. You should know me well enough to be sure that I would never force you to carry on if your present situation is abhorrent to you.'

Emily gazed down at the shapely hand reassuringly covering hers and felt her misgivings slowly ebbing. The truth of the matter was that, now he was with her to offer that un-failing comfort and support which he had so often given in the past, she almost felt as if she could play her part to the full.

'It isn't that exactly, Hawk. I want to help all I can,' she assured him. 'It's just…it's just that I wish there were some other way. I do so hate all the pretence. I realised yesterday evening that even your aunt believes the engagement genuine. How on earth do you manage to reconcile it with your conscience?'

His lips curled into a semblance of a smile. 'That's easy, Em. I simply do not look upon our engagement as false.' His smile widened at her look of astonishment. 'We were engaged to be married once before, remember? I didn't enter into that betrothal lightly either.'

'No, you did so because you felt obliged to agree to a dying woman's request.' Resentment like bile rose in her throat, leaving a bitter taste in her mouth. 'My mother should never have asked it of you, Hawk. It was the only thing she ever did of which I felt ashamed. She placed you in the most invidious position.'

'She did indeed,' he agreed, as the hand beneath his was pulled away sharply. 'But not for the reason you seem to suppose.' He regarded her in silence for a moment, easily recognising the reproachful glint in her eyes. 'Would I be correct in thinking that during these past years you have nurtured the belief that your mother asked me to marry you?'

Emily regarded him no less keenly. 'Do you deny it?'

'Most emphatically! It was entirely my own decision. I considered it far more agreeable than the alternative.'

For the first time doubts began to assail her. Could she possibly have been mistaken? Might he have truly wished to marry her? she wondered, experiencing a tiny glimmer of hope. 'I do not perfectly understand you, Hawk. What are you trying to tell me?'

He rose at once to his feet, and went over to the window. He seemed suddenly to have grown tense, his shoulders rigid as though bearing a great burden.

'Your mother knew she was dying,' he began softly. 'She

informed me, shortly before you returned home for Easter, that the doctor had told her she would live for a few months, but certainly no more. Her only concern was for you. She was fond of her father-in-law, but didn't consider him a suitable guardian, so she asked me to assume the role.'

He swung round to find her staring levelly across at him, her expression one of stunned disbelief, rather than anger. 'As you may or may not remember, my aunt Hester had brought Caroline for a visit. Such were my grave misgivings that I foolishly confided in them both. I was not five-and-twenty at the time. Too young, I thought, to be saddled with the responsibilities of a guardian, but not too young to become a husband.'

Emma recalled that particular Easter with disturbing clarity. How could she forget it! It was then, when she had called at his house the day before she was due to return to the seminary, that she had overheard the conversation between Sebastian and his cousin taking place in the library.

'Caroline, please reconsider. Farrington is not the man for you.' Sebastian's voice, clear and carrying, had filtered through to the hall, and Emily, about to enter the drawing-room in order to pay her respects to his aunt, had lingered to hear Caroline's reply, 'I do not believe half the stories I've been told about him are true. Besides, Papa is not opposed to the match.'

'Your father isn't a well man, Caroline. He wishes to see you comfortably established,' Sebastian had responded, a hint of desperation edging his voice. 'There is another who loves you… You must know that.'

'Yes, I do know. But he is not in a position to offer for me, and is far too honourable a man to go back on his word.'

There had been a slight pause before Sebastian had spoken again. 'I care for you deeply, Caroline. I've always loved you. If nothing else, at least promise me that you will take a little time before finally consenting to Farrington's proposal.'

Emily had been unable to remain to hear more. The servant who had admitted her to the house had unexpectedly returned, and rather than be caught brazenly eavesdropping, she had whisked herself into the drawing-room.

Sadly, she had never been able to forget that conversation, or the heartfelt dejection she had easily discerned in Sebastian's voice. That he loved his cousin, and had been deeply upset over the thought of her marrying Sir Courtney Farrington had never been in doubt. What she had never understood until now was why Sebastian had not been in a position to offer for Caroline at that time. After what she had learned this morning, however, the reason was crystal clear: he had already pledged his word to a dying woman to marry her daughter, and was far too honourable a man to go back on his word.

With that glimmer of hope now well and truly extinguished, Emily reached for her cup, her hand not quite steady, and hurriedly sampled its contents while mulling over what she had learned. Even if Sebastian had not decided to marry her out of some misguided sense of duty, could he have succeeded in persuading his cousin to change her mind and marry him instead? Had he ever attempted to do so weeks later, after he had been released from his obligations? These were questions that would continue to torment her, but she felt that now was not the time to attempt to discover the answers.

'I must say, Emily, you've taken it rather better than I could have hoped,' he announced, surprising her somewhat. His smile was clearly one of approval, as he resumed his seat beside her. 'I expected at the very least a strong rebuke for keeping my guardianship secret from you. But I thought it was better you learned about it from me than from my aunt. I wasn't one hundred per cent certain that she wouldn't let it slip at some point during your stay here in town.'

Mistakenly, he had taken her silence for docile acceptance of his authority over her and, glad of the opportunity to channel her thoughts in a new direction, she didn't hesitate to set him straight on the matter. 'Disabuse yourself of the notion that I'm overjoyed at the state of affairs.' She paused to reduce the contents of her cup still further, while trying to come to terms with his guardianship and striving to suppress the belated feeling of strong resentment. 'I suppose during these past years Grandpapa has always deferred to you, gaining your consent before agreeing to my requests?'

He wasn't foolish enough to deny it. 'Not that there were too many occasions. I was happy enough to allow you to do more or less as you wished and spend each summer with your mother's sister and her family in Brighton. I've done my utmost to interfere in your life as little as possible.'

If he had expected this admission to soothe any remaining ruffled feathers, he could not have been more wrong. If anything Emily's infuriation increased fourfold, not so much with his lordship as with herself for being such a naïve little simpleton as not to have suspected the truth long since. At the very least she ought to have realised during his recent short stay in Dorsetshire, when she had discovered he had been responsible for employing Finn, that his interest in her well-being was more than just casual.

Striving to be fair, Emily could quite understand why her mother had chosen Sebastian for the role of guardian. Her mother had been present at Sebastian's birth, and had watched him grow into a good-natured and sensible young man. She had admired the way he had dealt with life's cruel blows— the death of his mother, followed by his father's demise two years later, when Sebastian had just attained his majority. She had been full of praise for the way he had shouldered heavy responsibilities at such a young age, running his house and lands, and betraying a keen knowledge of good husbandry by attaining high yields from his acres.

It had to be admitted too that not many options had been open to the late Laura Stapleton. She had been, as Sebastian himself had remarked, immensely fond of her father-in-law, but had not been blind to his faults. An intensely private man, he had hardly been the ideal person to take charge of a lively sixteen-year-old girl. Neither had her sister Agnes who, with eight offspring of her own to rear, had had more than enough on her hands without the added burden of taking care of her orphaned niece.

Yes, Emily could appreciate why her mother had approached Sebastian. What she quite failed to understand was why her mother had chosen to keep his guardianship secret, and wasn't slow to seek the answer from the one person who might possibly know.

'I'm not certain, Emily,' he admitted. 'When next I visited your mother, shortly after you had returned to the seminary, we discussed the matter further, and I assured her that I honestly considered marriage preferable. She was overjoyed, openly confessing that it was what she had always hoped for. When next you saw her, she had deteriorated considerably, and was under the influence of laudanum for much of the time. And when you agreed to the match, I suppose she considered there was no reason to tell you that she had appointed me as your guardian.'

Yes, that was possibly the truth of it, Emily acknowledged silently, while vividly recalling that memorable occasion when she had acquiesced, in Sebastian's presence, to her mother's dearest wish. Undoubtedly she would have kept her word and gone through with the wedding if her mother had lived.

'In my arrogance it never occurred to me at the time that you didn't truly wish to marry me, and that you'd only agreed to oblige your mother and give her peace of mind,' he said, his voice surprisingly gentle and laced with a wealth of understanding. 'Quite naturally you considered that your mother's death absolved you from the promise you had made.'

'Yes, I did,' she freely admitted. 'I felt I ought to consider the feelings of those still living.'

'Not mine, Emily, you didn't,' he countered, his voice still gentle, yet edged now with faint reproach. 'I would quite happily have gone through with the ceremony.'

Yes, prompted by obligation, not love, she thought, but said, 'I dare say you would have done. But as I recall you didn't attempt to persuade me to change my mind when I called to see you that day.'

'True enough. And I have frequently asked myself why I didn't,' he astounded her by divulging. 'But at the time I considered your reasons fully justified. You were too young. Had you been eighteen or nineteen it would have been a different matter entirely.'

Listening to him anyone might be forgiven for supposing that he would have been quite happy to marry her, Emily decided. But how could this be so when he had loved Caroline?

'Well, think yourself lucky that I did change my mind.' Her gurgle of laughter sounded distinctly forced even to her own ears. 'Your guardianship has lasted a few years only, and will soon be over. Had we married you'd have been tied to me for life.'

He held her gaze with the sheer intensity of her own. 'Believe me, my dear, I would not consider that a hardship. But enough now of the past!' he continued with an abrupt change of tone, sounding almost businesslike. 'It is the future which concerns me, and whether you intend to remain a guest in this house?'

How could she refuse him? It was little enough to ask in recompense for what he had done for her—giving up the woman he loved in order to fulfil a dying woman's most ardent wish, she reflected, before echoing the answer she had given over two weeks ago in her grandfather's rose garden.

'I cannot tell you how much that relieves my mind,' he admitted. 'I did not relish the prospect of sending out notes cancelling our little party.'

'Party?' Emily experienced an unpleasant foreboding of

trouble to come, which the sudden wicked gleam in his eyes did absolutely nothing to alleviate. 'What party?'

Shapely brows rose in surprise. 'Why, the party to celebrate our engagement, of course! I felt sure my aunt would have mentioned it. She's spoken of nothing else since she arrived at this house, planning everything down to the last detail.'

'Well, she didn't,' Emily responded, annoyed with herself for not considering the possibility that the engagement would be celebrated in some way. 'It's reasonable to suppose that your aunt might have thought that I already knew.' She shrugged, quickly resigning herself to the ordeal ahead. 'I dare say I'll contrive to cope as it's only to be a small affair. But I shall need your full support, Hawk,' she warned. 'I'm no expert at dissembling.'

'Perhaps this might help.' From the pocket of his fashionable jacket he drew out a small, square box, and flicked open the lid to reveal a sapphire-and-diamond betrothal ring, nestling in a bed of dark-blue velvet. Then reaching across the table, he slid the ring down the third finger of her left hand.

'I hope you like it,' he prompted when all she did was to gaze down at the glinting stones in awestruck silence. 'We can always change it if you would prefer something else.'

'Oh, no…it's just perfect,' she assured him, finding her voice at last. 'But—but is it really necessary, Seb? It must have cost a great deal of money.'

'The Hawkridge males have for generations been renowned for showering their womenfolk with expensive trinkets.' His smile was distinctly tender, but there was no mistaking the earnest expression in his eyes. 'No matter what happens, Emily, that is yours to keep. And be assured that I shall not be the one to break off this engagement.'

She didn't doubt for a moment that he meant every word, and that he did look upon the engagement as genuine. Pray God that she did not foolishly come to do so, for the outcome for her could be nothing other than heart-rending!

Chapter Eight

A few hours later, when she left the house in the company of Lady Hester on the first of what was destined to be numerous visits to the fashionable shops during her stay in town, Emily was still trying to accustom herself to wearing that very special adornment on her left hand. The lady seated beside her in the carriage, being something of an expert when it came to judging the value of precious gems, had given an envious sigh when first setting eyes on the exquisite ring, and had subsequently passed some remark which had given Emily every reason to suppose that Sebastian's aunt was under the impression that her nephew had travelled into the West Country the previous month for the sole purpose of proposing marriage.

'I'm so pleased that you have taken to wearing your betrothal ring,' she had said in the next breath. 'I was hoping to see it yesterday. No doubt you chose to keep it somewhere safely hidden among your baggage during your journey. Very understandable! One cannot be too careful these days.'

What Lady Hester had gone on to reveal next had puzzled Emily even more. 'I must confess your engagement came as a slight surprise to me, even though I knew it would be only a matter of time before Sebastian asked you again. All the same, I did think he would wait a few more weeks, until you'd attained your majority. After all, the dear boy has waited almost five years.'

Frowning, Emily stared out of the carriage window, mulling over what her companion had said earlier. She could only assume that Sebastian must have given the impression that he'd had every intention of asking for her hand a second time. Lady Hester had been among the few who had known about the betrothal years before, and perhaps had quite naturally assumed, given that he had betrayed no obvious interest in any other female during the intervening years, that Sebastian had retained a *tendre* for his late godmother's daughter. Perhaps Sebastian had encouraged her in this belief in the hope that she'd reveal his long-standing devotion to the polite world at large. Yes, that must surely be it, Emily decided. After all, he had stressed that the engagement must appear genuine and in his aunt, whose acquaintance in town was large, he would have acquired a staunch, if unwitting, ally.

'You're very quiet, my dear. I trust you're not fatigued?' Lady Hester, always considerate to the needs of others, appeared concerned. 'I did hear, through my maid Watchet, that you didn't sleep too well and were up very early this morning.'

Undeniably the servant had been well named! Emily mused, before saying, 'No, I'm not tired, ma'am. I'm reliably informed that I shall very quickly accustom myself to town hours. And the noise.'

'Oh, dear me, yes. I did suggest to Sebastian that you might prefer a bedchamber at the rear of the house, but he wished you to be given that particular room because the decor matched your eyes. What a romantic the dear boy is! Why, he even chose a sapphire for your engagement ring!'

'Yes, he can even surprise me on occasions,' Emily admitted, smiling wryly as certain vivid recollections filtered through her mind. 'He was not always so romantically inclined, believe me, and was wont to treat me like some unruly young sister in dire need of schooling.'

Lady Hester frankly laughed. 'I dare say you will continue to find him domineering on occasions. It is in his nature, I'm afraid. And it has been my experience that a gentleman's character does not change to any significant degree after he has married. But you will never find his love wanting. I might not have visited the capital for several years, but I hear what goes on. Sebastian has been pursued relentlessly since coming into the title, but his devotion to you has never wavered.'

Oh, Lord! The poor woman honestly believed what she was saying. Emily only just succeeded in stifling a groan. It was simply dreadful. Somehow, though, she was going to have to accustom herself to such talk, and quickly, for she very much feared she was destined to hear a great deal more of the same while she remained in town.

Conscious that her companion's eyes were firmly fixed in her direction, Emily was able to utter the sentiment which was so obviously expected in the knowledge that it was not a lie. 'And be assured, ma'am, that my love for your nephew has never been found wanting. But I was far too young to marry when he first asked me.'

'I quite agree, my dear,' Lady Hester responded, with an understanding smile. 'I do not doubt Sebastian would have proved a very gentle and patient husband for the most part. But what you say is perfectly true. I happen to know that he thought so himself.'

As Sebastian had admitted as much that morning, this came as no very real surprise to Emily. What very much concerned her was what else he might have said to his aunt, and she made a mental note to see him alone at the first available opportunity. If they were to give a convincing performance of a happily engaged couple, then it was essential that their stories corresponded. In the meantime, she thought it might be wise to turn the conversation in a completely different direction, and did so by enquiring precisely where they were bound.

'The premises of one Madame Claudette Pérot for the final fittings of our ball gowns,' Lady Hester enlightened her. 'Anyone who is anyone has a gown made by Claudette. She is considered by many to be the foremost *modiste* in London.'

'*Our* gowns, ma'am?' Emily enquired, eyeing her companion with acute suspicion.

'Why, yes, my dear!' Lady Hester's expression betrayed a degree of smug satisfaction. 'My nephew, the dear boy, thinks of everything. Before he left Dorsetshire he even had the forethought to request your grandfather's housekeeper to furnish him with a list of your exact measurements. It was a simple matter then for me to consult with Claudette and select the style appropriate for your gown. Sebastian insisted that no expense be spared. You will look positively dazzling for your engagement ball.'

Emily easily managed to thrust aside thoughts of her possible appearance and concentrate on more important issues. 'But I understood that it was to be just a small affair.'

Lady Hester appeared nonplussed for a moment, then shrugged. 'Well, I suppose it will be when compared to some of the other events taking place this Season. But I consider three hundred guests a very sensible number. Any more and it would be in danger of being considered a sad crush.'

Small party, indeed! Emily inwardly fumed. Sebastian, the wretch, had deliberately misled her! Unfortunately common sense decreed that, as there was little she could do to change things at this late stage, she would be obliged to accept matters with as good a grace as she could muster.

'I suppose I shall require a new dress for such an occasion,' she was forced reluctantly to concede. 'But I have brought several evening gowns with me from Dorsetshire, so shan't require any more,' she added, and was puzzled by Lady Hester's slightly sheepish expression, until they arrived at their destination a few minutes later, and the reason behind the surprising look became crystal clear.

Honoured by the modiste's undivided attention, Emily was immediately ushered into a changing room where she spent some considerable time being fastened into an array of exquisite garments, which included four day dresses, three walking dresses, with matching accessories, and three evening gowns, one of which was none other than the exquisite creation of ivory silk and lace that she was to wear for the ball. At first Emily assumed that she was merely being offered the opportunity to view the modiste's extensive range of apparel, until it occurred to her that all the dresses were exactly her size and were receiving only the finest of adjustments under the modiste's highly critical eye.

Although having been blessed to live a very comfortable life thus far, Emily was neither avaricious nor extravagant, and in more recent years, since undertaking the day-to-day running of her grandfather's household, she had learned the benefits of practising economy, and was impatient of any form of wastefulness. Thus, she could be nothing other than appalled by the needless expense to which Sebastian had gone in order to deck her out in the latest fashions for what was likely to be a very short period in town, and was quick to air her views the instant she and Sebastian's highly satisfied aunt left the shop.

'But, my dear, one must dress!' Lady Hester protested, betraying a quaint snobbery in her nature. 'Watchet informed me, after helping your new maid unpack your things yesterday, that there is nothing in your wardrobe of which you need be ashamed, and that your evening gowns will do very well for the small, informal parties we will attend. But for the grand occasions you must be arrayed in the very best. After all, you are betrothed to Lord Hawkridge. My nephew has his reputation to consider.'

Clearly Lady Hester was one of those females who

believed that a lady could never have too many gowns, and had undoubtedly throughout her life been used to spending large sums in order to deck herself out in the prevailing mode. Which was perhaps understandable in the circumstances, Emily decided, striving to be fair, for Lady Hester Dawlish's parents had been Earl and Countess of Avonmore, and she had, therefore, been accustomed from birth to command every luxury money could buy. Emily could not recall Sebastian's mother being quite so extravagant, but then the late Lady Clarissa Hawkridge had been content living a quiet life in the country for the most part, well away from the fashionable throng. Furthermore it did not automatically follow that siblings held corresponding views or were in any way similar in character.

'By the by, my dear,' Lady Hester remarked, catching the eye of Sebastian's coachman who was awaiting them a little further down the street. 'How are you getting along with your new maid?'

Another needless expense, Emily thought, but decided to keep her opinion to herself this time, and merely said that she and Skinner were rubbing along together famously.

'I'm so glad. She was with her last employer for over twenty years, so I did wonder how she would take to caring for a new—'

Curious to know what had induced her companion to break off mid-sentence, Emily turned her eyes in the direction of Lady Hester's suddenly startled gaze to see a female alighting from a fashionable carriage. Then she noticed an equally astonished expression take possession of that female's gaunt face, when the woman raised her dark eyes and saw them standing a mere few feet away. However, several seconds passed before Emily realised that she was not staring at a perfect stranger.

Sebastian's cousin, the former Caroline Westcotte, would have been the first to admit that she had scant claim to beauty.

Her finest attribute by far was a pair of warm, brown eyes. Unfortunately even this striking feature had never quite atoned for a long nose, over-wide mouth, and hair of an unremarkable brown. What Sebastian's cousin had possessed in abundance, however, was vitality and charm, characteristics which had ensured that whatever social occasion she had happened to be attending, no one else present would ever have forgotten that she had been there.

There was precious little evidence of vivacity now in the forlorn-looking creature who moved listlessly across the pavement towards them. Clearly marriage and motherhood had taken their toll. She had lost considerable weight, there was even a suspicion of a stoop about her thin shoulders, and the sparkle had completely faded from her eyes, leaving them dull and lifeless.

'Why, this is a pleasant surprise!' There was precious little conviction in Caroline's voice and her smile was decidedly false. 'Courtney informed me that you were in town, Aunt Hester. Unfortunately I contracted a chill and have not been too well of late, otherwise I would have called to see you.' Dark eyes flickered in Emily's direction. 'And Miss Stapleton…I should never have recognised you had I passed you in the street. My, how you have changed!'

It took every ounce of self-control Emily possessed not to respond in kind. Fortunately Lady Hester intervened, thereby sparing her the necessity of formulating some innocuous response.

'How long have you been in town, Caroline?'

'Oh, just a few days. I'm afraid I've become very dull company, preferring the peace and quiet of the country, but Courtney insisted that I come up to town for the party.'

'And have you brought little Alicia with you? I should so love to see her again.'

Mention of her daughter's name brought a flicker of animation back into Caroline's mien. 'I'm afraid not, Aunt.

Courtney thought it better to leave her in the country. And he's right, of course. She's only just turned three, and the journey would have been too much for her.'

'Yes, perhaps you're wise,' Lady Hester agreed. 'I should dearly love to see her, though. I haven't seen her since her christening. Nor you for that matter.'

Emily certainly didn't miss the note of reproach in Lady Hester's voice, and seemingly neither did Caroline, if her faintly uncomfortable expression was any indication. Emily also noticed the decidedly wary glance Caroline cast up at the surly, thickset individual seated beside her coachman before she said rather hurriedly, 'Yes, we must arrange a visit, Aunt Hester, perhaps later in the year when you've returned to Bath. And now you must excuse me. I have an appointment with the dressmaker, and I believe Madame Pérot does not take kindly to being kept waiting.'

Lady Hester made no attempt to prolong the interview, but the instant she and Emily were comfortably settled in his lordship's carriage, and were heading back to Berkeley Square, she was quick to express her shock at her niece's vastly altered appearance. 'Furthermore I gained the distinct impression that she would have avoided us altogether if she could possibly have done so.'

Emily could well understand why Lady Hester felt so hurt. She, with the help of Sebastian's mother, had been virtually responsible for bringing Caroline up, after their sister had died shortly after giving birth to her only child. Caroline's father, a partner in a trading company, had travelled extensively after his wife's demise, and had been happy to leave the rearing of his baby daughter in the capable hands of his sisters-in-law. Caroline had spent several weeks each year in Hampshire with Sebastian's family, but for the most part had remained in Lady Hester's tender care. Having had no children of her own, Lady Hester had naturally enough eventually come to look upon her deceased sister's child as her own daughter.

'Am I correct in thinking that Sir Courtney's home is in Derbyshire, ma'am?' Emily enquired when her companion, uncharacteristically, fell silent and took to staring broodingly through the carriage window.

'Yes. And I do appreciate that it is a great distance to travel. But that is hardly reason enough never to make the effort to visit me in Bath, nor invite me to stay with her.' Lady Hester's sigh was clearly heartfelt. 'I was determined, after she married, not to interfere in her life. She knows where I am if she should have need of me.'

'Evidently, ma'am, you feel that she does.'

'You saw her, my dear!' Lady Hester did not attempt to conceal her dismay. 'Have you ever seen anyone so altered? She is not even seven-and-twenty and yet looks nearer forty!'

Emily had no wish to add to her companion's disquiet, but felt compelled to agree with this. 'But you heard her say yourself that she had been unwell of late,' she added.

'Pshaw!' Lady Hester scoffed, clearly revealing that the attempt to console her a little had singularly failed. 'It isn't a simple chill which has left her looking so haggard. It is much more likely to be a marriage which has failed miserably.' She shook her head sadly. 'Rumours reached me, of course, but I chose to ignore them, simply because Caroline's letters to me were always so cheerful. Furthermore some women are content to look the other way when their husbands stray.'

'You are suggesting that Sir Courtney Farrington has sought solace out of wedlock, ma'am?' Emily prompted, when her companion appeared disconcerted, as though she had sullied innocent ears with her revelations. 'I am not so naïve as to suppose that all men, once married, remain faithful to their wives and do not take a mistress.'

'If there had been only one! Farrington's name has been linked with a string of notorious women since his union with my niece. And there have been other unsavoury rumours about him over the years.' Lady Hester gave vent to a further heartfelt sigh. 'Perhaps I should have tried harder to dissuade Caroline from marrying him, but she had attained the age of two-and-twenty, hardly a chit out of the schoolroom, and she was intent on wedding him. And I must confess I always thought he was more interested in Caroline than her money. But I was wrong. I should have paid more heed to Sebastian and others who tried to warn me about Farrington's true character. It was a grave error of judgement on my part too that I didn't attempt to persuade Caroline to wait a while longer before tying the knot. Then she would have been in a position to wed one who really cared for her, and not just the money she was destined to inherit from her father.'

Emily experienced the pain of guilt, far more acutely searing than the stab she had suffered that morning. If she had known before, during the last Easter she had spent with her mother, she would not have hesitated to absolve Sebastian from all obligations then. At least he would have been given more time to attempt to win the woman he loved. Whether or not he would have succeeded in persuading Caroline to change her mind and marry him was anybody's guess, but at least he would have been granted ample opportunity to try.

Although Lady Hester, seemingly wrapped in her own unhappy thoughts, uttered nothing further throughout the remainder of the journey back to the house, Emily was convinced that the subject of Caroline would be raised again before the day was out, and sure enough, when she entered the parlour that evening, half an hour before dinner was due to be served, she discovered her chaperon and guardian with their heads together, deep in conversation.

They broke off abruptly the instant she entered the room, but Lady Hester didn't hesitate to enlighten her as to the topic under discussion. Nor was she slow to request Emily to corroborate her description of Caroline's vastly altered appearance.

'She certainly looked far from well,' Emily felt obliged to

concede, after accepting the glass of Madeira his lordship held out to her and his invitation to sit beside him on the sofa.

There was absolutely nothing in Sebastian's demeanour to suggest that he was in the least dismayed by what his aunt had revealed. All the same Emily was well aware that he was remarkably adept at concealing his feelings when he chose, and was possibly doing so now in an attempt not to add to his aunt's obvious concerns by betraying his own.

'Have you not seen Caroline yourself recently, Hawk?'

'No, my sweet life, I have not seen her since I attended her wedding to Farrington here in the capital, although we used to correspond from time to time,' he disclosed, before pausing to sample the contents of his glass. 'I'm rather surprised she decided to accept my invitation to the party, and came up to town. She's never been back since her wedding. Farrington himself has been here for several weeks.'

Lady Hester gave vent to what sounded suspiciously like a snort. 'Ha! When is he not in town?'

'He seems to spend a good deal of time here, certainly,' Sebastian concurred, smiling wryly. 'Surprisingly enough, even with his somewhat unsavoury reputation, he is invited everywhere. But then, it was ever so, was it not, Hester?'

'Oh, yes, for all your protestations to the contrary, I know you blame me for permitting the marriage to go ahead, Sebastian. And, of course, you're quite right.'

'You are in error, my dear,' he reassured her gently. 'You may have chaperoned Caroline during her Seasons in town, but she was no longer your responsibility. Her father, I clearly recall, had returned to England the year before the marriage took place, and did nothing to prevent the match.'

'He was dying, Sebastian,' his aunt reminded him. 'You know he wished to see his daughter settled. He was suffering from the same wasting illness as Emily's poor mother.'

Emily felt unaccountably moved as Sebastian reached out to clasp her hand and retain it gently in his own. Only on his broad shoulder had she wept bitterly, after her mother had passed away, even though two weeks later she had refused to marry him. Seemingly he was no less willing to offer comfort now. 'I did not realise that, ma'am,' Emily admitted, 'although I did read his obituary in the newspaper. It was very sad that he never saw his granddaughter.'

'It was indeed,' she agreed. 'And as I mentioned to you earlier, I have only ever seen the child once.'

'And I not at all,' Sebastian put in. 'But if Caroline wishes to ostracise herself from the members of her family it is entirely her own affair. If on the other hand she ever feels the need of our support, she need only ask. If you take my advice, ma'am, you'll let well alone, and not plague her with visits during her stay in town.'

If Emily had not known better she might have supposed from Sebastian's response that Caroline's well-being was of precious little interest to him, but she knew this could not be so. She very much suspected that he still retained a deep affection for his cousin. Unfortunately he was hardly in a position to reveal those feelings, especially not at the present time when he was striving to convince all and sundry that he had succeeded in persuading the girl he had always wished to wed to take the matrimonial plunge.

On the other hand, it was conceivable that he did not wish to interfere in his cousin's affairs, and was attempting by this display of indifference to dissuade his aunt from doing so, simply because he feared more harm than good might result. Only time would tell if he had been successful in influencing his aunt. And perhaps in due time the reason for the dramatic change in Caroline's appearance and personality might also become clear.

This of course did nothing to ease Lady Hester's obvious anxiety at this juncture, so Emily sought some topic which might improve that concerned lady's state of mind, at least in the short term, and swiftly hit upon the very thing.

'Of course everyone changes over the years, ma'am. I know I have.'

'Indeed you have, my dear,' Lady Hester agreed, unwittingly taking the bait. 'You used to be something of a hoyden as I recall, forever into mischief. But look at you now, quite the young lady! Your dear mama was very wise to persuade you to spend a year at that seminary in Bath.'

'Indeed she was, ma'am,' Emily concurred, inclined to be more amused than anything else by this severe description of her former behaviour. 'Truth to tell, though, she forced my hand, as you might say…gave me no choice.'

This admission induced the man seated beside her to regard her keenly, a hint of scepticism in his expression. 'Laura forced you to go? I don't believe it! Your mother simply doted on you, was far too lenient in my opinion.'

Emily shrugged. 'Believe it or not, as you will. It is true, all the same.'

A hint of uncertainty crept into grey eyes. 'May I be permitted to know what tactics she adopted? One never knows, the information might prove useful in the long term.'

It took a supreme effort, but Emily somehow managed to preserve her countenance at this deliberately provocative comment. 'She threatened to tell you about something I did of which afterwards I felt heartily ashamed, and which I was determined you should never discover.'

The hand raising the glass to Sebastian's lips checked for a moment. 'What precisely?'

He was nothing if not direct, but having attained his aunt's full attention, and succeeding in her aim, she decided to keep them both in suspense a while longer.

She turned her head on one side, as though considering the matter, and resembling nothing so much as a mischievous kitten debating what havoc to wreak next. 'Mmm, I do not know whether I should tell you even at this late stage.'

Lady Hester's gurgle of mirth was a relief to hear. 'Oh, it

would be too provoking of you not to do so now, after you've whetted our appetites.'

Emily risked a glance up at Sebastian through her long lashes, and easily detected that tell-tale twitch at one corner of his mouth. 'Do you recall that odious woman, Euphemia Bennington-Smythe, the local squire's wife?'

Clearly the name meant nothing to Lady Hester, but Sebastian, after a moment's thought, was aware to whom she referred. 'Go on,' he prompted.

Emily turned her attention to the lady seated on the sofa opposite. 'She was the most self-opinionated, hateful creature imaginable, ma'am. And forever calling upon Mama for the sole purpose of instructing her on the correct way to bring up daughters. Unfortunately she chose to pay one of her frequent visits to our house on a day when I was in a particular ill humour, owing to the fact that his high-and-mightiness here had strictly forbidden me to join the shooting party he had arranged for that afternoon.'

'I realise I'm in immediate danger of ageing ten years,' Sebastian muttered in failing tones, 'but pray continue.'

Emily was happy to oblige him. 'I happened to be in the study at the time, cleaning Papa's old pistol. It was a lovely warm afternoon, as I recall, and Mama was taking tea out on the terrace. The French windows were open, and I overheard every word that detestable woman said about me, so I decided to take my revenge and crept outside with the pistol.'

'Oh, my word!' Lady Hester appeared genuinely alarmed. 'You didn't shoot her, child, surely?'

'No, ma'am,' Emily hurriedly assured her, 'only the preposterous hat she was wearing. Lord! Feathers went flying everywhere. Anyone might have supposed a fox had invaded the chicken coop. Once Mama had succeeded in reviving Mrs Bennington-Smythe from her swoon, and had seen her safely on her way, she sent for me at once. Of course I tried to tell her that the person responsible must have been a member of the shooting party whose aim had gone sadly awry, but Mama was not fooled.'

Lady Hester and, surprisingly enough, Sebastian himself dissolved into laughter and were still chuckling when the butler entered a minute or so later to inform them that dinner was served. Emily made to rise from the sofa, in order to follow Lady Hester from the room, only to have a wrist captured and held fast.

'I shall take leave to inform you, Emily Stapleton, that you are an outrageous little baggage,' he told her, the severity of his tone tempered somewhat by the depth of warmth in his eyes. 'You don't need me to tell you that the incident itself does not redound to your credit. But the telling of the tale at such a time most certainly does. It was well done of you. Thank you, my dear, for restoring my aunt's spirits.'

Chapter Nine

It would have been foolish to suppose that her niece's welfare was no longer of great concern to Lady Hester. All the same during the next few days she only ever mentioned Caroline's name in passing, and never once attempted to pay her a visit. Emily was very certain of this, since she spent most of her time in that engaging lady's company, either paying visits to Lady Hester's wide circle of friends, or attempting to satisfy her chaperon's seemingly insatiable appetite for visiting those most fashionable emporia.

By the end of her first week in London Emily had met many of Sebastian's friends too, all of whom she liked without exception, and all of whom shared his lordship's predilection for outdoor pursuits. Visits to Gentleman Jackson's Boxing Salon in Bond Street, and other sporting venues, kept Sebastian away from the house a good deal, but he was always there to bear her company at breakfast, and never failed to return to the house in good time to join her for dinner, or squire Lady Hester and herself to a small and select party.

Emily swiftly realised that she was being carefully introduced to the polite world, but by the time her second week in town was drawing to a close she was very well aware that this gentle inauguration was fast coming to an end, and that commencing from the night of the engagement ball she would be expected to engage fully in the rigours of a hectic London Season.

Although middle-aged, Lady Hester quickly proved that she had hitherto untouched stores of energy, and attempted to sweep Emily along on a tide of enthusiasm, ensuring that no small detail had been overlooked and that everything was in readiness for the betrothal ball. Emily did her best to show equal eagerness for the forthcoming event. Unfortunately always at the back of her mind lurked the niggling fear that she would in some way betray the fact that the engagement was a complete charade, and this, in unguarded moments, induced her to show less fervour than might have been expected. Lady Hester was inclined to put this occasional display of apathy down to a mere irritation of nerves. Sebastian, however, knew better, and on the day the ball was to be held he insisted that Emily leave the servants to help his aunt with the flower arrangements, and accompany him out for a drive.

She swiftly discovered that travelling in an open carriage was by far the best way to view the capital. It was a glorious mid-spring morning, not oppressive, but warm enough to set forth without the added protection of heavy and constricting outdoor garments, though Sebastian had ensured, in his usual thoughtful manner, that she be provided with a lightweight rug to cover her knees.

As her daily jaunts about town had been thus far primarily to pay visits to the fashionable shops, Emily found plenty to interest her, and her attention was divided between viewing the numerous famous sights and staring with rapt attention at the seemingly effortless way Sebastian handled his spirited greys in the heavy London traffic.

'Several of your friends have referred to you within my hearing as a capital whip, and I now know they were not exaggerating in their praise. I should dearly love to handle a pair as skilfully as you, Hawk,' she remarked, after he'd tooled the curricle, with only inches to spare, between a cart and a lumbering coach.

'It's only practice, my sweet life,' he assured her, smiling to himself as he detected her suddenly heightened colour at the mild endearment. 'Now that you've settled in town, I shall take you out more often, and offer you the benefit of my no little expertise. And there's no better time to begin than the present,' he added, expertly turning into the park and drawing his greys to a halt.

'What?' Emily was astonished, and didn't attempt to hide the fact, as he handed her the reins. 'You'd trust me to tool a racing curricle? Then why in heaven's name didn't you allow me to have a sporting carriage of my own when you must have been told that it was what I really wanted?'

'You forced my hand, you little termagant! Be grateful that I agreed to an ordinary curricle. Now kindly do not leave my cattle standing.'

Thus adjured, Emily concentrated fully. However, after having successfully completed a full circuit of the park, and having attained a deal of satisfaction from the fact that only once did her tutor feel the need to touch her hand in order to correct a slight error, her mind returned to their former conversation, and she shook her head, wondering at herself for being so credulous all these years.

She ought to have suspected something when she had returned from her annual visit to Brighton late last summer. After witnessing a dashing young matron tooling herself about that fashionable seaside resort, she had been determined to have a light carriage of her own. Her grandfather's initial response had been decidedly noncommittal. Several weeks had elapsed before Emily had broached the subject again, and had received a curt refusal. Not one to be thwarted, she had then announced her intention of selling certain of her possessions in order to purchase the carriage for herself.

Then, lo and behold, the following day Jonas Finn had been dispatched hotfoot to London, and had returned two weeks later with her curricle and pair.

'So Finn told you of my intention to sell my jewellery in order to purchase a carriage, and you, having vast experience of my character, knew it was no idle threat.' Surprisingly she felt more amused than annoyed. 'I cannot tell you how satisfying it is to know that I did force your hand.'

'You very nearly forced me to come into Dorsetshire and reveal the authority I have over you, but I decided, on balance, that relenting on that occasion would prove more beneficial in the long run.'

Emily frowned at this. 'Why did you choose to keep your guardianship secret from me? Surely you didn't suppose that I'd throw some childish tantrum, and cause you a vast amount of trouble if I knew?'

Sebastian studied the perfect contours of her sweet profile in silence. 'No, I didn't suppose that for a moment,' he admitted at length. 'But as you didn't seem able to stomach me as a husband, I could not help wondering whether you'd feel any easier having me for a guardian.'

His lordship was surprised to see those slender fingers grasp the reins more tightly, as though a pain had suddenly shot through her. Before he was granted the chance to discover the reason behind the puzzling reaction, his attention was captured by a cheery voice calling his name, and he raised his eyes to discover a familiar figure, astride an equally familiar chestnut gelding, approaching, and immediately covered those tense little hands, drawing his curricle to a halt.

'By all that's holy! If it isn't Tobias Trevenen! What brings you up to the big city, you old rogue?'

'Been visiting a sick aunt in Cambridgeshire, and thought I'd take the opportunity of spending a few weeks in town. Young Michael Sutherland very kindly offered to put me up. Very nice young fellow, just like dear old Simon.'

'Yes, I thought I recognised Michael's gelding.' Sebastian saw his friend's eyes stray in Emily's direction and swiftly made the introductions. 'Toby and I were at university together, but I rarely see him these days. He's too busy looking after his mining interests.'

'Cornwall's a dashed long way away, old fellow,' Tobias protested, after doffing his hat to reveal a full head of bright red-gold curls. He then turned his attention back to his friend's companion. 'I didn't require the introduction to know who you were, Miss Stapleton. Not only have I heard a great deal about you over the years, but I know Hawkridge well enough to be sure that he would only ever entrust his cattle to a very special lady.'

Emily swiftly decided that she liked this fresh-faced gentleman. Like his lordship, he could by no stretch of the imagination be considered handsome, but there was unmistakably a depth of intelligence behind the seemingly mild, blue-eyed gaze, and he possessed an ease of manner which was most appealing.

'True,' Sebastian concurred. 'And this special lady and I are to celebrate our engagement tonight, of which I'm sure you must be fully aware as you're putting up with Michael. So I expect to see you there too.'

'My dear fellow, I'd be delighted, if you're sure I'll not be intruding.'

'Devil a bit, man! You'd have been one of the first to receive an invitation if I'd known you'd be in this part of the world,' Sebastian assured him. 'Furthermore I expect to see a great deal more of you before you return to your beloved Cornwall. We've a deal of catching up to do.'

'Why is it,' Emily asked, after a few more pleasantries had been exchanged, and Mr Trevenen had gone on his way, 'that none of your friends has betrayed the least surprise at your engagement?'

'Why should they?' Once again taking charge of the ribbons, Sebastian turned the carriage homewards. 'All of them have heard me talk about you often enough over the years.'

'Yes, I suppose there is something in what you say,' Emily conceded, after mulling this over. 'But I still think it rather odd. Furthermore, I have gained the distinct impression that all of them considered our engagement a foregone conclusion.'

'Yes, I must confess my friends are a discerning bunch of rogues.' His lordship took his eyes off the road to see a forehead marred by lines of concern. 'I know you're worried about tonight, Em, but there's absolutely no need for you to be. You'll sail through it, believe me. Everyone attending that ball will believe we're a blissfully happy newly engaged couple.'

Everyone except ourselves, Emily silently countered.

As soon as Sebastian had set Emily down before the steps of his town residence, he drove off again, pleading an urgent errand, and she was destined not to see him again until that evening.

After partaking of a light luncheon, she spent the best part of the afternoon helping Lady Hester, but the instant the last vase of flowers had been arranged she took herself off to her room in order to give Skinner, as promised, plenty of time in order to prepare her young mistress for the evening ahead.

From the first she had been impressed by Skinner's efficiency and unfailing attention to the smallest detail. The clothes Emily had brought with her from Dorsetshire now hung in the wardrobe, together with those which more recently had come from the famous Bond Street modiste, each one positioned in strict order, and each one containing not so much as a single crease. It was not until after she had bathed, however, and Skinner had washed and dried her hair, that she appreciated fully for the very first time the skill inherent in those long, workmanlike fingers.

With, seemingly, precious little effort, Skinner piled the long, dark hair high on Emily's head, arranging half in bouncy curls while leaving the rest to cascade down to the base of

Emily's neck in ringlets, before expertly threading an ivory-coloured ribbon through the finished *coiffeur*. Then, without so much as disturbing a single strand, she tossed the ivory silk and lace ball gown over Emily's head, and then coaxed her to study the overall effect in the full-length mirror.

Emily ran a critical eye over her image, from the topmost curl down to her satin slippers, and was forced silently to own that she had never looked so well. The lovely evening gown fitted perfectly. Its bodice, decorated with seed-pearls, was cut lower than she was accustomed to wearing, but not so low as to be considered unseemly. The matching gloves and evening slippers definitely added to the pleasing overall effect, as did the lip gloss and rouge she had been encouraged to don. Undeniably, though, it had been the attentions of an abigail, highly skilled in her profession, which had transformed her from the merely pretty into something quite out of the common way.

'Skinner, you are a credit to your profession,' Emily announced, once again seating herself before her dressing-table mirror in order to study the arrangement of her hair in more detail. 'A miracle worker, no less!'

'That I'm not, miss,' Skinner countered in her no-nonsense manner, although looking well pleased with this tribute. 'I can only work with the materials to hand, as it were. And, as I've said before, Miss Emily, you're an abigail's dream!'

Although touched by the accolade, Emily was beset by a strong sense of guilt, and paused in the act of rummaging through her jewellery case to watch her maid busily tidying the room.

'I cannot help feeling, Skinner, that your undeniable skills could be put to better use on a more worthy recipient. I live a quiet life in Dorsetshire. There will not be too many occasions when your expertise will be called upon.'

'A lady should attempt to look her best at all times, miss, not just when she's attending some grand party.'

'I couldn't agree with you more, Skinner. But at the same time I cannot help wondering how you'll like spending all year round buried in rural Dorsetshire. Until I attain the age of five-and-twenty, and come into my inheritance, there's not the remotest possibility that we can reside anywhere else, although I had considered eventually buying a house in one of the watering places, either Bath or Tunbridge Wells.'

Receiving no response, Emily paused in her perusal of the contents of her jewellery box to glance across at her maid, and was surprised to discover Skinner staring frowningly back at her, clearly troubled over something. 'What's the matter? Does the prospect of leaving the capital to live in the country not please you?'

'No, it isn't that, miss, exactly. But I thought his lordship's main country residence was in Kent. I didn't realise he had a house in Dorsetshire. And why should you be thinking of buying a property in Bath, miss? Is your wedding to his lordship not to take place in the near future?'

Lord, what a blunder! Emily silently cursed herself for every kind of a fool for so easily forgetting her role. At the same time it was a timely reminder to be on her guard throughout the evening ahead.

'We haven't fixed a date for the wedding yet, Skinner,' she admitted, striving to rectify the *faux pas* with the truth as far as she could. 'So naturally I shall return to Dorset to live with my grandfather until we do.'

What appeared to be an expression of relief flickered over the maid's face, considerably softening the harsh features. 'Yes, of course you will, miss, and I'll be only too happy to accompany you. Although I cannot imagine, if his lordship has any say in the matter, that we'll be there for very long,' she added, confounding Emily somewhat. Before she could query precisely what her maid had meant, there was a knock on the door, and a moment later Skinner admitted none other than Lord Hawkridge to the bedchamber.

After a nod of dismissal, Sebastian closed the door which the discreet Skinner had deliberately left open, and then sauntered across to the dressing table where Emily, regarding him with slightly raised brows, remained seated.

This was the first time he had ever entered her room since she had taken up residence in the house. He appeared completely relaxed, betraying no outward sign that he considered he was committing a grave solecism by being alone with her in her bedchamber, so Emily thought it prudent to bring this to his attention.

There was a suspicion of a twitch at one corner of his mouth. 'I've been alone with you in a bedchamber on scores of occasions before now.'

'Not since I was twelve years old,' she reminded him, and watched his eyes momentarily stray to the bodice of her gown.

He raised them again to discover a becoming hue, which had nothing to do with the contents of a rouge pot, suffusing delicate cheeks, and added to her obvious discomfiture by grinning wickedly. 'I would not dream of insulting your intelligence by suggesting that you are as safe with me now as you were then. But fear not, my sweet life. I have not come here with the intention of seducing you…at least not on this occasion.'

'Well? Why have you come?' she demanded pettishly, more annoyed with herself, if the truth were known, for so foolishly betraying unease at his presence. She couldn't imagine why an appreciative masculine glance at her figure should so overset her. It wasn't as if she was unused to receiving openly admiring looks from members of the opposite sex. Nor could she imagine why being alone with him should suddenly unnerve her either. After all, they had been alone together on numerous occasions during the past two weeks, and yet she had never been so conscious before of the raw masculinity he exuded.

After placing the square, leather-covered box that he had been carrying on the dressing table, Sebastian flicked open the lid to reveal its contents. 'My main purpose in being here is to present you with these.'

For several moments it was as much as Emily could do to keep herself from staring, open-mouthed, in astonishment at the sparkling gems resting on their bed of velvet. 'Oh, my!' she managed faintly. 'The Hawkridge diamonds. They must be worth a king's ransom.'

'They are certainly reputed to be worth as much as the other three necklaces in the set put together,' he informed her, removing the main item and placing it about her throat, his fingers as gentle and dextrous as those of any skilled lady's maid, but infinitely more disturbing.

Sebastian smiled to himself as he felt the tiny convulsive shudder ripple through her at his touch, but tactfully refrained from comment, and merely requested her to hold out her left arm so that he might fasten the bracelet above the elegant evening glove.

Mutely she obeyed, only finding her voice when he presented her with a second and much smaller box, which he drew from the pocket of his superbly tailored evening coat, and which contained a pair of diamond ear-drops. 'Are these a part of the collection too?'

'No, my darling. They are a separate gift from me. Now, do not argue,' he interrupted, when she was about to protest. 'It is quite in order for a gentleman to present his future bride with a present on the occasion of their engagement.'

'The way you talk sometimes, Sebastian,' she said softly, securing the ear-drops to her lobes with fingers which were far from steady, 'I almost imagine that you believe it is real.'

'But I do,' he assured her, his voice a soft caress, his breath fanning her cheek, as he raised her gently to her feet, while his eyes devoured every perfect contour of her upturned face, before finally coming to rest on lips slightly parted.

Emily wanted to say something, anything that might break the spell. This wasn't real. It couldn't possibly be! She was merely imagining that he was looking at her as though she were the most precious thing in the world to him, and that his face was drawing ever closer to claim the token that her role as his affianced bride demanded she should give.

His lips brushed against hers so fleetingly that she wasn't even certain in her own mind whether their mouths had truly met, but a moment later he was standing several feet away, his attention fixed on the door that was being thrown wide.

'Are you ready to come down, Emily?' With a swish of amber silk, Lady Hester appeared in the room. 'The dinner-guests will be arriving before long, so I—' She stopped short at the unexpected sight of her nephew. 'Sebastian...I didn't realise you were in here.'

He smiled easily at the unmistakable note of censure in her voice. 'I came merely to present my affianced bride with a token of my sincere regard,' he announced with aplomb.

Emily at last emerged from her dreamlike state to discover Lady Hester regarding her in a mixture of envy and doubt, the reason for which was swiftly made clear.

'Well, my dear, the adornments are truly magnificent. But do you not think they are just a mite too...too overwhelming for a girl of Emily's age?'

'A vulgar display of wealth, you mean,' Sebastian expounded, brutally frank. 'Yes, I suppose they are. But it is the custom for the head of my family to present the diamonds to his chosen lady. Of course it usually occurs after the nuptials have taken place, but I decided to dispense with tradition and present them now. I do not for a moment suppose Emily will rescind and break the engagement, and make off with the booty in the dead of night. Besides which, I wish no one in the polite world to be in any doubt that I have chosen my future Baroness.'

Emily once again felt as though she were descending into that dreamlike state. No one would have supposed for a moment that his lordship had been anything other than totally sincere. Clearly Lady Hester was in no doubt, for she beamed at him approvingly, before coming forward to examine the spectacular adornments more closely.

'They are truly breathtaking,' she was obliged to concede, after studying the upper part of the necklace, fashioned into a choker, and the larger, rectangular-shaped stones cascading in a thousand points of sparkling light across Emily's chest. 'I have heard much about the necklace, but this is the first time I've ever been privileged to see it.'

'Very few have set eyes on the Hawkridge diamonds in two generations,' he informed her while gazing fixedly at the wearer of the fabled item. 'I dare say they will arouse no little comment.'

'That goes without saying, my dear,' Lady Hester agreed drily, before a disturbing thought brought a flicker of alarm to her eyes. 'But surely you don't keep them in the house, Sebastian?'

'They have for many years been locked safely away in a vault at the bank. I ordered their removal two weeks ago in order to have them cleaned. I picked them up from the jeweller's myself earlier today.'

'And no doubt brought them back here without the least protection to yourself, you rash boy!' Lady Hester scolded.

'I was in no danger, Aunt,' he assured her. 'No one knew the nature of my errand.'

'But after tonight there won't be a soul in London who doesn't know that they're here,' she pointed out.

Which was precisely the intention, Emily mused, but refrained from comment, and merely picked up her fan, yet another present from the being who was giving a frighteningly realistic performance of a supremely happy, newly engaged gentleman, and accompanied him and his aunt down to the drawing-room to await the arrival of their dinner-guests.

Once the forty people invited to dine before the ball had eaten their fill, Sebastian led the way back up the stairs, where he positioned himself beside Emily and his aunt at the entrance to the ballroom in order to welcome the remaining two hundred and fifty-odd guests, who began to arrive almost immediately in a continuous, steady stream.

His lordship, who had earlier insisted that Emily be placed beside him at the dinner table, suggested that she leave him and Lady Hester to greet any latecomers, and lead the first set of country dances. As Michael Sutherland had been more than happy to deputise for Sebastian and partner her, Emily had readily agreed, for the young lord, possibly because he was the closest to her in age, had swiftly become her firm favourite among Sebastian's friends.

He favoured her with a wickedly teasing glance as they took up their positions in the set. 'Poor old Seb's getting a bit too long in the tooth for prancing about the room, I suppose.'

Although Emily knew better, she pretended to give the matter some thought. 'You may possibly be right, my lord. Truth to tell, I do not believe it is one of his favourite pastimes, and he's never once attempted to take to the floor since I've been in town. Oh, my! It bodes ill for me if he has suddenly developed two left feet. He's claimed the first waltz and the supper dance.'

'I don't think you need concern yourself, m'dear. I've yet to see Hawkridge perform any duty poorly.'

Although she did not know him that well, she didn't doubt that his admiration was genuine. 'You think highly of him, don't you, my lord?'

'He's the very best of good fellows, ma'am. I really don't know how I'd have gone on after dear old Simon's death if it hadn't been for Hawk. He above anyone else got me through that wretched time.'

This was the first occasion he had mentioned his late brother in her hearing, and she could not fail to detect the sadness in his pleasant voice. There was always that same sombre note whenever Sebastian spoke of his friend. He and the late Lord Sutherland had been so very close. That was perhaps why Sebastian had been willing to take his friend's sibling under his wing, although she did not doubt that he valued Michael for himself now. There was undeniably a wonderful camaraderie between them, a special bond which undoubtedly stemmed from their mutual loss.

It brought forcibly to mind the task Sebastian had entrusted her to perform. Yet where to begin? Surely there was much more that she could do than merely parade about in the Hawkridge diamonds in the hope of inducing the person indirectly responsible for the death of Michael Sutherland's brother to attempt to steal the necklace, thereby foolishly revealing his identity? He had neatly avoided exposure thus far, so it would not do to underestimate the villain.

And Sebastian certainly did not underrate the person he was bent on bringing to book for his nefarious deeds, of that she felt certain. He had already revealed that he suspected it was someone of his own class, perhaps even someone present tonight. But who? Had there been anyone in particular who had betrayed a vulgar interest in her adornments? Truth to tell she could not recall even one pair of eyes, masculine or feminine, which hadn't widened the instant they had focused on the glittering gems. It seemed a hopeless task.

'My lord, as I know so few people here tonight, would you be kind enough to identify one or two of the notables for me?' she asked when they came together once more in the set.

'Willingly,' he agreed, his attractive blue eyes sparkling with that boyishly teasing gleam, 'providing we dispense with formalities. With whom shall we begin, Emily?' he added, after she had willingly acquiesced to his request.

'You can start by telling me the name of the man who has just entered—the distinguished-looking gentleman now in conversation with Hawk.'

'That is Sir Giles Osborne,' he informed her, after the briefest of glances in the direction of the door. 'A somewhat reserved gentleman who, I believe, undertakes work on behalf of the government. Sebastian thinks highly of him.'

Well, it wasn't likely to be Sir Giles, then, Emily reflected, as she and Michael once again separated. By the time they had come together again Sebastian was greeting yet another pair of late arrivals, one of whom she did know well.

'I assume that the gentleman beside Lady Farrington is her husband?'

When Michael's light brows immediately drew together, Emily suspected that Sir Courtney Farrington did not number among his close friends. He didn't number among Sebastian's either, but his dislike was understandable in the circumstances, given that the strikingly handsome Baronet had won the woman he himself had wished to marry.

She turned her attention away from Caroline's tall Adonis of a husband in favour of her partner. 'You are not enamoured of the gentleman, sir?'

'Truth to tell, Emily, I don't know him that well. I do recall my brother never cared for him overmuch. Believe at one time Farrington wished to marry Elizabeth, but she turned him down flat, and married Simon instead. I know he's something of a gamester, who plays deep, and has earned himself the reputation of being something of a—a—'

'Rake,' she offered helpfully when he appeared to be struggling over finding the right word. 'Yes, I had heard.' She decided not to add to his obvious discomfiture by enquiring further into Sir Courtney's character, and requested him instead to remind her of the identity of the formidable-looking female who was holding Lady Hester in conversation. 'I've been introduced to so many this evening that I'm having the utmost difficulty in remembering names.'

A pained expression took possession of his boyishly handsome features, as he followed the direction of Emily's gaze. 'Oh, Lord! I didn't know she was here. That is none other than my esteemed great-aunt, the Dowager Lady Templehurst. Take my advice and avoid her if you can,' he added in a conspiratorial whisper. 'She's a fiendish woman, Em. Don't mind admitting she frightens me to death.'

'Your nephew appears to be entertaining Miss Stapleton right royally, ma'am,' Lady Hester remarked, after watching Emily throw her head back and gurgle with laughter.

Lady Templehurst had recourse to her lorgnette. 'Yes, he's an endearing young scamp.' She transferred her gaze to his partner, studying her progress, as Emily made her way down the set. 'And that young woman is certainly something above the norm. I had wondered just what type of female would eventually ensnare Hawkridge, and I was certain she would turn out to be someone with more than just looks to commend her. Both her figure and carriage are excellent, and she's lovely enough to capture any gentleman's interest. But those jewels, my dear…' she paused to bend a look of mild reproach in her companion's direction '…a little too much for a girl of that age, wouldn't you say? I think you might have tried to dissuade her.'

'I had little say in the matter, ma'am,' Lady Hester did not hesitate to enlighten her, feeling slightly resentful at being held to blame. 'Hawkridge himself insisted Miss Stapleton wear the set.'

'Did he now?' Lady Templehurst's wispy brows rose so high that they almost touched the rim of her ugly turban. 'That's tantamount to putting his stamp of ownership on her, the rogue!' Her appreciative bark of laughter induced several heads to turn in their direction. 'Well, and who can blame him? I might not wholeheartedly approve of such a vulgar display of gauds, but I cannot deny the girl can carry the gems. She has a queenly bearing, and is altogether very pleasing on the eye. Which is more than can be said for Lady Farrington,' she added, once again peering through her lorgnette in the general direction of the door, 'who is surprisingly bearing that philandering husband of hers company tonight, unless I much mistake the matter.'

Lady Hester, who hadn't noticed her niece's arrival, quickly excused herself and rose to her feet, just as the first set of country dances came to an end. Emily, catching sight of her chaperon, watched her hurriedly making her way towards the entrance and guessed that her niece was her quarry. Unfortunately she was unable to witness the meeting, for no sooner had Michael escorted her over to the table at which a footman stood dispensing glasses of refreshing fruit punch than a softly spoken voice from behind requested an introduction.

'You may safely leave Miss Stapleton in my care,' Sir Giles Osborne said smoothly, 'for unless I much mistake the matter your esteemed great-aunt is attempting to gain your attention, Sutherland.'

Emily could not forbear a smile as Michael, muttering under his breath, moved away. She watched him until he had reached his redoubtable aunt's side, and then turned to discover Sir Giles studying the arrangement of jewels covering her throat.

'Shall we find ourselves a quiet corner, my dear, where we can be private for a few minutes?' he suggested, and Emily automatically found herself accompanying him across the room to two vacant chairs, not quite certain whether the glint she had detected in his eyes moments before had been avarice, admiration or faint alarm.

'Tell me, my dear, how does that grandfather of yours go on? I have not seen him for…oh, it must be twenty years or more.'

'He is keeping well, sir, considering he has turned seventy.'

'And does he still indulge in his hobby? Collecting butter-lies, if my memory serves me correctly.'

Emily had not been quite certain whether or not the gen-leman now seated beside her was in fact acquainted with her grandfather, but she was no longer in any doubt and began to elax. 'Sticking pins into butterflies was merely one of his arbaric pastimes.'

Sir Giles smiled grimly. 'I visited his home only once, long before you were born, but I seem to recall that ornithology was another of his hobbies. He kept several stuffed specimens about the place. As I recall, birds of prey interested him most of all.'

Emily, who had been absently studying the painted figures on her fan, was suddenly alert, and looked directly into her companion's eyes, which were of a similar hue and betrayed the same depth of intelligence as a certain other gentleman's of her acquaintance. Unless she was very much mistaken Sir Giles Osborne was none other than the person with whom Sebastian worked closely.

'Yes, sir. That is correct…his particular favourite, and mine, being the kestrel.'

Thin lips curled into an appreciative smile. 'Clever girl,' he murmured. 'Now that we understand each other, we can be comfortable.'

He took a moment to stare about the room at the assembled throng, before favouring Emily with his full attention once more. 'You have beautiful eyes, Miss Stapleton, use them wisely whilst you remain in town. Try always to look beneath the surface, for people are not always what they seem.'

'How very true, sir. And you, if I may say so, are a prime example.'

Once again Sir Giles smiled appreciatively. 'You have a ready wit, child. My friend Hawkridge chose wisely.'

'I sincerely trust I am able to live up to his expectations, sir for I've been of precious little help thus far. I was hoping that someone present tonight would betray a marked interest in the necklace. But the truth of the matter is that everyone has.'

'Hardly surprising, child. But do not be disheartened, and do not make the mistake of underestimating your quarry. He's a cunning rogue and will not betray himself easily.'

'I suppose it is safe to assume that it is a man behind it all, sir?'

'Yes, I think we can safely assume that much, simply because it is more difficult for a woman to move about so freely. But do not rule out the possibility that he might well be in league with a female. He seems to have the knack of discovering the whereabouts of these expensive items of jewellery when they are most easily purloined. It is quite feasible that he attains information from a lady who moves in polite circles. Anything is possible, so be on your guard at all times.'

Sir Giles, ever alert himself, noticed the tall, immaculately attired figure of their host heading purposefully in their direction, and rose at once to his feet. 'Your fiancé evidently feels that I have monopolised you for long enough, so I shall tactfully withdraw and leave you in his care.'

The instant the Baronet had moved away, Emily revealed without hesitation that she now knew Sir Giles was the one with whom Sebastian was collaborating, but could not resist adding, as Sebastian took a hold of her wrists and gently pulled her to her feet, that he might have told her this himself.

His lordship was not slow to detect the note of resentment in her voice, nor had he any difficulty in understanding the reason behind it. 'Disabuse yourself of the least notion that I do not trust you, Em. I would trust you with my life, my darling,' he assured her. 'It was simply that Sir Giles considered it might be prudent to keep his involvement in my personal crusade secret, but seemingly he chose to take you into his confidence. He's an extremely astute judge of character, Em. Evidently he made up his mind swiftly that you could be trusted. I assured him you could. None the less the decision to confide in you had to be his.'

He could see at once that this had gone some way to soothe her ruffled feathers, but was not unduly surprised when she said, 'I wish you would confide in me more, Hawk. I'm certain there is much you've chosen not to reveal. For instance, do you suspect the person you're seeking is present tonight?'

'He could well be, yes,' he conceded. 'I have a list of names in my library, any one of whom might turn out to be the miscreant. I'll show it to you tomorrow. In the meantime I have a far more pleasurable task to undertake, namely partnering my future bride in a waltz.'

Emily was immediately conscious of the fact that they were the focal point of many pairs of interested eyes, as they made their way on to the dance floor. Most looked on with indulgent approval, while a few others, especially the older female guests, were frowning dourly, and it didn't take Emily many moments to appreciate the reason why.

'I do believe I'm in the gravest danger of ruining my reputation by standing up with you, my lord,' she announced, secretly hoping that he had not detected the little convulsive shudder which had rippled through her the instant his hand had grasped her waist. 'I might spend most of the year buried in the depths of rural Dorsetshire, but I am not completely ignorant of the ways of the polite world,' she added, striving to ignore the tingling in her fingers as that other shapely masculine hand clasped hers. 'The waltz is still very much frowned upon in certain quarters, and any young lady caught performing it is instantly labelled fast.'

'Have no fear, my child. I assure you your reputation will not suffer as a consequence of standing up with me now. The dance is increasingly performed at private functions here in the capital, and those fearsome patronesses of Almack's are forced to turn a blind eye. I did, however, take the added precaution of attaining the consent of one of them, the loquacious Sally Jersey, no less, whose company, thankfully, we have been spared this evening.'

The lady in question was not universally liked, and clearly Sebastian was one of those who did not hold the Regent's ex-mistress in the highest regard. Nevertheless he wasn't above making use of her, it seemed, when it served his purpose.

Emily couldn't suppress a gurgle of mirth at his sheer

audacity which unfortunately induced her to miss a step as the dance began. Determined not to disgrace herself further, she concentrated hard, focusing her attention for several moments on the glinting diamond nestling between the folds of his expertly tied cravat, before studying the rest of his immaculate apparel.

Smiling to herself, she recalled how acutely disappointed she had felt when first setting eyes on him at the party held at Deverel Hall a few weeks before, but this was no longer the case. She could not deny that she preferred to see him more casually attired in riding garb, but she was forced to concede that he was the epitome of sartorial elegance in his long-tailed black coat and tight-fitting trousers. She had long since considered that his features were too ruggedly masculine for him to be deemed handsome by the vast majority of her sex, herself included, but any discerning female would readily acknowledge that his physique was excellent and that he wore his clothes with an air of refinement which set him quite apart from most other gentlemen in the room.

She raised her head to discover grey eyes glinting no less brightly than the diamond nestling in his cravat, and a wicked smile about his mouth which suggested strongly that he was very well aware that he had just won her stamp of approval, so she did not hesitate to confirm the fact.

'Why, thank you, my dear! And you do not need me to tell you that your own appearance leaves nothing to be desired.'

'If that is so then you have Skinner to thank,' she returned, striving not to blush like a gauche schoolgirl at the compliment.

'Skinner?' he echoed, before enlightenment dawned. 'Ah! Your new maid. How do you find her? Looks a bit of a dragon to me.'

Emily hastened to assure him that she was very well pleased. 'I should like to keep her if possible, and I believe she will be content to return to Dorset with me, only I do not feel that I could ask Grandpapa to pay her wages.' A thought suddenly occurred to her. 'I suppose, as my guardian, you have control over my money too, and that I must apply to you for an extra allowance in order to pay for Skinner's services?'

Here again Sebastian wasn't slow to detect the hint of resentment in her voice. 'So that rankles, does it? Well, never mind. We can discuss it at a more appropriate time. And as far as your maid is concerned…if you wish to keep her you may do so.'

The arrival of another latecomer caught his attention. 'Ahh! So, he decided to put in an appearance, after all. I half suspected that he might not.'

Following the direction of his gaze, Emily saw Mr Tobias Trevenen being greeted by Lady Hester who instantly guided him towards the vacant chair beside her niece. The next moment, he was bending to retrieve the fan Caroline had inadvertently dropped on the floor.

'Interesting,' Sebastian murmured, smiling to himself.

Emily was curious to know precisely what he had meant, but at that moment she just happened to notice a rent in the hem of her gown, undoubtedly the result of her slight falter at the commencement of the dance. Consequently the instant the waltz came to an end, she didn't hesitate to excuse herself and slipped quietly away along the passageway to the chamber set aside for the female guests' private use.

Deciding not to waste time in ringing for assistance, she settled herself behind one of the screens, and had all but completed the simple repair when she detected the click of the door, quickly followed by what sounded suspiciously like muffled weeping. Curiosity swiftly getting the better of her, she pressed an eye to the gap in the screen and had no difficulty whatsoever in recognising the woebegone figure who had seated herself on one of the couches, and whose thin shoulders were shaking with the sobs she was incapable of suppressing.

'Why, Caroline! Whatever is the matter?'

With a tiny gasp of dismay, Lady Farrington let her hands fall, and looked wildly about her, clearly distraught to discover that she was not alone. Emily, however, did not allow this to deter her. Having slipped from behind the screen, she seated herself beside Sebastian's cousin on the couch.

'Whatever has happened to overset you?' Emily could not recall that Caroline had been given to weeping for no reason. Obviously something had upset her deeply.

'I'm sorry. So…so stupid of me. It's nothing, really,' she managed faintly, after delving into her reticule for her hand-kerchief and making use of the piece of fine lawn. 'There, I'm better now,' she went on, with a very weak attempt at a smile. 'I'm just being a foolish, brooding mother, missing my little daughter, and being stupidly sentimental over coming face to face with a…a dear friend again.'

Regarding her dispassionately, Emily decided that Caroline's appearance had not improved since their encounter in Bond Street. If anything, she looked even worse now. She was a mere shadow of the vivacious young woman whose dress sense, Emily clearly remembered, had always been above reproach. This unfortunately was no longer the case, for she had chosen to wear a gown of lavender silk which suited her ill and did little to improve her slightly sallow complexion; her hair, dull and lifeless, had been plainly arranged, and her only adornments were her wedding band and a velvet ribbon about her neck upon which a fine cameo had been pinned.

Her continued scrutiny undoubtedly caused Caroline some disquiet, for she raised a trembling hand, inadvertently dislodging the length of lavender velvet to reveal a nasty lesion to her throat.

Emily was appalled, for the injury must have been causing no little discomfort. 'Heavens above! Whatever have you done? Did you burn yourself?'

'Oh, it is nothing…I'm becoming so very clumsy of late.' If possible Caroline appeared more disconcerted than before, as she tried with little success to reposition the velvet band to cover the blemish.

'Here, let me.' Emily had removed the ribbon before Caroline had a chance to stop her. Her concern swiftly mounted as she saw the full extent of the injury which completely encircled Caroline's neck, the skin red raw and bearing a distinct and regular diamond-shaped impression. It was most strange and definitely not the result of a burn.

'How did you come by this?' she asked, striving to be gentle as she repositioned the ribbon so that the strange wound was once again completely hidden. 'One might almost suspect that you had attempted to hang yourself with some kind of cord,' she prompted when she received no response.

Caroline's laugh was distinctly shaky. 'Why, yes! How very clever of you to guess! That is precisely what I very nearly did do. I—er—was taking a length of cord, which I use to tie back the drapes about my bed, downstairs with me. It had become sadly frayed and I was hoping to purchase a further length in the same shade of blue. Foolishly I placed it about my neck, tripped on the stairs, and it became entwined round the balustrade. I was very lucky not to be throttled.'

'You must take more care in future,' Emily advised, not wholly convinced that the explanation was the true one. 'There…it is completely hidden now.'

'Thank you so much.' Caroline began to twist the strings of her reticule nervously round her fingers. 'Please do not mention it to anyone, Emily. Courtney would be so cross with me if he knew. I'm such a trial to him of late with all my megrims. He would not like it above half, either, if he knew I'd been weeping.'

'In which case we'll not tell him. Although I think it might be wise to remain here a while longer,' Emily advised gently. 'Your eyes are still a little red. I shall remain with you and bear you company.'

It was not very long before Emily was regretting this act

of kindness, for Caroline, in an obvious attempt to appear perfectly restored, began to prattle away on a wide variety of subjects, her tongue running on wheels. 'Have you perchance read Miss Austen's *Sense and Sensibility*?' she asked, once again changing the topic without pausing for breath. 'It is strongly rumoured that the Regent himself is an admirer of her work.'

'No, I haven't,' Emily responded, finally managing to edge in a word.

'Oh, you really must. I have brought my copy to London. You may borrow it if you like.'

'That is most kind of you. In the meantime—' Emily hurriedly rose to her feet before her patience was stretched to breaking point '—I think we ought to return to the party, otherwise our continued absence might give rise to comment.'

Caroline acquiesced readily enough, appearing more than willing to return. Consequently Emily was somewhat surprised when she found her companion dragging her heels, as they headed back along the passageway towards the ballroom, and raised her eyes to discover Sir Courtney Farrington, not looking altogether pleased about something, hovering near the entrance.

'Where on earth have you been, Caroline?' he demanded sharply, his voice betraying impatience, before Emily drew his attention by introducing herself.

Undeniably he was strikingly handsome, tall and broadshouldered, and, unlike his wife, faultlessly attired. Yet there was something about him that Emily did not quite like. The smile came too readily to lips that had a distinctly cruel curve, and lines of dissipation were already visible about the vivid blue eyes which lacked any vestige of warmth, even though they glinted now with quite blatant masculine appreciation as they rested upon her.

'Introductions are unnecessary, Miss Stapleton,' he assured her, bowing with studied elegance over her hand, and retaining his clasp on her fingers for just a fraction too long. 'Your engagement to Hawkridge is the talk of the Season. I would have known you anywhere.'

'Yes, I'm afraid the jewels clearly reveal my identity to the world at large,' she responded lightly, and noticed that his gaze flickered only momentarily over the gems before resting upon her face once more. 'Caroline, of course, I have known since I was a child,' she went on hurriedly, feeling slightly uncomfortable beneath the unsubtly admiring masculine scrutiny, 'but we have not seen each other for years, so you must forgive me for monopolising her for so long.'

One fair brow quirked. 'I was under the impression that you bumped into each other in Bond Street the other week.'

'Oh, yes we did,' Emily hurriedly affirmed, presuming Caroline herself must have told him this. 'Unfortunately time was pressing and we were unable to chat for long.' She chose not to add that his wife seemed disinclined to do so on that occasion. Caroline for some reason was looking decidedly uneasy now, as though she wished she could find herself a quiet corner and be alone, and so Emily decided not to prolong the conversation, but could not resist adding, 'I sincerely hope that your wife and I can make up for lost time and see a good deal of each other during the forthcoming weeks.'

'I can safely promise you, Miss Stapleton, that we shall both be delighted if you were to honour us with a visit in the near future.'

Caroline was not slow to confirm this, but Emily, moving away to refresh herself with a glass of fruit punch, was not so certain that the assurance had been genuine.

Over the rim of her glass Emily saw Sir Courtney disappear into the room set out for cards, before watching his wife's progress, as Caroline made her way down to the far end of the room, where fewer guests were congregating. Why was it, she wondered, frowning heavily, that she experienced not an atom of animosity towards that woman, not even a twinge of jealousy? If anything, that short interlude in the ladies' withdrawing-room had left her experiencing deep concern.

'If you continue to look so troubled, no one will suppose for a moment that you are enjoying your engagement ball,' Sebastian murmured unexpectedly in her left ear, almost making her jump out of her skin. 'What has put your nose out of joint?' he prompted, when all she did was to favour him with a disapproving glance. 'You're not still nettled over the fact that, as your guardian, I have control over your money, I trust?'

'The only part of your guardianship which I find irksome is your persistence in treating me as though I were still a child,' she replied shortly, and his brow rose sharply.

'Is that how you imagine I view you?'

An odd expression, impossible to define, flickered in his eyes. It was neither anger nor irritation, though Emily could not have blamed him if he had been annoyed. She was here for a purpose, and must fulfil her promise and play her part of a happily engaged young woman to the full.

Her gaze automatically straying once more to the lady in the lavender-coloured gown, Emily could only hope that her performance was a deal more credible than Caroline's had been a short while before, for she was now firmly convinced of two things—Lady Farrington had lied about the way she had come by that injury to her neck, and she was very much afraid of the man whom she had chosen to marry.

Chapter Ten

It was hardly surprising, considering she had not climbed into the comfortable four-poster bed until the small hours, that Emily woke much later than usual the following day and, on discovering from Skinner that his lordship had already break-fasted and had left the house, she decided to break the habit of a lifetime and ordered the first meal of the day brought up to her on a tray.

Nibbling her way daintily through a hot buttered roll, Emily began to reflect on the events of the previous evening. Extraordinarily enough she had very much enjoyed the occasion, but it had certainly left her with plenty to mull over, not least of which had been Caroline's behaviour.

Undoubtedly the Farringtons' marriage was an unmiti-gated disaster, and given Sir Courtney's reputation where the fair sex was concerned it wasn't too difficult to understand why. Yet Emily was forced to concede that not once through-out the entire evening had she seen Sir Courtney paying undue attention to any particular female guest, least of all his wife. He had behaved with the utmost propriety, spending much of the evening in the room set out for cards, leaving his spouse for the most part to her own devices. Even so, on the few oc-casions when he had been close by, Caroline had appeared to withdraw completely into her shell, eyes lowered, saying not a word. Only once had she betrayed a glimmer of that old liveliness of spirit, and that had been when Mr Tobias Trevenen had escorted her in to supper.

Puzzling too had been Sebastian's behaviour towards the great love of his life. Except on the occasions when he had welcomed her to the ball, and, later, when he had bidden the Farringtons farewell, he had not once attempted to approach Caroline.

Of course it would have caused a deal of speculation if he had singled her out for particular attention, given that he was supposed to be a newly betrothed man, and Emily was forced to own that he had maintained his role of devoted fiancé wonderfully well by never remaining for very long away from her side. All the same, she would have expected him to show at least some interest in his cousin, as he must have known, being acutely perceptive, that Caroline was not herself.

Yes, Sebastian's attitude had been most odd, she decided, tossing the bed covers aside, and swinging her feet to the floor. 'Do you happen to know if Lady Hester is up and about yet?'

'Most unlikely, I should say, miss,' the maid answered with a wry grin. 'I cannot imagine she'll bestir herself much before early afternoon.'

'Yes, you're probably right. In which case I think I shall go out for a walk. Would you care to accompany me, or would you prefer I acquire the services of one of the housemaids?'

'I'd be delighted to come with you, miss.'

Emily suspected that Skinner's answer derived more from tact than honesty, but later, as they set out together, she realised she had done the abigail a disservice in thinking her less than sincere. Skinner was happy to keep pace and not dawdle along, as many of her younger counterparts were inclined to do, though she continued to remain deferentially that step or two behind until Emily insisted that she walk beside her. Clearly she was enjoying the exercise as much as her young mistress and appeared happy to converse whenever called upon to do so, while at the same time remaining vigilant, ready to repel the unwanted attentions of any waggish fop.

Fortunately her conscientious maid's heavy, repellent frown was not brought into play too often, as Emily sensibly chose not to stray beyond the fashionable area of town. She had set out with no clear destination in mind. Yet, whether through a subconscious desire to have her curiosity satisfied, or mere chance, she eventually found herself in the thoroughfare where the Farringtons' elegant town house was situated, and paused on the corner of the street to stare at that certain dwelling which Lady Hester had pointed out during their return from one of those numerous shopping expeditions.

Emily had gained the distinct impression the previous evening that Lady Farrington did not receive too many visitors to the house. Her husband, on the other hand, had earned himself the reputation of being highly sociable. There was no carriage waiting outside now, which suggested that the occupants were not entertaining at the present time, although it was quite common for visits to be made on foot.

Emily hesitated only for a moment, then marched resolutely up to the front door. She was admitted to the house by none other than the thickset individual who had accompanied Caroline to Bond Street two weeks before, and invited to take a seat in the hall, where she looked about with interest. The house was nowhere near as large as Sebastian's residence in Berkeley Square. Even so it was tastefully decorated and elegantly furnished, and undeniably the dwelling of a gentleman of some means.

Common report suggested strongly that Sir Courtney was something of a gamester who played deep. If that was so, and she had no reason to doubt it, Emily could only assume that

Lady Luck favoured him for the most part; either that or he had inherited wealth enough to satisfy his expensive tastes.

A light step on the stairs drew her attention, and she looked up to see Caroline descending. Dressed in a high-necked muslin gown, with the flimsiest of shawls draped around her thin shoulders, she appeared more composed than she had the evening before, and succeeded in at least giving the impression that she was pleased by the visit, even if she was not, by placing a slight salute on Emily's cheek and greeting her warmly.

'I dare say it is the wish to read the book I recommended which has brought you here,' she announced, momentarily startling Emily who had completely forgotten the kind offer.

'Why, yes, that's right!' she responded, with a flagrant disregard for the truth. 'If you are certain you don't mind?'

'Not at all. I believe I left it in the library.'

Automatically following her across the hall, Emily noted the slight hesitation before Caroline grasped the doorknob, and then led the way into the masculine sanctum lined with books and smelling faintly of leather and brandy. Undoubtedly this was Sir Courtney's private domain, which perhaps accounted for the slight diffidence on Caroline's part. Emily could not in all honesty say that she had ever experienced the least reluctance to enter her grandfather's retreat, or indeed the library in Berkeley Square, whether the master of the house happened to be occupying the room or not.

While Caroline began to search the shelves, Emily once again studied her surroundings, her gaze finally coming to rest on the object secured to the wall above the fireplace. 'That's rather an odd sort of adornment to have above a mantelshelf,' she remarked, moving across to study the whip more closely. 'One usually finds a mirror or a favourite painting in such positions.'

Detecting the sound of a faint gasp, Emily turned in time to see the book fall from Caroline's fingers, her other hand clasping her throat, her face now ashen. 'Why, whatever is the matter?'

Receiving no response, Emily turned again to stare intently

at the object of Caroline's horrified gaze, noting this time the ornate design on the handle and the diamond-shaped pattern in the leather coils. The truth hit her with stunning clarity. 'My God!' she murmured. 'It was this that caused the injury to your neck, wasn't it?'

For answer Caroline swooped to retrieve the book, before hurrying over to the door. 'Come, let us repair to the parlour. We shall be more comfortable in there.'

Prey to the most disturbing conjecture, Emily was relieved to see a semblance of colour return to thin cheeks as they repaired to the sunny front room overlooking the street, and made themselves comfortable in two of the chairs. Even so she didn't hesitate to interrupt Caroline when she betrayed alarming signs of attempting to strike up a trivial conversation, painfully reminiscent of that inane one in which she had indulged the evening before.

'You are fooling no one by these displays of light-heartedness, Caroline, least of all me,' she announced, and was rewarded by a genuinely spontaneous smile, albeit a wry one, before Caroline rose to her feet and went to stand before the window to gaze out upon the street.

'I had forgotten just how forthright you could be on occasions, Emily. You were never afraid to speak your mind.'

'Very true,' she agreed. 'Moreover I do not object to others speaking theirs. So you may tell me to mind my own business if you wish, but kindly do not insult my intelligence further by endeavouring to appear perfectly contented when it's painfully obvious that you are anything but. And little wonder when you are riveted to a man who attains some perverse pleasure in trying to throttle you!' she added, guessing at the truth.

'It isn't as bad as that,' Caroline responded, thereby confirming Emily's suspicions. 'It has happened only once before. I'm afraid it is a wife's lot to put up with her husband's foibles. It just so happens that Courtney enjoys inflicting pain at times when—when tenderness might be expected. All gentlemen enjoy their little peculiarities, you know.' She raised trembling fingers to her forehead. 'What am I saying…? Of course you don't know. And it is most improper to be speaking of such things in your hearing.'

'Perhaps,' Emily agreed. 'But it is as well that I know what to expect if I'm ever tempted to take the matrimonial plunge.'

'If…?' Clearly puzzled, Caroline looked back across the room. 'When, I think you mean. And you've nothing to fear from Sebastian.' She could not have sounded more sincere. 'He absolutely adores you, Emily. He always has, you know.'

'Yes,' she responded hollowly. 'He's truly very fond of me.'

Emily noted the lingering look of puzzlement in those brown eyes, as Caroline resumed her seat opposite, and quickly steered the conversation back to the former topic. 'But it isn't my future well-being that's in question, it is yours. If you're so desperately unhappy, why don't you leave him? Lady Hester would be more than happy for you to live with her in Bath. You must know that she looks upon you as her own daughter.'

'Yes, I do know,' Caroline acknowledged softly. 'But how could I forfeit mine? Alicia is my life, Emily. I could never bear to be parted from her for long. And I know Courtney's character well enough to be certain that he would never permit me to take her.'

'He is fond of his daughter?'

'Ha!' Caroline scoffed. 'He's never paid her the least attention. He wanted a son…still wants a son. That is the only reason why he pays the occasional visit to Derbyshire. But for the most part he remains in town, leaving me to my own devices. And I am very content to have it that way. Believe me when I tell you that I have never experienced an ounce of jealousy towards any one of those women who have offered inducement enough for him to remain away from me. If anything, I've been immensely grateful to them.'

Emily, experiencing little difficulty in understanding this viewpoint, frowned as something odd occurred to her. 'Why, then, are you here now?'

'I really don't know,' Caroline admitted, once again looking puzzled. 'Needless to say I didn't wish to come to town, and wrote to tell him so. I could quite easily have written a letter of congratulations to Sebastian. But Courtney sent Sloane, his henchman, to Derbyshire to fetch me, giving me no choice.'

Emily was appalled, for the implication was clear. 'You are not obliged to take orders from a servant, surely?'

Caroline's smile was bitter. 'Sloane is no ordinary servant, Emily. He is devoted to Courtney, and has been assigned to protect me during my stay here in town.'

'You mean to spy on you,' Emily countered, as forthright as ever, and received a nod in response.

'He informs his master of precisely whom I see on the odd occasion I do venture forth. He is not above turning visitors away from the house either, if he suspects Courtney might disapprove.'

'I assume he is the one who admitted me today?' Emily received a further nod in response. 'He appeared happy to let me enter.'

'Yes, he must have received instructions from his master to do so. Courtney, I noticed, appeared eager for you to call.'

'Well, let us hope he is as eager for your aunt to visit because I cannot imagine she will refrain from doing so for much longer. She's very concerned about you, Caroline.'

'Yes, I do know. We spoke at length at the party last night.' The sombre note in her voice suggested strongly that she had found the tête-à-tête something of an ordeal. 'It's perfectly true that I haven't been well of late, Emily,' she continued softly. 'I suffered a miscarriage a few weeks ago, and have not been easy with myself since. May God forgive me, but i wasn't the loss of the child which upset me so much as the knowledge that I would be forced to suffer again my husband's attentions in order to beget the heir he's so determined to have.'

'Oh, Caroline, I'm so sorry,' Emily said softly, and Lady Farrington, seemingly believing the sympathy genuine, smiled.

'You must not pity me, Emily. My lot is not so bad. And really I have only myself to blame. Sebastian, to name but one, tried to warn me against Courtney, but I was too stubborn to listen. I allowed myself to be beguiled by a handsome face, and discovered to my cost that my husband's character was nowhere near as perfect as his physiognomy.' A further sigh escaped her. 'If I had only listened…if I had only waited, I might have married a man who truly cared for me.'

'Yes, I know,' Emily murmured, if possible feeling more guilty than ever before. If only she had realised sooner! If only she had known about Sebastian's promise before she had returned to the seminary for that final term!

She raised her eyes to discover a questioning look in Caroline's. 'Believe me, I too wish you had waited those few weeks. If only there was something I could do… something to make your lot a little easier to bear.'

'You have,' Caroline surprisingly divulged. 'I've never spoken to anyone about this before, Emily. But I knew last night, when you assured Courtney that you were to blame for my long absence, that I could trust you. It's a great comfort to know I have at least one friend and ally here in town. But there, that is enough about me,' she went on. 'Tell me about yourself, and what you've been doing during these past years.'

Emily obligingly did so, and gained a deal of satisfaction from hearing Caroline give vent to several spontaneous gurgles of mirth, thereby proving that her unhappy marriage had not, thankfully, succeeded in destroying her vivacity completely.

'Your grandfather sounds a real character, Emily. Little wonder you've been so happy. And soon you are to be Lady Hawkridge…so your continued happiness is assured. Sebastian's a wonderful man. And so generous too!' A further gurgle of laughter escaped Caroline. 'Those diamonds you were wearing last night must be worth an absolute fortune. Dear Aunt Hester must be pea-green with envy! She is one for expensive trifles, you know.'

'Yes, I had already gathered that. Although,' Emily added, 'I'm not so certain she's very keen on their remaining at Berkeley Square. If she has her way they'll be dispatched to the bank without delay!'

Sebastian's return to the house coincided with the long-case clock in the hall solemnly heralding the arrival of two o'clock. 'Has my fiancée or my aunt risen yet?' he asked, handing Clegg his hat and gloves.

'Lady Hester, so I understand, has now broken her fast, but has not as yet emerged from her room, sir. And Miss Staple-ton left the house some time ago to enjoy a walk.'

'Not alone, I trust?'

'No, sir. She was accompanied by her personal maid.'

'In that case, would you inform her on her return that I wish to see her?'

Certain that his major-domo wouldn't fail to carry out his instructions, Sebastian didn't wait for a response, and entered the room where he had spent much of his time before his aunt and Emily had taken up residence in the house.

He smiled wryly as he poured himself a glass of Madeira and carried it across to the desk. How his life had changed with the advent of the ladies' arrival, most especially Emily's. Having her under his roof was proving to be a sweet torment, increasingly a strain. Each night, before he retired, he found himself pausing outside her bedchamber door, fighting the desire to enter. It was perhaps fortunate that his aunt was taking her duties as chaperon seriously. None the less he couldn't deny that he wished her elsewhere for much of the time.

Ideally it would have been far better to have rented a house for them for the duration of their stay in town, but he had been given insufficient time to do so. He had not travelled into Dorsetshire with the intention of becoming engaged. He had been prepared to be patient and wait a while longer, and then woo Emily in the established fashion. All the same, when the idea had sprung into his mind on that sunny afternoon when they had ridden to the coast, he hadn't hesitated to grasp the opportunity which Emily's quite innocent offer of help had presented.

Perhaps, though, in one way he might yet come to regret embarking on this charade, for if the events of last night had taught him anything then it was that his darling fiancée was intent on playing her part to the full in the hope of aiding him to uncover the identity of the devil who had been indirectly responsible for Simon Sutherland's demise.

Foolishly he hadn't taken into account her innate doggedness. Once she had made up her mind to do something, nothing could sway her; her determination to drive herself about in her own carriage was proof of this. Undeniably she had been both resentful and suspicious after her conversation with Sir Giles Osborne the previous evening, and once again had succeeded in forcing his hand. God only knew he didn't want her embroiled in the affair. None the less for the time being it might be as well to allow her to continue to believe that she was being of use to him in his endeavours in the hope that she would eventually acknowledge that they were so wonderfully compatible, and that becoming the future Lady Hawkridge was what she truly desired.

The sound of an arrival put an end to these musings, and Sebastian had only just begun to browse through the pile of letters awaiting his attention, when the door opened and the young woman who occupied his thoughts for much of the time stood on the threshold, one fine brow raised in a questioning arch.

'The lord and master demanded to see me?'

'I wished to speak with you, yes,' he corrected. 'Come in and close the door, Em.'

He waited for her to do so, before searching through the top drawer of his desk for a certain sheet of paper, and then joining her on the sofa where she had seated herself. 'I promised to let you see this.'

The instant she had placed the book that she had been holding on the table beside her, and had begun to scan the list of names he had written down, the surprising hauteur she had displayed on entering the room vanished and was replaced by an expression of deep concentration, as she ran her eyes down what had become over many months an ever decreasing list of names.

'I recall being introduced to several of these people yesterday evening. Were they all at the party?'

'Only the four whose names have not been struck through. The others, over a period of time, I've eliminated as possible suspects.'

'I see Sir Courtney Farrington remains on your list.' One finely arched brow rose. 'Is your reason for including him justified, or is it merely a case of sour grapes on your part?'

Sebastian had little difficulty in affecting the same haughty expression as she had worn on entering the room. 'And what precisely is that supposed to mean, young lady?'

She had the grace to blush. 'Well, you don't like him, do you, Seb?'

He had forgotten that one of her most winning traits was peering up at him through those ridiculously long lashes of hers when she suspected she had displeased him in some way, and found it impossible to suppress a smile. 'I didn't realise I was quite so transparent. No, I have never liked him, not since we were at school together.'

She appeared surprised to learn this. 'Why, what did he do to give you such a distaste of him?'

Disposed to satisfy her curiosity, he revealed, 'It was on one of those occasions when Simon Sutherland and I went into the local town to buy our stock of cakes that we came upon Farrington and his cronies watching a dog fight. Farrington had tied the animals together, and was attaining a deal of pleasure in watching the smaller and weaker dog being torn to shreds. Simon and I put a stop to it and cut them loose, not without, I might add, sustaining several injuries ourselves.'

A look of intense dislike took possession of her features as she turned her head to stare at the landscape painting on the wall above the grate. 'I cannot say that I'm surprised,' she admitted. 'There is something distinctly unpleasant…cruel in that man's expression. I noticed it last night.'

He was surprised to hear this. 'Most women find him devilishly attractive, Em.'

'Yes, it must be said that a great many females are sadly undiscerning—credulous, too. Most believe marriage is preferable to spinsterhood. I wonder if they would continue to do so if they were made aware of the indignities they might be forced to suffer once the knot was tied?'

Eyes narrowing, Sebastian took a firm yet gentle grasp on the pointed little chin, giving her no choice but to look at him again, his suspicion that something was troubling her instantly confirmed by the sheepish look she cast him before lowering those delicate lids.

'Why should you imagine females suffer indignities in marriage? Who has been filling your pretty head with such pernicious rubbish, my little one?'

'It is true. You know it is,' she responded, thereby neatly avoiding revealing the source. 'All men have their…their peculiarities.'

She looked so deliciously embarrassed with the sudden eruption of colour suffusing her cheeks that he could quite easily have given way to mirth had he not known she was in deadly earnest.

'Yes, I suppose we do,' he agreed, preserving his admirable self-control. 'But what I suspect you are referring to specifically is the more intimate side of marriage. Which, it is true, some women find an unpleasant duty. But certainly not all, Emily. A great many wives are blissfully happy, and welcome their husbands' attentions, simply because they attain equal pleasure from lovemaking.'

Although she raised her eyes only briefly to his, Sebastian could not fail to detect the puzzlement and lingering doubt in the clear blue depths. 'I can see you're not wholly convinced that what I say is true,' he said softly, his gaze focusing on the sweetly curving outline of her mouth. 'Perhaps a practical display might serve the purpose better.'

He detected those striking blue orbs widening in startled anticipation of the assault, as he lowered his head, and then felt the delicious tremble rippling through her as he covered her lips with his own, but even so she made not the least attempt to turn her head away, or break free from the gentle hold he retained on her chin. He raised his other hand to cup her face, thereby denying her any further opportunity of escape, and began to caress the soft hair curling behind her ears and at the base of her neck with his fingertips, while his lips, exerting only the gentlest of pressure, induced hers to part, swiftly winning the sweetly satisfying response he had been determined to attain.

Well versed in the art of lovemaking, Sebastian wisely suppressed the very natural desire to take the gentle initiation a good deal further, and released her before the temptation to do so became too strong.

'Now, can you honestly say that you found anything the least distasteful in that?' he demanded, his voice husky with the lingering desire he was unable to suppress.

'W-well, n-no, not exactly,' she admitted, before the colour returned to her cheeks with a vengeance, and she shot up from the sofa as though she expected its soft fabric to burst into flames at any moment. 'No, I… Oh, my,' she muttered, and sped from the room, leaving Sebastian to revel in the highly satisfying knowledge that he had banished some of her fears at least, even if he had replaced them with delicious confusion

His pleasurable contemplation of her further indoctrination was brought to an abrupt end by the arrival of his aunt who regarded him with a deal of suspicion, and a certain amount of reproach. 'What have you been saying to that poor girl? I passed her on the stairs, and was about to remind her that we are bound for the theatre tonight, when she sped on her way, just as though I were not there.'

'Don't concern yourself, Aunt,' he advised, returning to his desk in order to collect his glass of Madeira. 'emily's a tenacious little thing. She'll recover presently, I assure you.'

Lady Hester flashed him an impatient glance. 'I do not doubt that you've been teasing her again. It is high time you realised that she's not a little girl any longer.'

A slow and satisfied smile curled his lordship's mouth. 'Be assured, ma'am, I am fully aware of it. More importantly, Emily can no longer be in any doubt that I am.'

Chapter Eleven

By the time she had taken her seat in the box at the theatre
that night, Emily had managed to regain much of her lost composure, even though she continued to dwell on the interlude in
the library with a certain amount of bewilderment and shame.

It had been all her own fault, of course. There was little
point in trying to deny that. She had realised his intention, and
could easily have avoided the contact by simply breaking
free from the gentle clasp he had held on her chin. But, no,
foolishly she allowed curiosity to get the better of her, and
was now having to come to terms with the rather disturbing
fact that she could never look upon Sebastian in quite the
same way again. Their association was rapidly moving on to
a different plain, where deep friendship and respect remained
but where a purely platonic relationship was left behind.

From the moment his lips had touched hers, she had been
aware of the vibrant sensual male beneath the gentlemanlike
outward trappings. She hadn't experienced the least revulsion
at his touch. In fact, if the truth were known, he had awakened
some deep, fundamental physical need that even in her innocence she realised could not be satisfied with a mere kiss
alone. Ashamed though she was to admit to it, she had wanted
those sensitive fingers, which had teased the hair about her

neck and ears, to caress far more of her, and could only be thankful that Sebastian at least had appeared to maintain full control over himself, for she had experienced not the least inclination to retain hers.

'Oh, is that not young Sutherland over there, with Lady Templehurst, Sebastian?' Lady Hester asked after scanning the row of boxes opposite, one or two of which had yet to be occupied. 'And I do believe it is that charming Mr Trevenen too. I've always liked him immensely. Such a tragic loss the poor boy suffered! But he seems to have recovered now.'

Thankful for the opportunity to turn her thoughts in a new direction, Emily enquired precisely what Lady Hester had meant, and felt genuinely saddened when Sebastian himself disclosed that his friend's fiancée had died in a riding accident just a month before their wedding was due to take place.

'She was the daughter of his nearest neighbours,' he went on to divulge. 'They had known each other all their lives, and it was generally expected that they would one day marry.'

'How terrible,' Emily murmured. 'He's such a very personable gentleman, as you say, Lady Hester. I do so hope he one day meets someone else, don't you?'

Much to Emily's surprise neither of her companions attempted to respond this time. They were both staring fixedly into the box directly opposite, where Sir Courtney Farrington was lowering himself into a seat beside a handsome lady in a bright crimson gown, which did absolutely nothing to conceal her ample charms. Behind them sat a portly, middle-aged gentleman and a young woman of about Emily's own age whose fixed, simpering expression made her appear singularly foolish.

Lady Hester's unladylike snort clearly betrayed her feelings. Emily had noticed at the ball the previous evening that she had not made the least attempt to engage her niece's husband in conversation. Which had come as no real surprise, as Lady Hester had not been slow to reveal that she now held Sir Courtney in the lowest esteem.

Sebastian, on the other hand, was faintly smiling, as though at some private thought. 'Dear me,' he murmured. 'Louisa Mountjoy's taste would appear to have deteriorated of late. Pity really, she used to be such a discerning creature, so very discreet. Perhaps, though, she has her reasons for being seen in such company.'

'Yes, I suppose she must,' Lady Hester agreed, tight-lipped, and visibly bristling with disapproval. 'But I should certainly not wish to be seen in the company of that dissolute rake Lord Hewley and that idiotic schoolroom chit he married.'

'His wife…?' Emily didn't attempt to hide her astonishment 'I thought it must surely be his daughter. She must be my age!'

'Younger, my dear,' Lady Hester didn't hesitate to reveal 'She's a wealthy Cit's daughter. Needless to say, Hewley married her for money. And no one would have blamed him for that if he hadn't done so in such disgusting haste. His late long-suffering wife was not even cold in her grave, poor woman!'

Masterfully suppressing a chuckle, Emily turned her attention to the stage, where the curtain was about to rise. Lady Hester knew a good deal about the comings and goings o Society's leading figures, and those not so high on the social ladder, even though she had resided in Bath for several years She possibly knew a good deal about the bejewelled handsome brunette seated beside her niece's husband, and Emily experienced the uneasy feeling that Lady Hester had tactfully refrained from comment simply because her nephew was, or had been, on friendly terms with the lady.

Emily might have succeeded in thrusting the suspicion that the relationship might have been more than that of mere friends from her mind completely had Lord Sutherland dragging Mr Tobias Trevenen with him, not paid a visit to their box at the end of the first act.

'My aunt asked me to come across, Lady Hester,' he an

nounced, after pleasantries had been exchanged. 'Would appreciate a word with you. Wants to ask your advice about—' He stopped short as his attention was caught by several persons invading the box opposite. 'Good gad! Ain't that your old flame, Louisa Mountjoy, Hawk, holding court to half the theatre?'

Lady Hester, noting her nephew's understandable frown of annoyance, hurriedly rose to her feet before the irrepressible young Viscount could utter any further tactless remarks. 'Perhaps you would be kind enough to offer me your escort, young man?' she said, slipping her arm through his, and very nearly hauling him from the box.

Mr Trevenen was not slow to put an end to the awkward silence which followed their departure by politely asking Emily if she would care to take a little exercise by strolling in the passageway before the commencement of the second act.

'I should be delighted, sir,' she told him, grasping the chance to be away from Sebastian until she had gained some control over the all-consuming emotion which had gripped her after Michael's artless disclosure.

Emily whisked herself out of the box, thereby successfully denying Mr Trevenen the opportunity to enquire whether his lordship would care to join them. This, she swiftly discovered, had never been his intention, as he declared that he was delighted to obtain a quiet word alone.

'I was not granted the opportunity of offering my heartfelt congratulations yesterday evening, Miss Stapleton,' he explained, when she raised a questioning brow. 'There was little time for much private conversation, but I should like you to know that I sincerely wish you every happiness. Hawkridge is the best of good fellows.'

As Emily's opinion of Sebastian at that moment was vastly contrasting, she wisely refrained from comment, and merely remarked, for want of something better to say, 'You were a good deal occupied as I recall, sir. I was not aware that you were upon friendly terms with the Farringtons.'

'I am not well acquainted with Sir Courtney. But Caroline and I met the year before she married. We discovered we had much in common and became friends.' A troubled look appeared in his kindly eyes. 'Are you perhaps well acquainted with her, Miss Stapleton?'

'I have known her all my life, sir. But I would be less than truthful to claim a close friendship,' she answered, and saw at once that he seemed disappointed. 'Why do you ask?'

'Well, it was just I felt that she…that she didn't seem herself, not the Caroline I remembered. Has she, perhaps, been unwell of late?'

Clearly he was concerned, and Emily would dearly have liked to relieve his anxiety of mind, but he was far too astute a gentleman to believe that nothing was wrong. The problem besetting her was that she had pledged not to reveal what Caroline had disclosed earlier that day to a living soul, and she had no intention of breaking her word. Yet at the same time she felt that Lady Farrington could only benefit from the support of worthy friends like Mr Trevenen.

'She has not been well, it is true,' she admitted, swiftly settling on a compromise. 'Sadly Caroline experienced a miscarriage earlier this year, and quite naturally is suffering the loss. But it just so happens,' she added, in an attempt to relieve a little of his evident concern, 'that I paid her a visit earlier today, and discovered her spirits much improved.'

Mr Trevenen appeared about to utter something in response, but checked when the door to one of the boxes opened, and a tall, immaculately attired figure stepped out into the passageway.

Emily was immediately aware of a change in Mr Trevenen's demeanour. He visibly stiffened, and there was a definite hard set now to his jaw. He might well have been speaking no less than the truth when he had disclosed that he was not well acquainted with Caroline's husband. Evidently he had no desire for that state of affairs to change.

'Sir Courtney,' she greeted him, offering her hand, and hoping that her smile disguised the contempt in which she now held the handsome Baronet, 'are you following our example by taking the opportunity to exercise your limbs?'

Unlike the evening before, he retained a hold on the slender fingers for a few moments only. 'I'm afraid my companion, Lady Mountjoy, is a popular figure. It has become a sad crush in our box,' he divulged before acknowledging Mr Trevenen's presence with the merest of nods, and receiving a salute of no greater warmth in return. 'As your own box, sir, is just a little further along, perhaps you would allow me to return Miss Stapleton to her own?'

Sensing that Mr Trevenen was about to deny the request, Emily hurriedly intervened by accepting Sir Courtney's offer with spurious enthusiasm. Heaven only knew she had no wish to be in the company of a man whom she utterly despised, but for Caroline's sake she was prepared to conceal her antipathy.

'I am grateful for this opportunity to thank you, Miss Stapleton, for taking the trouble to visit my wife,' he surprised her by announcing, the instant Mr Trevenen had moved away, and they turned to walk in the opposite direction. 'Her spirits, which have been low of late, were much improved after you called, I noticed. My one regret is that I was not at home to receive you, and can only hope that you will grant me the opportunity to do so in the near future.'

'I shall be only too delighted to oblige you, sir,' Emily assured him, hoping that he had not detected her flinching reaction to his touch, when he placed his fingers momentarily on her elbow in order to guide her past a couple loitering in the passageway. 'In fact, Caroline might have mentioned that I suggested we might take walks in the park together, weather permitting. Perhaps you could persuade her? Walking is such excellent exercise. Nothing better for restoring the bloom to one's cheeks, do you not agree?'

'You may safely rely on my full support, Miss Stapleton, for my wife's well-being is my prime concern.'

Emily was forced silently to concede that the lying, adulterous rogue's performance was equal to that given by any one of those thespians taking part in the play. Had she not known the truth she would have believed his solicitude genuine.

'I cannot tell you how relieved I am to hear you say so, sir,' she responded, hoping that her powers of dissimulation were equal to his, as she favoured him with a dazzling smile. 'Your wife and I have not seen each other for such a long time. We have much catching up to do. I only hope that I do not prove to be a nuisance by invading your home too frequently.'

'Be assured, dear young lady, that your visits will always be welcomed…and not only by my wife.'

Thankfully Emily was spared the necessity of attempting to appear flattered by this unsubtle admission by none other than Sebastian, who unexpectedly emerged from their box. Her relief, however, was short-lived. His lordship's expression was sombre, and became markedly more so when his eyes fell upon her companion.

'The second act is due to begin shortly.' His voice distinctly lacked its customary warmth, and became cooler still when he informed her companion that his services as an escort were no longer required.

Sir Courtney, thankfully, appeared to receive his *congé* with a good grace, merely bowing slightly before swinging round on his heels. Emily, on the other hand, found his lordship's lofty attitude annoying. Evidently he disapproved of her choice of escort, a fact that he made perfectly plain the instant they returned to their seats.

'I should be obliged in future, young woman, if you would refrain from encouraging that particular person's attentions.'

Unaccustomed to having her actions criticised, Emily's annoyance increased. Even so, she might well have succeeded in suppressing her vexation at his high-handed attitude, and allowing the matter to drop, if she had not just happened to look up at that moment in time to catch the vivacious widow in the box opposite bestowing a seductive smile in his lordship's direction. His slight nod in acknowledgement only succeeded in stoking the fires of her wrath.

'For your information I did not offer any encouragement. He merely volunteered to escort me back to this box and I accepted,' she hissed between gritted teeth. 'And might I remind you that how I choose to conduct myself is entirely my own affair.'

'And might I remind *you* that I am not only your fiancé but also your guardian,' he countered, the tender mouth which earlier in the day had wrought such havoc on her senses now set in a straight line, hard and uncompromising. 'You would do well to remember it in future, for I shan't brook any acts of defiance on your part.'

Her smile could not have been sweeter, but the challenging gleam in her eyes was unmistakable. 'And *you* would do well to remember that thus far I have caused you no real concern… That, of course, might well change if you continue to provoke me, Lord Hawkridge.'

It was perhaps fortunate that Lady Hester returned to the box a moment later. She was in no good mood herself, as she had been forced to swallow her pride and exchange a few pleasantries with her niece's husband whom she had been unable to avoid in the passageway, and yet she was immediately aware of the tense atmosphere in the box. Her nephew, grim-faced, was scowling fixedly down at the curtain on the stage, while Emily appeared to be finding the toes of her satin evening slippers of immense interest.

Undoubtedly there had been some sort of disagreement between them which sadly neither appeared willing to put right. Lady Hester had no intention of prying, but she could not help wondering whether young Michael Sutherland's unfortunate reference to Sebastian's association with a certain vivacious widow might not be at the root of the trouble.

The situation between them might well have improved if Sebastian, after curtly excusing himself at the end of the second act, had not left the box. Lady Hester, in an attempt to divert Emily, only succeeded in making matters worse when she suggested a stroll in the passageway, for they discovered his lordship loitering there, deep in conversation with Lady Mountjoy. Not surprisingly Emily's reaction was to turn sharply on her heels and return to her seat, and Lady Hester decided that, all things considered, it might be wise if they did not go on somewhere for supper as originally planned, but returned to the house, a suggestion which gained her seething charge's wholehearted support.

But later that night, as she lay in bed, Emily could only wonder at herself for succumbing to a fit of the sullens. When Sebastian had returned to their box, in good time for the commencement of the third and final act of the play, his mood had obviously improved and he had tried to make amends for his bout of ill humour, but she would have none of it, and had answered him only in monosyllables. He had raised not the least objection to their returning home early, declaring that he himself would go on to his club. Whether he had done so or not was open to speculation, but whatever entertainment he had sought had not induced him to remain away from the house for long, for Emily had detected that familiar tread in the passageway a short time before, when he had passed her door, heading in the direction of his own suite of rooms.

Jealousy, of course, had been the force behind her show of petulance, she silently acknowledged, now feeling utterly ashamed of herself for allowing the unpleasant emotion to take such an overwhelming grasp on her, adversely affecting her judgement, and inducing her to behave in a thoroughly immature manner. After all, it wasn't as if she had been so naïve as to suppose that Sebastian had never enjoyed intimate relationships with members of her sex. During their years apart his name had been linked with more than one female of dubious morals. It was simply that she had never once found herself having to ward off the appalling influence of an emotion quite foreign to her nature, and she was forced to admit she had been ill equipped to deal with the unpleasant experience.

Finally accepting that she would never succumb to the re-cuperative powers of sleep in her present disturbed frame of mind, Emily threw back the bed covers and swung her feet to the floor. She managed to locate the candle on the bedside table and light it with precious little effort. Unfortunately she was nowhere near as successful in finding the book that Caroline had kindly loaned her, and searched her bedchamber in vain for several minutes before she recalled leaving it downstairs in the library, after that memorable interlude with Sebastian.

Why was it, she wondered, after donning her robe and slipping quietly out of the bedchamber to discover the stair-case and hall below cast in eerie, menacing shadow, that a house's normal creaks and groans, which one would ignore during daylight hours, always seemed so sinister and threat-ening the instant darkness fell? Of course it was all in the mind, she told herself, striving to hold her candle steadily and not spill hot wax, as she stretched out her fingers to clasp the knob on the library door. Then she detected what sounded sus-piciously like splintering glass, a noise which she simply could not dismiss as the normal settlement of a house.

Could one of the servants still be up and about…? Surely not! Sebastian did not encourage any member of his staff, not even his valet, to wait up for him, and she felt sure the house had been quiet for some little time before his return. She was striving to convince herself that she simply must have imagined it, when she distinctly heard a further sound, a scraping one this time, coming from behind the breakfast-parlour door.

Her first impulse was to rouse the household, but she

curbed it. If the sound had been made by a rose bush scraping against the window, or the kitchen cat, perhaps having stealthily found its way into this part of the house, endeavouring to escape, she would have caused a disturbance for no purpose. It would be far better for her to investigate, she decided, swiftly steeling herself to do just that.

The butler's conscientious approach to the smallest detail of his work, ensuring all doorhinges were kept well oiled and squeak free, coupled with the fact that her feet were clad in the softest of slippers, resulted in her entering the breakfast parlour without a sound. For a few moments it was as much as she could do to gape in astonished disbelief at the unexpected sight of an intruder straddling the window-sill, then pure instinct took over and she hurled the candlestick, which she had been holding aloft, across the room. A low groan, a further shattering of glass and a muffled expletive following in quick succession suggested strongly that she had hit her mark, as did the miscreant's immediate departure. Then Emily resorted to what any self-respecting female would do in the circumstances and screamed for all she was worth.

No sooner had the last echoes of her shrill cry died away than sounds of doors opening and running footsteps filtered down from above, and all at once she was being protectively cradled in those strong arms which had offered such comfort on more occasions than she cared to remember in her formative years.

'Well, now,' his lordship murmured, still retaining his comforting grasp on slender shoulders, while surveying the damage and disorder by the open window, 'this is most unexpected.'

Chapter Twelve

In view of the fact that she had been involved in a somewhat unnerving incident, Emily managed to drop off to sleep remarkably quickly once the hammering in order to board up the window and make all safe for the night had been completed, and she awoke the next day feeling not a whit the worse for having experienced the disquieting ordeal.

Discovering from Skinner that Clegg had already engaged the services of a glazier to effect the necessary repairs to the parlour window, Emily decided once again to eat breakfast in bed. The tray, which arrived promptly, not only contained a delicious repast but also a note from his lordship inviting her to join him for a ride in the park. Good relations having been fully restored between them, after the events of the night, Emily did not need to think twice about it, and dispatched Skinner with a message that she would be ready to accompany him out in an hour.

'One of your many fine qualities, my angel,' his lordship remarked, emerging from his library at the appointed time to discover her descending the last few steps into the hall, 'is that your timekeeping is impeccable. A rare virtue in a female, believe me!'

'I dislike being kept waiting myself, and do not approve

of the present vogue for keeping a gentleman kicking his heels,' she admitted, preceding him outside to discover Jonas Finn walking his lordship's fine bay and a darling chestnut filly round from the mews.

Sebastian saw those beloved features positively light up before Emily ran down the steps. 'I trust you approve my choice? I purchased her yesterday.'

'Need you ask?' she answered, gently making the filly's acquaintance. 'She's utterly adorable.'

'She certainly is,' his lordship agreed, his gaze not straying from a perfectly proportioned, trim figure. 'A trifle head-strong on occasions, but that only seems to enhance her charm.'

Emily detected her groom's shoulders shaking in silent, appreciative laughter as he assisted her to alight, and cast a suspicious glance in his lordship's direction as he mounted his favourite hack. 'I sincerely trust you were referring to your latest acquisition?'

Grinning wickedly, Sebastian remained silent as they rode out of the Square, secretly admiring the way Emily handled the frisky filly with comparative ease. By the time they had reached the gates of Hyde Park he would have defied anyone to suppose that horse and rider were not friends of long standing.

'I suspected that she was merely playful and not ill-natured when I made the purchase yesterday. And I'm delighted to be proved right.'

A disturbing thought suddenly occurred to Emily. 'Oh, Hawk, you didn't go to the expense of buying her especially for me, did you? I was certain you'd have some animal in your stable suitable for me to ride.'

'Two or three as it happens. But I wanted you to have a mount of your own. Now, for heaven's sake don't set up a fuss, Em!' he went on when she was about to protest. 'If it disturbs you so much then look upon her as an early birthday present.'

A tender smile replaced the troubled frown. 'You have never once forgotten my birthday, Hawk, in all the years we were apart. I was always most touched by the gifts you sent me.'

'Mere trifles, my angel.'

'But you can hardly call this lovely girl a trifle,' she countered, leaning forward to stroke the sleek chestnut-coloured neck. 'She must have cost you a great deal. What's her name, by the way?'

He grimaced. 'Buttercup, would you believe? It might be as well to rename her. Do by all means give it due consideration. But not at the moment, for I should like you to turn your thoughts to what occurred last night.'

Emily regarded him keenly. He appeared as undisturbed now as he had been shortly after he had burst into the breakfast parlour and taken control of the situation in his usual, highly efficient way, ordering the young footman who had followed closely at his heels to rouse all the male members of his household staff, and ensure that temporary repairs to the window were put into effect immediately. He had then escorted Emily back up to her room, saying nothing, except that she was not to worry, and that he would ensure that a vigil was kept throughout the night to ensure the miscreant didn't pay a return visit.

The one thing he had said that she had considered odd at the time filtered through her mind again, and she immediately sought an explanation. 'I remember you saying that you were surprised by the break-in, Seb. But surely that was what you expected to happen?'

'I'd have been amazed if an attempt to purloin the Hawkridge diamonds hadn't been made before the Season ended, but I must admit I was surprised that it occurred quite so soon.' He stared fixedly ahead, his intelligent brow slightly furrowed. 'As I've mentioned before, I don't underestimate my quarry, Em. He's a cunning devil. That is why he's escaped detection for so long. So I cannot help wondering what prompted him to make an attempt so quickly? He must surely have suspected that a strict vigil would be maintained, at least for a while.'

'And has it?'

'Oh, yes. Young Thomas has been sleeping in my dressing-room, as an added precaution.'

Up until that moment Emily had never given a thought as to where the necklace was being kept. 'So it is safely locked away somewhere in your bedchamber, is it?'

He nodded. 'Behind the mirror on the wall,' he enlightened her without giving the matter a second thought. 'Apart from myself, only Clegg, Thomas and my valet know the safe's whereabouts. And now, of course, you.'

'Well, I shan't divulge it to anyone,' she assured him, 'though I cannot help but think your aunt is right and it would be sensible to return the necklace to the bank.'

'That would defeat the object somewhat,' he countered, slanting her a mocking glance. 'The idea, my little love, was to draw the villain out. And we succeeded. But why did he act so soon? That's what defeats me.' After a moment's intense thought he thrust the conundrum to the back of his mind to puzzle over later, and asked, 'I don't suppose for a moment that you recognised our uninvited guest, or perhaps sensed that you'd seen him somewhere before?'

Emily paused to consider before shaking her head. 'No, I cannot say that I did. But he was there for a few moments only. I threw my candlestick at him and he—er—departed instantly.'

Exerting masterly self-control, his lordship managed not to laugh. His Emily, as always, had shown great presence of mind. He recalled that, apart from looking a little pale, she had been none the worse for the ordeal, although she had seemed to attain a deal of comfort when he had placed his arm about her. Which had come as a great relief, after their sense-less disagreement earlier in the evening.

'I don't suppose he'd considered that he'd be confronted

by an intrepid virago,' he couldn't resist saying, his voice shaking only slightly. 'Your aim, by the way, was unerringly accurate. I noticed a reddish-brown stain on the candlestick.'

'Ahh! I thought I'd hit him,' she disclosed with simple pride. 'The impertinent rogue had the effrontery to swear at me.' Ignoring his lordship's bark of laughter, she added, 'When I was speaking to Sir Giles Osborne the other evening, he advised me not to rule out the possibility that a woman might be involved, not directly in the crimes themselves, merely passing on information. Do you think that's a possibility?'

Sebastian nodded. 'But I would imagine it's unwittingly done. The man I'm seeking has proved beyond doubt that he has precious little respect for your sex, so I think it highly unlikely that he'd trust a woman with information which could put a noose around his neck.'

Emily was forced to agree. 'Yes, you're right—it isn't likely he'd place his trust in a mistress.'

His lordship slanted her a further mocking glance. 'My dear girl, mistresses to do not go about in polite society.'

'Some do,' she countered without pausing to consider what she was saying, but it was already too late. Those shrewd grey eyes had narrowed and were firmly fixed on the rapidly heightening colour she was powerless to suppress.

'Louisa Mountjoy is no lightskirt,' he freely disclosed, reading her thoughts with distressing accuracy. 'She's an immensely sensible woman who has always conducted her affairs with the utmost discretion.' He did not fail to notice one fine brow arch sceptically. 'Lady Mountjoy and I were once very close,' he admitted, swiftly accepting that it would be immensely foolish to attempt to deny their past, more intimate association, 'and I still consider her a friend now, and always make a point of speaking to her if we should happen to attend the same function. But I hope you would know me better than to suppose that I would ever flaunt a mistress of mine in front of you.'

By great good fortune Emily was spared the humiliation of having to respond, for Sebastian's attention was immediately captured by a couple strolling down the path towards them.

'Why, Toby, you old dog! I do believe you are acquiring a taste for town life.' He then turned to his friend's companion, and smiled approvingly. 'Good to see you out and about enjoying yourself, Cousin.'

If Caroline was discomposed by this unexpected encounter she certainly betrayed no sign of it as she returned his lordship's greeting with an easy smile, before turning to Emily and suggesting that she might like to walk for a while.

'I came to the park in the hope of seeing you, and bumped into Mr Trevenen instead,' Caroline disclosed after Emily, dismounting without assistance, had fallen into step beside her. 'I understand that you were attending the theatre last night. Courtney mentioned that he'd seen you there.'

Emily hardly knew what to say. To have denied it was impossible. At the same time she had no intention of revealing that the Baronet had been in the company of the Dowager Lady Mountjoy. Something in her expression, however, must have betrayed her slight feelings of unease, for Caroline smiled, assuring her that she had known all about her husband's visit to the theatre.

'Louisa Mountjoy is one of the few members of Society with whom I have kept up a correspondence since my marriage, Emily,' she revealed. 'We were at school together, and had our come-out in the same year. Her first Season was a success. She married Lord Mountjoy when she had just turned nineteen. Their marriage, though tragically short, was happy and fruitful. She has a young son. It was she who hired the box at the theatre in the hope that I would be there.' She raised a hand briefly to her throat. 'But of course that was impossible.'

Emily had the grace to look a little shamefaced. She had allowed personal concerns to cloud her judgement to such an extent that she would have been happy to believe that Lady Mountjoy was none other than the very one aiding and abetting the murderous jewel thief. 'Oh, dear. It would seem that I did indeed jump to several wrong conclusions where Lady Mountjoy is concerned.'

Caroline did not pretend to misunderstand. 'Oh, no. Louisa is not my husband's mistress, Emily. I strongly suspect that she doesn't even like him, though she's never admitted as much, and she does manage to conceal her feelings remarkably well. No, Louisa is my friend, and a good one. I'm not trying to suggest that she hasn't enjoyed a close relationship with certain privileged gentlemen since her husband's demise. But why should she not? She is still young.'

Emily might have wholeheartedly agreed if she hadn't known for a fact that Sebastian had numbered among the favoured few, so she wisely refrained from comment, lest she betray her lingering, less than charitable views on the vivacious widow, and changed the subject slightly by revealing the identities of the two other persons sharing Lady Mountjoy's box.

'Good heavens!' Caroline exclaimed, sounding genuinely surprised. 'I do not believe Lord Hewley numbers among Louisa's particular friends, and I'm equally certain his wife does not. I can only imagine that they were there at Courtney's invitation. How odd! I cannot recall that Hewley is a particular friend of my husband's either, although they both enjoy playing for high stakes.' She shrugged. 'Perhaps it's his wife who is proving the attraction.'

Caroline seemed not to care whether this was so or not, but once again Emily tactfully changed the subject by remarking that the fresh air seemed to be doing her the world of good and that a healthy bloom was returning to her cheeks.

'If that is so,' Caroline responded, smiling wryly, 'then I have you to thank for it. Courtney informed me earlier, before he left the house, that I was to enjoy your company as much as possible. Needless to say I was for once happy to comply with his wishes, and doubly so when I discovered that his faithful watchdog, Sloane, is indisposed.' Caroline's full lips were curled by a wickedly satisfied smile. 'The loathsome creature walked into a door, by all accounts, possibly eavesdropping, and suffered a cut forehead and a black eye for his pains. Serves him right!'

Emily could not prevent a gurgle of mirth at her companion's understandable vindictiveness. She might not have found it quite so amusing had she appreciated fully what she had just learned, but she was not destined to do so until her stay in the capital was fast drawing to a close.

No sooner had they arrived back at Berkeley Square than Sebastian went out again almost immediately to keep an appointment with one of his friends at the famous boxing salon in Bond Street; and Emily, discovering his aunt was at last awake, went upstairs to change out of her habit, before going along to Lady Hester's room to discover her chaperon propped up in bed, sipping a cup of sweet hot chocolate.

'emily, my dear!' she greeted her with every evidence of delight, whilst patting the edge of the bed invitingly. 'My maid assured me that you were none the worse for your ordeal. And I see that Watchet was being perfectly truthful. What a to-do! But, there, didn't I warn that nephew of mine that we would all be murdered in our beds if he insisted on keeping that wretched heirloom in the house?'

Emily, accepting the invitation to sit on the edge of the bed, couldn't forbear a smile. If the intruder had, indeed, had murder in mind, Lady Hester would have known precious little about it. She had slept, so Skinner had amazingly divulged, through it all, unbelievably not even stirring when the window had been receiving temporary repairs.

'And it was you, so I understand, who confronted the villain!' Lady Hester continued, her expression a quaint mixture of admiration and disapproval. 'What on earth were you doing wandering about the house at that time of night, child?'

'I couldn't sleep, and so went downstairs to collect the book your niece very kindly loaned me.'

Lady Hester's gaze grew noticeably more intense. 'I didn't realise you had called on Caroline.'

'Oh, didn't I mention it?' Emily feigned surprise. 'It must have slipped my mind. Yes, I paid a visit yesterday morning. I saw her again today, as it happens, whilst I was out riding with Sebastian. She was taking the air with Mr Trevenen.'

The intense look in Lady Hester's eyes was replaced by a speculative one, but she refrained from comment, and merely said after a moment's quiet deliberation, 'And did she appear well?'

'Very much better, yes,' Emily was pleased to assure her. 'Sir Courtney, it seems, is concerned for her health, and is keen for her to take more exercise in the fresh air.'

'Fagh!' Lady Hester dismissed this with an impatient wave of her hand. 'When has that lecherous rogue ever given a thought to my niece's well-being? Look at the way he behaves—out every night, enjoying himself and leaving Caroline to her own devices.'

'I think, ma'am, that she prefers it that way,' Emily responded, careful not to divulge too much, thereby betraying Caroline's trust. 'The invitation to the theatre was issued by Lady Mountjoy and included Caroline. Seemingly they have been friends for some time, and from what I gather Lady Mountjoy doesn't hold Sir Courtney in the highest esteem.'

'You may possibly be right,' Lady Hester agreed. 'Sebastian hinted as much, did he not?'

That was true enough. Even so, Emily had gained the distinct impression that Caroline wouldn't have cared a whit if it had been quite otherwise. And therein, she silently acknowledged, was the difference between them. Loving Sebastian as she did, Emily had been consumed with jealousy at the mere thought of his having enjoyed a close relationship with Lady Mountjoy. Perhaps Caroline was the sensible one. Love, after all, could be extremely painful. Perhaps it was better not to care…

'I don't suppose Caroline mentioned whether she is to attend Lady Pilkington's rout this evening out at Richmond?' Lady Hester asked, thereby forcing Emily to abandon her unsettling reflections.

'No, she didn't, ma'am, although she gave me every reason to suppose that she intends to accept invitations in the near future.'

Lady Hester appeared relieved to learn this. 'I shall pay her a visit later. It's high time I did. No doubt my nephew will wish you to bear him company?'

'Yes, he did suggest that when we went out for a drive in the curricle. I very much enjoyed our ride this morning. He very kindly acquired a mount for me, a darling chestnut filly whom I've decided to call Hera. Sebastian spoils me.'

'And so he should.' Lady Hester beamed approvingly. 'You are remarkably well suited, you know. Everyone remarks upon it. And the fact that he's head over heels in love.'

Yes, Emily thought hollowly. But not with me.

Lady Hester might not have been sensible to the fact that Emily's spirits had slumped, but Sebastian, far more sensitive to her moods, was instantly aware that all was not as it should be with her the instant he returned to the house. He refrained from comment during their excursion in the curricle, when he allowed her once again to handle his fine greys, but that evening, after they had travelled out to Richmond to attend Lord and Lady Pilkington's rout, he made up his mind to discover what was causing her such concern.

'Shall we forgo our dance,' he suggested, successfully managing to catch her before yet another male guest could claim her as a partner, 'and take a stroll in the delightful garden before that false smile of yours begins to crack under the strain?'

Blue eyes darted a distinctly wary look in his direction, but she accompanied him readily enough, even going so far as to link her arm through his as they strolled down the path towards a rose arbour.

It was a fine late May evening, warm and with the lightest of breezes, a circumstance which had induced several couples to take advantage of a little fresh air. Eventually, however, his lordship managed to discover a secluded spot, where he could commence his inquisition without fear of being overheard.

'Why should you suppose that there is something amiss with me?' she said in response to his gambit. 'It's a delightful party, and a perfect evening. And more importantly, as I'm sure you've noticed, all four of your remaining suspects are present. Perhaps you oughtn't to have taken heed of your aunt's advice and permitted me to wear the diamonds. When all is said and done, that is the reason for my being in the capital.'

He easily put an end to her seemingly rapt contemplation of a particularly fine specimen of a white rose by taking a firm clasp on her shoulders and turning her round to face him squarely.

'You'll be trying to suggest next that it was my decision not to permit you to wear the diamonds which has put your nose out of joint. Save your breath, my darling,' he advised gently. 'It won't serve. I've known you too long not to be very certain that something has upset you since we parted company after our ride.'

His lordship could easily discern the wariness in her blue eyes, before she lowered them and released her breath in a tiny sigh of resignation. 'Yes,' she admitted at last, 'something did. It was something that your aunt said which made me realise that maybe I'm beginning to enjoy this stay in town with you more than I ought and that I might resent it very much when it comes to an end, and I am obliged to resume my former life.'

One of the facets of her character which he had always admired was her innate honesty, and he was convinced that she was speaking the truth, as far as it went, but could not quite rid himself of the uneasy feeling that there was something more fundamental at the root of her malcontent. Even so he refrained from pressing her further, and merely chose to remind her of something that he had disclosed before. 'It will be your decision to end it, Emily. I have no desire to do so. I have been happier during these past few weeks than I have been for years. And it is all because you are now back in my life, where you belong.'

He watched those small, white teeth begin to gnaw at her bottom lip, but not before he had noticed it trembling, and placed his fingers beneath her chin, swiftly deciding that actions, here again, would serve his purpose far better than words.

Her instant response to his kiss was sweetly satisfying, and more so when she betrayed no reluctance whatsoever in wrapping slender arms about his neck so that he could replace tenderness with passion, and hold those softly feminine curves against him in a way that he had never done before without fear of causing her the least alarm. Nevertheless, he knew his limitations and reluctantly brought the highly satisfying embrace to an end while he still maintained sufficient control over his ardour.

'Well now,' he murmured, while he stared down into eyes still hazy with desire. 'That was most revealing. How very satisfying it is to know that my patience all these years has finally been rewarded.'

Still slightly dazed by the sudden eruption of passion which had taken such immediate control of both mind and body, Emily was hardly aware of what he had said. She only knew that she was eager for him to repeat the embrace, and experienced a stab of disappointment when his hands went to her shoulders holding her firmly away, before he allowed them to fall to his sides. Then she heard it too—the crunching of gravel and a shrill, high-pitched titter.

'Oh, my!' a deep voice drawled. 'We appear to have

stumbled upon a trysting place, Lady Hewley, and are clearly *de trop*. If you take my advice, Hawkridge, you'll tie the knot as soon as possible before the strain becomes too much for you.'

Emily could easily detect the look of disdain flicker over Sebastian's features, before he turned to face the unwelcome intruders. 'For once, Farrington, I find that you and I are in complete accord. My marriage cannot take place quickly enough for me.'

Emily couldn't fail to notice, either, the look of intense dislike which, for one unguarded moment, glinted in the handsome Baronet's ice-blue eyes, before his highly amused companion thankfully brought the uncomfortable silence to an end by announcing, 'Oh, such impatience!' Once again that shrill, high-pitched titter shattered the tranquillity of the garden. 'Do allow me to accompany you back inside, Miss Stapleton, before your fiancé frightens you with his ardour.'

Although Emily had no wish to spend the least amount of time in the company of a female whom she had stigmatised as foolishly immature when they had conversed briefly earlier in the evening, she didn't hesitate to take immediate advantage of the invitation to return to the drawing-room where the party was being held.

It was patently obvious that the gentlemen's antipathy was entirely mutual, so the sooner they went their separate ways the better. More urgent still was the need for a few minutes' quiet reflection to assess what might possibly be the repercussions of her sad lack of control. That Sebastian now viewed her as a desirable young woman could not have been made more clear. But did this automatically mean that his feelings for her had deepened too? She needed to be sure; needed to evaluate what had truly induced him to utter those sweet sentiments and that tenderly spoken desire to wed her, and if the only way to achieve this was to spend a brief period in the company of the loquacious Lady Hewley, then it was a small price to pay.

Unfortunately things did not go quite as Emily might have wished. Although Sebastian and Sir Courtney obliged her by taking refuge in the card room, at different tables, needless to say, Lady Hewley betrayed no sign of wanting to mingle with the other guests. She accompanied Emily across to where Lady Hester sat with the dowagers, and commenced to regale them both with the latest *on dits,* which included scurrilous remarks about several of those present.

Emily had discovered soon after her arrival in town that Sebastian's engaging aunt wasn't above indulging in gossip herself, most especially when it came to criticising the outrageous behaviour of the more colourful members of Society. Even so Emily had never once heard Lady Hester utter an unkind word about those more vulnerable members of her class, or those who, lacking natural vivacity, did not go about attempting to scandalise the polite world.

Consequently it came as no great surprise to Emily, when Lord Hewley's immature young wife, having exhausted her supply of gossip, began to pass some quite unnecessary and highly critical remarks about the daughter of the house, to hear Lady Hester immediately defend the hapless victim of such childish spite.

'It is true that Miss Pilkington has little claim to beauty,' she agreed stiffly. 'Yet no one could deny that her carriage is excellent, and her manners are pleasing. Breeding shows.' She sniffed pointedly. 'Believe me, my dear, there is no substitute for it.'

The gibe was clearly lost on Lady Hewley who gazed about her seeking further prey. 'I must say that I consider Lady Pilkington a handsome woman, even though she is well past her prime. And I should willingly die just to possess those rubies she's wearing.'

Lady Hester, though wishful to move away in order to find more genial company, could not resist voicing her opinion on Lady Pilkington's famous rubies. 'Such a sacrifice on your part would be self-defeating, I fear, for once in your grave, you would never attain the pleasure of wearing them. None the less I am forced to agree that they are quite magnificent.'

Lady Hewley gave vent to one of her high-pitched giggles, though whether this stemmed from appreciation of Lady Hester's wit or some private thought was hard to judge. 'Would you believe she keeps her jewels in a box at the bottom of her wardrobe, simply because she is forever misplacing the key to her safe!'

By this time Emily, like her chaperon, had had quite enough of the frivolous young matron's company, and had listened with only half an ear. However, the following day she was given every reason to recall the interlude with Lady Hewley and to wonder who had been close enough to overhear their conversation.

Chapter Thirteen

Clegg, having positioned an arrangement of flowers to his
satisfaction on the largest of the three tables in the hall,
grimaced as the doorknocker was applied with quite unnecessary vigour, and moved sedately across the chequered hall to
answer the summons. In his experience only one young
person ever set up such a hammering. Consequently he was
somewhat taken aback when he was almost rudely thrust
aside a moment later not by young Lord Sutherland, as
expected, but by Emily, who dashed past him in her eagerness to enter the house.

After dispensing with her outdoor garments, tossing both
bonnet and pelisse into Skinner's arms, Emily wasted no time
in discovering from Clegg the whereabouts of his master
and then went striding purposefully across the hall.

When she had first arrived at Berkeley Square, Emily
wouldn't have dreamed of entering Sebastian's sanctum
without knocking and gaining permission to do so first. That
of course had changed once the wonderful camaraderie which
they had always enjoyed had been swiftly re-established, dispensing with the need for polite formality.

She discovered him seated behind his desk, busily engaged
in reading his correspondence and, more importantly, quit

alone, a circumstance which she would have ascertained first from Clegg had she not been so eager to impart her news.

His lordship looked up as she entered, and although he smiled readily enough, Emily had little difficulty in detecting uncertainty in his eyes. And who could blame him for being wary? After all, what was he to make of a young woman who had willingly responded to his embrace one moment, matching his passion with her own, and then had spent the rest of the evening doing everything humanly possible to keep him at a distance? She had remained on the dance floor for much of the time, with a variety of partners, and had even gone so far as to feign sleep throughout the entire carriage journey back to Berkeley Square in order to avoid conversation.

He was no fool. And neither was she! An indifferent night's sleep, when she had spent many hours soul-searching, had forced her to acknowledge that attempting to avoid him was no answer to her heart-rending dilemma, and impossible to achieve while she remained under this roof. She had been forced to acknowledge too that when Sebastian touched her, held her in those protective, masculine arms of his, her body and heart took control, swiftly silencing the cautionary little voice which urged continued circumspection. She rather feared, though, that it was too late for discretion now. She had betrayed herself and he couldn't possibly be under any illusion about just how deeply she loved him.

And he loved her too; there was no doubt in her mind about that any longer. When he had declared his wish to marry her as soon as possible, he had meant every word. When he had admitted to having been happier during recent weeks than he had for a very long time, he had been totally sincere. But did that necessarily mean that his feelings for his cousin had lessened over the years? If not, would she, the girl who had loved him all her life, from somewhere manage to find the strength to refuse to marry him a second time…? She might possibly, yes; but she was under no illusion that it would be immensely hard to do so, given that she no longer retained the remotest desire to refuse.

'I have to admit to misjudging you, my darling,' he remarked drily, as she came across to seat herself in the chair positioned by the desk. 'When you failed to appear, as arranged, for our ride this morning, I was convinced you were doing your utmost to avoid me still.'

He was nothing if not direct, but at least she was able to hold that faintly quizzical gaze as she said, 'I own to being somewhat contrary on occasions, Sebastian, and sometimes stubborn, but I am not so foolish as to suppose that I would succeed for any length of time in trying to avoid someone residing under the same roof. The simple truth is that I passed an indifferent night and, in consequence, rose late. When I discovered you had gone out for a ride alone, I decided to go for a walk. And you will be glad I did not await your return, when you learn what I have discovered.'

His expression changed to one of polite interest. 'You find me positively agog with curiosity, my angel. Pray do enlighten me.'

Emily experienced a certain satisfaction in divulging her startling news. 'Lady Pilkington's ruby necklace is missing. Purloined sometime during the night when, would you believe, she left it in full view on her dressing table. Apparently she has earned herself the reputation for being somewhat lax where the care of her valuables is concerned.'

The expressive masculine brows once more came into play as he arched them quizzically. 'Oh, and from whom did you glean all this information, may I ask?'

'From Caroline. I went for a walk in the park with Skinner. Caroline mentioned yesterday that she had every intention of taking the air again there today, so I was hoping to see her.'

Sebastian regarded in her in silence, his expression now difficult to read. 'You seem to have acquired a partiality for my cousin's company, Emily. I noticed yesterday that you appeared wondrous close, walking on ahead, and chattering away like two lifelong bosom bows.'

Was that an element of censure in his voice? she wondered. 'You do not object, surely?'

He shrugged. 'Merely an observation. I cannot recall, you see, that you ever betrayed a partiality for her company when she paid numerous visits to my parents' home years ago.'

One of the most irritating things about him, Emily reflected, was that he never forgot a dratted thing. And he was absolutely right, of course. Yet she could hardly explain why she was displaying such a keen interest in Caroline now without breaking her word.

'I suppose because years ago she always seemed so very much older, very much the young lady, whereas I was a sad scamp. Consequently we had very little in common. That quite naturally has changed now.'

He appeared to accept this readily enough, and she was relieved when he didn't press her further. Unfortunately his observations had succeeded in jogging her memory, reminding her of something that had been puzzling her slightly in recent days. She hovered for a moment, uncertain whether to have her curiosity satisfied, then decided that, no matter the answer, it was better to know the truth.

'If I have been taking an interest in your cousin, Sebastian, you, considering how very close you and Caroline were at one time, have not. Even your aunt chose to pay her a visit yesterday. But you haven't attempted to go out of your way to see her once since she arrived in town.'

His only response was to rise from his chair and go over to stand before the window, staring out across the patch of green in the Square. Emily thought she was destined to remain in ignorance, but then he surprised her by admitting, 'I interfered in her life once before, the result of which possibly did more harm than good. I vowed never to do so again.'

Emily frowned at this surprising disclosure. She knew, of course, that he had been very much against Caroline's marriage to Farrington. Which was not hard to understand when he had wished to marry her himself! Yet Caroline had chosen to marry the handsome Baronet against his advice. It was entirely her own choice, so why should Sebastian blame himself for that?

'I do not perfectly understand, Hawk.' She had no wish to reopen old wounds which just might, blessedly, have now healed. At the same time she was forced to accept that it was better to know the truth, better to know precisely how she stood if they ever were to marry. 'I know you were against your cousin's marriage, that you tried to dissuade her, but surely that was advice, kindly meant, not interference?'

'True, but what I did afterwards cannot be termed as anything other than deliberate meddling.' He turned to discover her regarding him in frowning silence, head on one side, fine brows meeting above the bridge of the straight, little nose, assuming that endearing pose which she always adopted whenever puzzled by something.

'I went to see Caroline's father shortly before he died, confided my fears for his daughter's future well-being and succeeded in persuading him to make certain alterations to his will. It had been his intention to leave everything unconditionally to Caroline, which of course would have found its way directly into her husband's purse. In the new will Henry Westcotte left half his fortune in trust for any children Caroline might have, and the remainder to his daughter which she would be unable to touch until she attained the age of forty or became a widow before reaching that age. If, however, anything happened to Caroline in the meantime the money would automatically be transferred to her offspring. Naturally Farrington attempted to contest the new will, but without success, as I was one of the executors and was not silent in my assurances that Henry Westcotte was in sound mind when he had made the adjustments.'

'So that is why Farrington dislikes you so much,' she murmured, clearly recalling the hostility in those ice-blue eyes.

'One of the reasons, yes,' he concurred as he resumed his seat. 'But as I believe I mentioned once before, we never liked each other from the first.'

He shook his head, still not sure whether he had done the right thing by interfering and echoed his thoughts aloud. Emily, on the other hand, had no doubts whatsoever. She could still recall that vivid red mark, evidence of Sir Courtney's uncertain temper, around his wife's throat. He might or might not be capable of murder, but it was perhaps fortunate for Caroline that it was in her husband's best interest to ensure that she remained hale and hearty until she came into her fortune.

'But you did it for Caroline's sake. Surely she must understand that?'

'Perhaps…I'm not sure. Before her father's demise she wrote to me on a regular basis. I have received one letter only from her since, the one she wrote in response to my missive informing her of our engagement, and inviting her to the party.'

'I do not believe she bears you any ill will, Hawk,' Emily assured him gently, certain in her own mind that it was more likely to have been Sir Courtney himself who had forbidden her to write.

'Maybe not. But what I do know is that she seemed happy in her marriage up until her father's death. It was only afterwards that Farrington began to neglect her, leaving her in Derbyshire while he resided for much of the time here in town, squandering money on gambling and women.'

Emily stared intently across the desk. 'And you are wondering where he acquires the money to do so. Is that why he remains high on your list of suspects?'

'One of the reasons, certainly,' his lordship freely admitted, 'although I happen to know Caroline's dowry was considerable.'

Leaning back against his chair, Sebastian raised his arms to place his hands at the back of his head, and in so doing drew

Emily's attention to the waistcoat beneath his jacket, straining across his broad chest. He saw the faint flush touch the delicate cheeks before she quickly lowered her gaze to stare intently at the standish on the desk. He experienced a deal of satisfaction and smiled to himself, sensing that she was remembering the highly enjoyable interlude in the Pilkingtons' garden the previous evening, and sensing too that the memory was not unpleasant for her. It most definitely wasn't for him, and he quickly channelled his thoughts in a new direction before he was tempted to repeat the delightful experience.

'You said that it was Caroline who imparted the news about Lady Pilkington's missing rubies. How did she come by the information when it is not generally known? I encountered several of those present last night when I went out for my ride, and no one mentioned anything.'

'She heard it from her husband. He, apparently, was among the few who remained at the Pilkingtons' overnight.'

Sebastian's eyes narrowed. 'Was he now?'

'Yes, but don't jump to the wrong conclusion,' Emily advised. 'Lord Kelthorpe also stayed over with his wife, and so too did Mr Wentworth, both of whom are on your list of suspects, and both of whom have unsavoury reputations equal to that of Sir Courtney Farrington, if not a deal worse. The one who didn't remain was Skeffington, so I suppose you can cross his name off the list, even though in my opinion he's as disreputable as the others.'

'He was never high on the list to begin with,' Sebastian admitted. 'I have never rated his intelligence above average. And our quarry is shrewd.'

'Well, I think you can cross Sir Courtney off too. According to Caroline it was he who suggested calling in the Runners this morning, as soon as the necklace was discovered missing. And he also insisted that both he and his baggage were searched before he left the house. Apparently the other guests set up a fuss over that, but not he.'

'Yes, clever devil,' Sebastian murmured, eyes narrowing. 'I'm not prepared to rule him out quite yet. There's no saying that he didn't throw the booty out of his window to one of his accomplices. We know the person we're after doesn't work alone.' He was silent for a moment then bethought himself of something else. 'You mentioned that Lady Pilkington is very lax when it comes to the safekeeping of her jewels. How came you to know this?'

'It was something Lady Hewley remarked upon. And I've been racking my brain to think of who might have overheard our conversation. I wish I'd paid more attention at the time. Sir Giles Osborne thought the man you're after was assisted by loose talk, and I'm beginning to think that he isn't far wrong. But I don't for a moment suppose that Clara Hewley is involved. She's such a simpleton!'

'You are always so beautifully candid, my darling,' Sebastian remarked, shoulders shaking with suppressed laughter. 'And perfectly correct in this instance. The devil is far too astute to take bird-witted females into his confidence, but I suspect that he isn't above using their lack of intelligence to his advantage.'

Raising his eyes, Sebastian contemplated the filled shelves behind Emily's head. 'But he took a risk… Why, I wonder? Never before has an item been stolen on the night of a party. The robberies have always been carefully planned. He's no opportunist thief. Is he so desperate for money at the moment that he considered the risk worth taking? Or is he now so supremely confident that he believes he will always escape detection? Or was it perhaps merely frustration at not getting his hands on the Hawkridge diamonds which prompted this latest rash act? We must hope that is the case. It could result in a further reckless move which might lead to his capture.'

'If you seriously suppose that it is indeed the Hawkridge diamonds which he covets most of all, is it not time we offered him the golden opportunity to try his luck once more by my wearing them again? Apart from this evening, our calendar is pretty full until the end of the Season.'

Emily considered it a splendid notion and was surprised when he shook his head. 'No, Hester is right—they ought to be returned to the bank. You don't know how deeply I regret involving you in all this.'

Emily felt both hurt and angry. 'But why?' she demanded to know, desperately striving to keep both emotions under control. 'I thought I had been of some help.'

'You have, my darling,' he hurriedly assured her. 'But you are too precious to me. If anything should ever happen to you… No, my mind is made up,' he went on, his determination unshakeable. 'The wretched necklace will be returned to the bank, and we shall enjoy what little remains of the Season together, like the happily engaged couple we are.'

Emily could only stare at him in wonder, as he rose to his feet, and came round the desk, her throat so constricted by emotion that she dared not speak. If she had needed further proof of the depths of his feelings for her, she was being given it now, as he took a gentle hold of her arms and pulled her to her feet, so that he could trail a path of feather-light kisses down her face.

'Will you give me your word that you will not involve yourself further?' he husked against one corner of her mouth. 'Can you forget that I ever suggested such a thing in the first place and just be content to be with me here where you belong, in my home…sharing my life?'

Emily didn't need even a moment to consider, but before she could give voice to the dearest wish of her heart, there was an interruption, and Clegg unexpectedly entered, an expression of abject apology on his features for the intrusion. 'I'm sorry to disturb you, my lord, but Sir Charles Deverel has called to see you.'

Sebastian checked the refusal he had been about to utter and instructed his butler to show the unexpected visitor in. 'I wonder what could have brought him to London?'

Neither he nor Emily was destined to be kept wondering for long. Charles came striding into the room, his face positively beaming with happiness, and announced that he and Sarah were to be married later in the year.

Sebastian looked on indulgently as Emily, squealing with delight, placed a sisterly salute on one of Charles's slightly flushed cheeks. 'I do not think you need me to tell you that your news has been well received,' he said, shaking his friend warmly by the hand, before slanting a glance of mock severity in his fiancée's direction. 'There, you see, what did I tell you? All your little stratagems were unnecessary. You would do well to take heed of your lord and master in the future, young woman, and leave well alone.'

Charles's fair brows rose. 'Eh? What's this, what's this?'

'Pay no attention, Charles,' Emily advised him, swiftly dispensing with polite formality. 'All he's trying to say is that I always considered you and Sarah would deal well together.' She reached for his hands. 'I couldn't be more happy! But why didn't Sarah mention anything in her most recent letter?'

'She wished me to tell you in person, and persuade you to return to Dorset before the end of next month when we plan to hold the engagement party.'

'I wouldn't miss it for the world!' she assured him, before turning to Sebastian for corroboration.

'When have I ever been able to refuse you anything you had your heart set on, you little baggage? Of course we shall be there.' He turned again to his friend. 'How long do you intend staying in town?'

'A couple of weeks. There are a few things I need to attend to. Most importantly, I'm here to buy Sarah's betrothal ring.' Charles cast a look of appeal in Emily's direction. 'I'd appreciate some advice. You know Sarah's taste far better than I do. You wouldn't help me to choose, would you?'

'Nothing would give her more pleasure,' Sebastian answered, taking the words out of Emily's mouth. 'As you're staying in town, come and dine with us tonight, and you can fill us in on all the latest news from Dorset.'

Dinner that evening was a relaxed and enjoyable affair. Emily, still bubbling with happiness over her friend's engagement, was looking forward to accompanying Charles out to a certain notable jeweller's the following day. Lady Hester too, given that she had earned herself the reputation of being a sociable animal, was surprisingly in high spirits at the prospect of returning to her comfortable little house in Bath as soon as the Season was officially over. Even so, until they all left London their diary was pretty full, with hardly a free evening. Consequently it came as no real surprise to Sebastian that both ladies took advantage of this rare evening at home by retiring early.

He then decided to leave the elegant drawing-room for the more relaxed, masculine atmosphere of the library, where he soon had his friend comfortably settled in a chair by the hearth, glass of brandy at his elbow, happily reminiscing about the years they had spent up at Oxford together.

'But those times have gone, and we're no longer carefree young men. We both have responsibilities, and will soon have many more once we're both wedded. Have you fixed on a date yet?'

'No, not yet,' Sebastian admitted, after silently contemplating the liquid in his glass. 'But I have every reason to believe that she'll not experience a change of heart this time.'

Charles was puzzled by the disclosure and didn't attempt to conceal the fact. 'I'm sorry, Hawk, but I do not perfectly understand you. Were you and Emily engaged once before?'

'It was never officially announced. But we were to be married, yes. The date had been set, the banns had been read, then just a matter of a couple of weeks before the ceremony was due to take place she came to see me and said that she'd changed her mind and wished to live with her grandfather.

Even after all this time he still found the memory painful. 'She was very young and, all things considered, I thought it was for the best.'

Charles, regarding his lordship in silence, could easily detect the concern flickering in those intelligent grey eyes. 'But surely you don't suppose that she'll change her mind a second time? It's clear that she absolutely adores you.'

This assurance in no way improved his lordship's troubled state of mind. 'Yes, I know she does... But then she always has, and it didn't stop her from calling a halt to proceedings before.' He took a moment to fortify himself from the contents of his glass. 'Not that I think for a moment she would change her mind a second time. If she agrees to marry me, then I'm positive she'll go through with it this time.'

Once more Charles found himself at a loss to understand. 'But of course she'll marry you! I do not know Emily nearly half so well as you do, but she has never struck me as in any way capricious. In fact, I would say the opposite is true. She's a young woman who knows her own mind. Why else did she agree to the engagement if she didn't wish to marry you?'

'Well may you ask!' His lordship's smile was distinctly rueful. 'You might say that I tricked her into agreeing to an engagement between us.'

If anything Charles looked more puzzled than ever and, after a moment's indecision, Sebastian decided to confide in him fully, divulging what he himself had been doing during the past years, since he knew Charles was one of the few who knew the full facts surrounding Simon Sutherland's death. 'Needless to say, Charles, what I have just told you is in the strictest confidence.'

'Of course. And I hope you know me well enough to be sure that I'd never breathe a word to a living soul, not even to Sarah.' He smiled wryly. 'I can only wonder at myself for not suspecting something before. I thought it deuced odd when you suddenly changed your mind and decided to accept the invitation to my sister's birthday party.'

Sebastian had the grace to look a little shamefaced. 'Yes, I'm sorry about that, but once I discovered that it was none other than Emily who had come across that fatally injured agent, I knew I had to see her.'

Rising from his chair, his lordship went over to the decanters to replenish both their glasses, taking his own across to the grate to stare down at the empty hearth. 'It wasn't until Emily refused to marry me five years ago that I realised just how much she meant to me. I had always been dashed fond of her. But it wasn't until after she'd spent a year at that seminary, returning a young woman and not the mischievous child I remembered, that I realised I'd fallen in love. So, as you can imagine, her refusing to marry me came as a bitter blow. But I was forced to acknowledge that she was very young, and it would be wrong to go through with the wedding if she had any misgivings.

'My guardianship was an added burden,' he continued, glancing over his shoulder in time to catch his companion's startled expression. 'Yes, I am her legal guardian, not her grandfather. Emily now knows that, and took it rather better than I would have expected. But during our years apart she had no notion. The last thing I wanted was for her to become resentful, so I kept a discreet watch on her from a distance. Then fate took a hand and brought us back together a little sooner than I had planned. But from the moment I saw her at your sister's birthday party, I knew I couldn't bear to be parted from her again, at least not for any length of time.'

'Does she now know that you were in earnest over the engagement all along?' Charles queried gently.

Once again Sebastian's mouth was tugged by a rueful smile 'Yes, I believe she does. More importantly, I truly believe tha she is very contented with her role as my affianced bride.'

'Then I don't see that there's a problem,' Charles responded reasonably. 'As I've already mentioned it's clear to anyone that she loves you. It is there in her eyes for anyone to see.'

'Yes, I have seen it. I have also glimpsed something else there too, less frequently of late, it is true. Nevertheless, I still from time to time detect that shadow of uncertainty and hurt—a look I well remember from years ago. Only then I was too stupid to suppose the reason she had given for not wishing for our marriage to take place was not the true one. Something occasionally returns to trouble her deeply still, but for the life of me I cannot imagine what it can be.'

'Sarah might know,' Charles offered helpfully. 'They are wondrous close, more like sisters. If she confided in anyone, then you can lay odds that it was my Sarah. Would you like me to ask her when I return home?'

'No.' There was no mistaking the note of resolve in Sebastian's reply. 'I want Emily to confide in me herself. So I must be patient and wait, though the good Lord knows for how much longer I can restrain myself. I've found it no easy task having her living here under this roof. Sometimes I marvel at my powers of self-control.'

Charles gave a shout of laughter. 'You do not need to tell me, old fellow. I am having similar problems. There are times when I could wish my mother and sister elsewhere. If you take my advice you'll broach the subject of a wedding day as quickly as possible.'

'Yes, that's good advice,' Sebastian agreed. 'It is just a simple case of picking the right moment.'

Chapter Fourteen

Sebastian's powers of restraint were severely tested during the following days, although he did somehow manage to exert sufficient control to stop himself from imprisoning Emily in his arms and kissing her breathless whenever they happened to find themselves alone together, which unfortunately was not nearly often enough for his liking.

Soon after her arrival in London Emily had won the approval of the vast majority of the polite world. Having been spoken for, as it were, she was not seen as a threat by matrons with daughters of marriageable age and, in consequence, was invited everywhere, her company frequently sought both by day and by night.

If she wasn't walking in the park, usually with Caroline Farrington, she was accompanying Lady Hester about the capital, repaying calls. The only time Sebastian ever seemed to get her to himself was when they rode out together, though he hardly considered sharing the park with the rest of the fashionable world as precisely having her to himself. Nevertheless he was, all in all, very happy with his lot, and gained a deal of satisfaction from the knowledge that Emily increasingly seemed blissfully contented with hers, that tell-tale flicker of uncertainty having disappeared completely from her eyes.

Selecting the right moment to broach the subject of marriage was never far from his thoughts, but towards the end of their penultimate week in the capital, when they were attending a rout party at the home of one of the most famous London hostesses, pinning Emily down to select a date for their wedding was not at the forefront of his mind. In fact for once she was not precisely basking in the sunshine of his approval, for he was now very certain that she had not abandoned her attempts to assist him in his determination to uncover the identity of the murderous villain who had brought such misery to so many lives.

'Why, that damnable little minx!' he muttered, staring fixedly through the doorway leading to the card room. 'I swear I'll have her liver and lights!'

His lordship hadn't realisèd that he had given voice to his barbarous desires, until he detected a rumble of masculine laughter and turned to see Sir Charles Deverel at his elbow.

'You're not by any chance plagued by a fit of jealousy, old fellow?' he enquired in some amusement. 'I know Farrington is a handsome devil, but take it from me that Emily is interested in no one but you.'

This assurance in no way mollified his lordship. 'If I thought for a moment that she had fallen victim to that inveterate womaniser's overblown charms, it would be a relief, believe me!' Sebastian responded somewhat enigmatically, and then, leaving Charles to puzzle over precisely what he had meant, went striding into the card room.

'Ah, Hawkridge!' Sir Courtney favoured him with a half-mocking glance before returning his attention to the cards in his hand. 'Have you come to rescue your lovely fiancée from my pernicious influence? Rest assured that you're in no danger of losing your shirt,' he continued when he received no response. 'Miss Stapleton is a worthy opponent, and the stakes have remained very low.'

'Which is just as well,' Emily put in, 'as you have won every hand comprehensively thus far.'

A provocative gleam brightened ice-blue eyes. 'Might I remind you, ma'am, that I suggested we play for love, but you would have none of it.'

'Yes, a wise decision on my part. Had I done so I would have been in grave danger of losing my virtue several times over.' Emily turned her attention to Sebastian, noting that he, unlike Sir Courtney, was not in the least amused by the light-hearted banter. 'Did you have a specific reason for seeking me out?'

'Indeed, I did,' his lordship squeezed through tightly compressed lips. 'You promised me the next dance?'

'Did I?' She made not the least attempt to conceal her surprise. 'I thought we were engaged for the supper dance.'

'And this one too,' he returned, grasping her wrist and giving her no choice but to rise from the chair, and little time to bid adieu to her card-playing partner either.

'What are you about, Hawk?' she demanded, the vice-like grip tightening about her wrist, as he headed purposefully towards the French windows, which led outside to a large terrace and the delightful garden beyond.

'More to the point, what are you about, young lady?' he returned, coming to such an abrupt halt in the shadowed area at the end of the terrace that Emily cannoned into him. 'You gave me your word that you would cease involving yourself in the business of the robberies.'

'I most certainly did not,' she countered, deciding his expression was about as tender as the grasp he retained on her wrist. She could feel the heat from those shapely fingers penetrating her long evening glove, surprisingly causing a very pleasant sensation to ripple up and down the length of her arm.

'Maybe you didn't,' innate honesty forced him to acknowledge. However he steadfastly refused to concede more than this. 'But you were in no doubt that I didn't want you ferreting around any more,' he went on, reminding her of nothing so much as an irate father castigating a recalcitrant child

'And what do I find you doing? Last evening you went out of your way to encourage the attentions of Skeffington and Lord Kelthorpe, both of whom, as you are very well aware, are on my list of suspects. And tonight it is none other than Farrington!'

'Yes, and what a trio of oily, dissolute wretches they are too!' she agreed, not noticeably chastened. 'I swear Skeffington wears a corset. At least something was creaking when I was dancing with him yesterday evening, and I'm certain it wasn't his back. And that debauched roué Kelthorpe is nothing more than a bully. You did mention once that your quarry had scant regard for my sex. And there's a strong rumour circulating this evening that the reason his wife isn't present tonight is because she's sporting a black eye.'

'I'm beginning to appreciate just why a gentleman might be driven to such lengths,' he confessed, but Emily was not fooled by the husky hint of malicious intent in his voice, and twinkled provocatively up at him.

'A gentleman would surely not, Hawk... All right, all right!' she capitulated, half-laughing as the clasp on her wrist, if anything, became marginally tighter and his eyes flashed that clear warning she well remembered from years ago which was sufficient to convince her that to tease him further might not be wise. 'I shan't involve myself any more. Besides which, I don't suppose I'll achieve anything if I do. I couldn't choose between your suspects. They are all equally obnoxious, and I wouldn't trust any one of them an inch. And the only reason I bore Sir Courtney company tonight was to keep him well away from his wife,' she went on to explain. 'Not that he ever pays her much attention, but he always seems to know precisely where she is and with whom. And now that Caroline has begun to socialise again, I see no reason why she shouldn't enjoy herself a little. And she always appears so happy and relaxed in Tobias Trevenen's company. I've observed that on several occasions. So I think it was a wonderful ploy of mine to keep Farrington occupied whilst they danced together.'

If she hoped that this would placate him, she was swiftly to discover her mistake. 'Do not interfere, Emily!' he ordered, and there was no mistaking the steely element in his voice now. 'God!' He released his hold on her to clap a hand over his eyes. 'How I could have been so stupid as to involve you in the first place, I'll never know! The sooner I get you away from London the better!'

Had he admitted as much even a week or two before she would have been devastated, heartbroken. Now, however, this was not the case. She was wholly convinced that he loved her, but even so a small part of her still desperately craved reassurance. 'Is it the engagement you regret, Hawk?' She kept her gaze firmly fixed on the intricate folds of his cravat. 'Because if it is you have only to say so, and I'll—'

'You know it is not!' His voice might have been harsh, but his touch now could not have been more gentle as he curled his long fingers about her upper arms. 'Look at me, Em!' he ordered, and then waited for her to obey. 'The means by which I persuaded you to agree to our engagement doesn't precisely redound to my credit. But do not ever doubt that it was the dearest wish of my heart. I love you, Emily Stapleton, and fully intend to spend the rest of my life with you.' He placed one hand under her chin, holding her head up so that she could not mistake the sincerity in his eyes, even if she quite failed to detect it in his voice. 'I allowed you to back out once before, remember…? I shall never permit you to do so again.'

'And who suggested that I would ever wish to?' she murmured, raising one hand to touch his cheek.

Sebastian's triumphant shout seemed to hang in the air long after his mouth had covered hers in a kiss that showed more clearly than words ever could that he considered her wholly his. 'I've been patient for almost five long years,

Emily,' he murmured, reluctantly dragging his lips away to bury them in her hair. 'Do not be cruel and expect me to wait for very much longer. I'm only flesh and blood, and I'd be less than honest if I didn't admit to feeling the strain.'

As if to add credence to his words, he held her firmly away, his ragged breathing further proof, had Emily needed any, that he was indeed a gentleman battling to maintain his control. She too was not oblivious to the sensations his touch never failed to arouse in her, an addictive brew of tactile pleasure, excitement and anticipation which never failed to leave her craving further intimate contact.

'I cannot see any reason why the wedding should not take place soon after our return to Dorset,' she assured him with complete sincerity, little realising that within the space of twenty-four hours she would discover something which would force her to revise her opinion and which would send her toppling from the pinnacle of happiness to the very depths of despair.

The ball which the Dowager Lady Templehurst had managed to organise in so short a time was one of the last major events of the Season, and the first party to be held at the Sutherland mansion since the tragic demise of the former head of the family.

It didn't take Emily very long to realise that poor Michael, dutifully standing beside his formidable great-aunt at the entrance to the ballroom, was not precisely enjoying the experience of playing host to the cream of Society. More than once Emily caught him mopping his young brow, and his fixed smile was beginning to show definite signs of cracking under the strain.

'Poor Michael isn't at all comfortable with his role,' she remarked, as she and Lady Hester found themselves two vacant chairs by the wall. 'I wonder at you, ma'am, for encouraging Lady Templehurst to hold such a grand event in her nephew's home.'

A hint of pure mischief sprang into her chaperon's eyes. 'Well dear, I was forced to agree when she sought my advice on the night we visited the theatre that, now having attained the age of four-and-twenty, Michael ought to be thinking of the future. I'm not suggesting that he should be considering marriage seriously quite yet, but it wouldn't hurt to think about the kind of girl he might one day wish to wed. Undeniably Lady Templehurst is a domineering female, but she's genuinely attached to her nephew and has only his best interests at heart. She doesn't wish to see the title go to another branch of the family.'

'And I for one do not doubt for a moment that such a determined woman will achieve her objective,' Emily responded, glancing about the crowded ballroom. 'Considering she didn't organise this affair until very late in the Season, she has certainly succeeded in persuading many leading figures to attend, although there are some notable absentees too.'

'Little wonder, dear. The very warm weather has induced several families to return to the country early. And many more are planning to leave within the next few days.'

'And some have remained longer than originally planned,' Emily returned, catching sight of Mr Tobias Trevenen heading towards the spot where Sebastian stood amid a group of gentlemen. 'I suppose Michael must have persuaded him to remain to bear him company for this ordeal.'

Lady Hester did not comment, and merely glanced across the room at her niece, who was conversing with none other than Lady Hewley. 'I'm pleased to see Caroline is once again present tonight, and is at least appearing as though she's enjoying herself. I cannot imagine she'll wish to remain in town for very much longer, although the poor child must abide by her husband's wishes, I suppose.'

Until that moment Emily had not considered it strange that Sir Courtney had seemed happy for his wife to remain with him in the capital. He must have had his reasons, but she very much doubted that a sudden desire for her company was one of them.

'You are about to be offered the opportunity to discover that, ma'am,' Emily remarked, as she noticed Caroline heading in their direction, with a look of comical dismay flitting over her features.

'Lady Hewley is an unconscionable gabble-monger,' Caroline declared the instant she reached them. 'Why Courtney chooses to associate with such persons I cannot imagine. I have just been informed by that loquacious young woman that she is to dine with us tomorrow evening.'

'That is something for you to look forward to, my dear,' her aunt responded wryly. 'You must hope that you can look forward to a swift return to Derbyshire too.'

'I wish I could say that I was, Aunt. But Courtney has yet to inform me of his plans. I understand that you and Emily are leaving next week.'

'Yes, and I cannot say that I'll be sorry to go. It has grown so insufferably warm of late. Although I must say,' she added, giving Emily's hand a fond pat, 'that I have very much enjoyed myself.'

'Yes, thanks to Emily and…and a few others, so have I,' Caroline admitted.

Emily was surprised to catch a rather wistful expression flit over Lady Hester's features. Unfortunately she wasn't able to discover just what might have prompted the odd look, for her hand was claimed for the first set of country dances, and by the time she returned Caroline had moved away and Lady Hester was happily engaged in conversation with a matron of about her own age.

No sooner had Emily resumed her seat than none other than their beleaguered young host slipped into the chair beside her own, and was nervously tugging at his cravat and bemoaning the fact that his shirt points had wilted.

'Poor Michael. Are you finding it such an ordeal? I know

you put your name down on my card for the next dance, but would you prefer to find a quiet spot and sit for a while?'

He accepted the suggestion with alacrity, escorting her across to a secluded little alcove at the far end of the ballroom. 'If that fiendish aunt of mine supposes she's going to put me through this ordeal every year, she's something to learn,' he muttered, favouring the formidable dowager, who was still hovering near the entrance, with a basilisk stare.

Emily could quite understand his resentment, and yet she could understand his aunt's concerns too. He was now head of the family, and must one day take steps to secure an heir. 'I know you felt no desire to hold the title, Michael. Sadly, though, your brother's demise instantly made you a matrimonial prize. Lady Templehurst is only trying to prepare you for the years ahead when you will be pursued by every matchmaking mama.'

'Dear Lord! What a prospect!' He grimaced before staring gravely down at his hands. 'I do not mind the responsibility so much, Emily, especially as I have good friends like Hawkridge and Toby Trevenen to turn to for advice. But I cannot deny that I would have preferred a career in the army. Still—' he shrugged '—brooding about it won't change what has happened.'

'No, that's true enough,' she agreed, sympathising. 'It's just a pity that the persons responsible for changing the course of your life were never apprehended.'

'It's unlikely now, I suppose, but I refuse to give up hope. It isn't so much Simon's death I would like avenged as sweet Elizabeth's. I'll never forget what they did to my sister-in-law, nor the look on poor Simon's face when he saw the extent of her injuries and knew what she must have suffered.'

Emily looked at him closely. 'I'm sorry, Michael, I didn't realise that you had accompanied your brother to the scene of the crime.'

'Yes, I'd been sent down from Oxford for indulging in some lark. Simon wasn't best pleased, but managed to soothe things over, and I was to be allowed back in the autumn. I was staying with him in London when news reached us. Sebastian was present too. The information we received was a little vague, and at first we all thought that Eliza's carriage had been involved in some accident. It wasn't until we saw the bodies of Elizabeth and her maid that we knew.' His gaze remained fixed on a certain spot on the ballroom floor. 'Even now I can still see that frightful red mark about Eliza's neck, and that strange diamond-shaped imprint in the skin. Must have been made by a rope, or something. I've never seen anything like it before.'

More or less at the exact moment that Emily began to assimilate what she had just learned, Caroline, partnered by Mr Trevenen, crossed her field of vision as they joined the set now forming on the dance floor. 'Oh, my God,' she murmured, as the scene before her began to fade, and her mind's eye conjured up a vision of a coiled whip on a certain library wall.

'emily…Miss Stapleton, are you all right? You look dreadfully pale.' Michael's concerned voice eventually penetrated her trance-like state, successfully drawing her back to the present. 'What a clodpole I am! I should never have spoken of such things to you.'

'Oh, yes you should, Michael,' she countered, though feeling as if icy-cold fingers had just encircled her heart. 'I might not like what I have just learned… But, believe me, it is as well that I do know.'

Much later, after dismissing Skinner, Emily sat on the window sill in her bedchamber, staring sightlessly out across the deserted Square. The evening had seemed interminable, and she could only wonder just how she had managed to get through it all without betraying what she was increasingly believing was true—that Sir Courtney Farrington was the brains behind the spate of robberies, the very one responsible for inflicting so much suffering by needlessly taking innocent lives.

Her initial reaction, understandably enough, had been to seek out Sebastian and reveal at once what she had discovered. Wiser counsel, however, had swiftly prevailed. Sebastian, with good reason, loathed the very ground Sir Courtney Farrington walked upon, and although a level-headed being for the most part, Sebastian was not above giving vent to his feelings on occasions. Furthermore, he hadn't a cowardly bone in his entire body, and Emily very much feared that, if sufficiently roused, he wasn't above engaging in a duel, thereby extracting a swift and very personal revenge for the loss of his friend Simon Sutherland. But even this very real possibility, she was silently forced to concede, might not have succeeded in holding her mute if she had not happened to witness Sebastian dancing with his cousin a short while after listening to Michael's startling disclosures.

During the past few weeks Emily had been highly gratified to see that haunted, almost fearful look fading from Caroline's dark eyes, and a semblance of that vivacity of yore returning; and that night she had looked positively radiant, almost pretty, as she had swirled about the room on Sebastian's arm, laughing up at him and smiling so brilliantly that Emily's heart had given a painful lurch.

Any fool could see that there was a bond of genuine affection between them which the past few years had done little to diminish. But how strong was that regard now? Did Sebastian, in some secret corner of his heart, still retain a deep and unwavering love for his cousin which he had successfully managed to conceal from the world at large? Would he, if given the opportunity, choose Caroline as his life's companion? There was only one way, Emily reflected, releasing her breath in a heartfelt sigh, that she was ever going to find out for sure.

She couldn't deny that the temptation to remain silent, not to reveal to a living soul what she had inadvertently discovered, was still strong. She and Sebastian could marry as planned, and she didn't doubt that they would be happy together. Sadly, though, she knew herself too well. Throughout her life, lurking there at the back of her mind, would remain that tormenting little doubt—given the choice would he still have chosen to marry her? No, she couldn't live with that. She must release him from his obligations and leave him free to choose. But how?

Her conscience having at last mastered pure self-interest, Emily was determined to settle on the best course of action before she finally retired. Her resolve not to involve Sebastian remained firm. Living without him playing any part in her life was a risk she was prepared to take; she was not prepared to place his life in jeopardy by revealing what she knew. Fortunately there was one other in whom she could confide. But would Sir Giles Osborne act on what might easily be perceived as mere coincidence? He was an astute, very careful man, and perhaps would require more proof before he could arrange for Sir Courtney Farrington to be taken into custody. After all, a wife could not give evidence against her husband in a court of law, and without Caroline's testimony there was precious little to link Farrington with the crimes.

Therefore more proof was needed, Emily decided, at last climbing into her comfortable bed. Her stay in the capital was swiftly drawing to a close, and time was not on her side, but somehow she must find a way of attaining the proof needed to enable Sir Giles Osborne to act.

Chapter Fifteen

Although Emily woke the following morning with no very clear idea of how to set about exposing Sir Courtney Farrington and bringing about his downfall, her resolve to do so had not diminished. Nor had her determination not to involve Sebastian unless totally unavoidable lessened either. It wasn't merely a matter of not wishing Sebastian to place his life in jeopardy, but also a desire to protect him from scurrilous, wagging tongues.

Her experience of the polite world might not have been vast, but she knew enough to be sure that the tattle-mongers would have a field-day, wondering if there were more behind his determination to see Sir Courtney brought to book, most especially if he betrayed an amorous interest in the Baronet's widow soon after justice had been served.

As she completed her toilette, and then made her way downstairs to the breakfast parlour, Emily chose not to dwell on the possibility that Sebastian's undeniably tender regard for her might prove wanting should he be offered the opportunity to marry his first love.

Although blissfully unaware of the fact himself, Sebastian could not have done more to try to dispel that niggling uncertainty lurking in the corner of her mind, when he rose to his feet the moment she joined him in the parlour to brush his lips lightly across her cheek. Emily could not fail to note the look of tenderness which accompanied the chaste salute. All the same she knew herself well enough to be sure that misgivings would return to plague her if she denied him the opportunity to form an alliance with his cousin. Unwittingly she had deprived him of that chance years ago. For her own peace of mind she must right that wrong, no matter how heartbreaking the outcome might turn out to be for her.

'You're very quiet, sweetheart,' his lordship remarked, after resuming his seat and helping her to coffee. 'I noticed you appeared a little subdued from time to time yesterday evening. Nothing troubling you, is there?'

Emily managed to effect a careless shrug, but the mild query was a timely reminder. No one knew her better than the man seated beside her. It was uncanny the way he could almost read her mind on occasions. She would need to be so very careful from now on, for just one careless word, one unguarded look might alert that large brain of his to the fact that she was plotting something.

Her lack of response only served to stoke the fires of suspicion. 'I hope you are not peeved because I chose to dance twice with my cousin last night.'

Emily almost choked, but recovered in an instant, and found herself immediately on the defensive. 'Is there reason for me to be?'

'No, certainly not.' He could not have sounded more sincere. 'And might I remind you that it was you who suggested that I should pay Caroline more attention.'

That, Emily was forced silently to acknowledge, might yet prove to be a grave error of judgement on her part. 'I don't object to your dancing with your cousin, Hawk. In fact it was a pleasure to see her looking so happy. Five minutes in your company and the old sparkle was back in her eyes.'

'I cannot accept the credit for that,' he countered, his lips curling into a secretive half-smile, before he changed the subject by revealing that he would be unable to accompany her out for a ride that day. 'I've received an urgent summons from Sir Giles Osborne. He wishes to see me without delay.'

Sebastian observed slender fingers tremble slightly, as Emily reached for her coffee-cup and raised it to her lips. 'Are you sure nothing is troubling you, my darling? You do seem a little on edge this morning.'

She forced a smile. 'I'm fine. I was just wondering what Sir Giles can have to tell you that's so urgent.'

'I've no idea.' Finishing off the dregs in his own cup, Sebastian rose to his feet, and then paused by her chair to capture her chin and raise her head. 'But whatever it is doesn't concern you. I've already told you I don't want you involving yourself further in the business.' The delicate lids lowered, but not before he had glimpsed a wary look in those strikingly lovely blue eyes. 'And I shall be most displeased if you do.'

Torn between guilt and resentment at the high-handed tone he was adopting, Emily risked a fleeting look up at him again. 'Must I attain your permission before I do anything? I shall be heartily glad when your guardianship comes to an end and I can do as I please.'

'Don't raise your hopes too high,' he warned, releasing her chin to flick one cheek gently with a careless finger. 'I shall make a far stricter husband.' He went over to the door, thereby missing the wistful expression flitting over her delicate features. 'How, by the way, do you intend occupying yourself until my esteemed aunt decides to leave her bedchamber?' he turned back to add.

She managed with a reasonable amount of success to affect an air of innocence. 'Oh, I thought I might just pay your cousin a visit.'

'Do so by all means. I've absolutely no objection,' he assured her with infuriating superiority.

'Good. Because I have every intention of doing so, with

or without your permission,' Emily muttered, the instant he had closed the door behind him.

Remaining only for the time it took to consume a buttered roll, and swill it down with a second cup of coffee, Emily returned to her room to collect her bonnet and, after securing Skinner's services as chaperon for the proposed visit, returned downstairs in time to see Clegg admit Mr Tobias Trevenen into the house.

'I'm afraid his lordship went out a short while ago, sir, and did not inform me when we might expect his return.'

Easily discerning the look of disappointment on the visitor's face, Emily came forward, thereby instantly drawing Mr Trevenen's attention to her presence. 'Perhaps you would care to leave a message, sir? You may be sure that his lordship will receive it.'

'That is most kind of you, Miss Stapleton. The fact is I am about to leave London. I received news late last night that there has been an accident in one of my mines.'

'Oh, I am sorry,' Emily responded with total sincerity. 'I hope it wasn't serious?'

'Blessedly there was no loss of life, but even so I feel obliged to return without delay. I wonder,' he added, drawing her a little to one side, 'if I may ask a very great favour of you, ma'am? I am unable to remain to make my farewells, so I would be very grateful if you would explain to Sebastian the reason for my hasty departure.' He paused to draw a letter from his pocket. 'Also might I importune you further by securing your promise to ensure that Caroline…Lady Farrington receives this. I do not wish to send it to the house in case it should fall into the wrong hands and cause any embarrassment.'

'Be assured, sir, that I shall hand it to her personally,' Emily promised, relieving him of the missive, and slipping it into her reticule for safekeeping. 'It so happens that I was on the point of leaving to pay a visit to Caroline when you arrived.'

'In that case, ma'am, I shall detain you no longer.'

'Nor I you, sir.' Emily accompanied him outside to the waiting carriage. 'I shall pass on your farewells to his lordship.'

She waited until the carriage had moved away before setting off on her own visit, her mind too occupied with her own immediate concerns to give any thought at all as to why Mr Trevenen should feel the need to take such pains to inform Caroline of his unexpected departure from town.

When she arrived at her destination Emily had no very clear idea of just how to proceed in her attempt to bring about Sir Courtney's downfall. Nevertheless certain lingering doubts about his guilt were considerably reduced when his henchman answered the summons, and she saw the healing cut on Hector Sloane's forehead, and the faint, lingering evidence of a black eye.

She gained some satisfaction from the knowledge that she had in all probability been responsible for inflicting the injuries, and his look of resentment, not sufficiently disguised, was further proof had she needed any that he bore a grudge. Even so the gratification she attained was tempered somewhat by a sudden surge of annoyance at her own stupidity for not having suspected something when Caroline had mentioned the servant's mishap on the very morning after the attempted break-in.

'You appear to have been in the wars, my good man,' she remarked, successfully suppressing a smile as his look of intense dislike manifestly increased. 'You should take more care.'

'Walked into a door, that's all,' he muttered sourly, before disappearing into the parlour, and returning a moment later, holding wide the door for Emily to pass into the sunny front room.

'Why, this is a pleasant surprise!' Caroline greeted her with every evidence of delight, coming forward to place a sisterly salute on her cheek. 'I was hoping to see you in the park later.'

Emily took the precaution of closing the door which, by accident or design, had been left ajar by the disreputable manservant, before announcing that she was unsure of her plans for the afternoon. 'Much will depend on what Lady Hester might have arranged. I possibly mentioned that we leave the capital at the end of the week. Lady Hester might wish me to accompany her when she bids farewell to certain of her friends before she becomes involved in the final arrangements for her journey to Bath. Which reminds me…'

Delving into her reticule, Emily drew out the letter. 'The exodus from the capital has begun in earnest. Mr Trevenen left today and asked me to give you this.'

There was a noticeable dimming of the sparkle in dark eyes as Caroline took the missive. Before she could apprise herself of its contents the door opened once again, and she consigned the letter to the safety of her pocket only moments before her husband entered.

'Ah! Miss Stapleton! I was delighted to discover that you had called,' he announced, his ready smile fading as he turned his attention to his wife. 'Caroline, it is extremely remiss of you not to have offered our guest refreshment.'

Emily could hardly believe her great good fortune in finding the Baronet at home. He had always been out on the rare occasions she had paid a visit to his house. Caroline, on the other hand, was not so gratified by her husband's presence. The instant he had entered the room her demeanour had altered. She had grown quiet, markedly so, and the impatient glance he cast in her direction before moving over to the decanters did nothing to lessen her obvious unease.

'Your wife has hardly been granted the opportunity to do so, sir,' Emily assured him, not reticent to come to Caroline's defence, as she accepted the glass of Madeira he held out and made herself comfortable in one of the chairs.

'I understand that you are to leave the capital soon, Miss Stapleton?'

Emily smiled to herself as she watched her silver-tongued host move with an easy grace to join his wife upon the sofa.

Not too many, she supposed, would imagine that a gentleman who had been blessed with the physique of a Corinthian and the features of some classic Greek statue could harbour the soul of a viper. No, not many would, she reiterated silently. But the woman seated beside him was under no illusion about his true character. The problem was how to trick him into revealing it to the world at large.

'It is becoming daily more stifling here in the capital. I cannot say that I'll be sorry to get back to the country again.'

'Nor I,' Caroline agreed, thereby earning herself a further impatient glance from the man seated beside her.

'Our plans are uncertain,' her husband reminded her. 'I have yet to decide whether to accept Hewley's invitation to pay a visit to his estate in Somerset.'

By Caroline's expression the prospect of doing so did not precisely please her. That, quite naturally, was only to be expected. It was with her young daughter she wished to be, so why did Sir Courtney not allow her to return? It was not out of any desire to enjoy his wife's company, Emily felt sure. No, it was much more likely that the loathsome creature derived some perverse pleasure from keeping mother and daughter apart.

'Aunt Hester has led me to believe that you intend to return to Dorsetshire in order to attend an engagement party, is that not so?'

Emily's heart went out to Sebastian's cousin. The poor woman was doing her level best to behave naturally and not betray unease or unhappiness. But she was daily facing an uphill struggle. What must it be like to be tied to someone who paid you only scant attention when it suited his purposes? Surely Caroline would find it a blessed release if one day she was freed from the loveless union, even if she chose never to remarry?

'Yes, Lord Deverel himself is returning tomorrow, I believe, to lend a hand with the preparations,' Emily divulged, casting the poor woman whom she had against all the odds come to look upon as a friend a smile of encouragement. 'H intends to celebrate his betrothal in fine style and it sounds as if it is to be a grand affair. I'm very much looking forward to it.'

'I for one shall be sorry to see you go.' No one could have doubted Caroline's sincerity. 'Our walks together in the park have very much added to the enjoyment of my stay here in town.'

'I too shall be sorry to see you leave, Miss Stapleton.' Sir Courtney's sentiment was less believable until he added, 'I shall be deprived of the sight of your perfect neck adorned by those splendid gems again. Or shall you be favouring us all with one last display before you desert us?'

It took a monumental effort but somehow Emily managed to suppress a shout of triumph, and remain calmly seated in her chair. Of course, the necklace was the very means by which she might induce Sir Courtney to place himself in a position whereby he risked exposure! But how?

As those ice-blue eyes continued to regard her keenly, Emily was forced silently to acknowledge that it would be a grave mistake to underestimate his intellect, so it might be wise to stick to the truth as far as possible.

'Unlikely, sir,' she responded, after fortifying herself from the contents of her glass. 'The few invitations Lady Hester has accepted while we remain in town are all small affairs. Besides which, Lord Hawkridge, I believe, has had the necklace returned to the safety of his bank's vault.'

'Ah, yes. I believe Caroline did mention something about a break-in at his lordship's house. A very wise precaution, if I may say so.'

Lord, how plausible he was! Emily silently acknowledged. No one would believe for a moment that he wasn't totally sincere. She would enjoy pitting her wits against him. One thing she must not do, however, was to allow her guard to weaken. He would strike without mercy any man, woman or child who attempted to cross him.

'Indeed it was, sir,' she agreed, and waited a moment before adding, with a flash of inspiration, 'but I am hoping to persuade him to allow me to wear it for the engagement party.'

'Do you think that wise, my dear?' Caroline put in. 'Dorsetshire is a good distance from the capital. Anything might happen on the journey.'

'Do not be ridiculous, Caroline!' Sir Courtney snapped, momentarily losing his customary aplomb. 'No doubt Hawkridge himself will be travelling with Miss Stapleton, together with an army of servants.'

'It would make no difference if it were quite otherwise, sir,' she informed him, resolved not to put Sebastian's life in danger. 'Lord Hawkridge would never take the risk. He would arrange for the necklace to be conveyed by special, private messenger to arrive possibly on the day of the party, thereby reducing the risk of it being stolen.'

Emily dared not say more lest the cunning rogue become suspicious. More importantly, though, if by some miracle he had taken the bait, how on earth was she to proceed? One thing was certain, if she stood the remotest chance of carrying her plan through to a successful conclusion she was going to need help. Before she attempted to approach Sir Giles Osborne, however, she was still going to need further proof of Farrington's guilt, so she must be patient for the time being and wait to see what, if anything, transpired during the next few days.

Unfortunately her machinations were to receive a setback the instant she returned to Berkeley Square, and was apprised by Sebastian that his appointment that morning had been urgent because Sir Giles planned to leave the capital later that day, with no very firm idea of precisely when he would be returning.

Emily tried not to be too downhearted. However, the following day two visitors to the house forced her to re-evaluate the situation, and acknowledge that she might well have placed herself in no little danger.

The first important caller arrived just after noon, when Lady Hester had not emerged from her bedchamber, and Sebastian had taken himself off to the city to visit his bankers. Emily was in the library, occupied in writing a letter to Sarah, when Clegg, looking distinctly disapproving, entered the room.

'Sir Charles Deverel is here, Miss Stapleton.' He sniffed quite pointedly. 'I informed him that his lordship is out, and should be back shortly, but he insists that he cannot wait, as he plans to leave town, and is wishful to see you.'

Emily raised an enquiring brow. 'Well, what's the problem, Clegg? Show Sir Charles in.'

His expression wooden, the butler made no attempt to carry out the instruction, and suggested instead, 'Perhaps I might show him into the front parlour, Miss Stapleton, while I make enquiries to see if Lady Hester is ready to leave her room?'

Emily wasn't slow to follow the very correct butler's train of thought, but in this instance she considered he was adhering too strictly to social convention.

'As you are very well aware, Clegg, it is unlikely that Lady Hester will show her face for at least another hour. Besides which, his lordship would not object to my seeing Sir Charles alone, so you may admit him with a clear conscience.'

She could not help but smile when the butler, betraying a marked degree of reluctance, finally did as bidden, although pointedly leaving the door ajar after showing the visitor into the room. She made no attempt to close it, and merely came round the desk, holding out her hands in welcome.

'It is good of you to see me, Emily, in view of the fact that Sebastian isn't here,' Charles announced, proving that he was well aware of the breach of propriety. 'But I could not leave the capital without saying goodbye.'

'I'm very glad you did not,' she assured him. 'I've begun

a letter to Sarah. If you'd wait a few minutes while I finish it, I'd be very grateful if you would take it with you.'

Not wishing to delay him for longer than necessary, Emily returned to the desk, leaving Charles to make himself comfortable in one of the chairs. 'It is really only to assure Sarah that I shall be home well in time for the party, and that I'm very much looking forward to it,' she informed him as she signed her name at the bottom with a flourish.

'Not surprisingly, so am I,' he responded, with that boyish grin which made him appear considerably younger than his nine-and-twenty years. 'It is likely to be a repeat of the one we held a few weeks ago, with far more people invited than originally planned. And I'm the one to blame this time,' he surprisingly divulged. 'I've found myself inviting one or two others since my arrival in town.'

'Have you indeed,' Emily responded betraying a mild interest. 'Anyone I know?'

'Young Michael Sutherland, for one. Apparently he's escorting his aunt back to her home in Gloucestershire, and said that he'd be delighted to come along, if his aunt leaves the capital as planned. And then there's Sir Courtney Farrington.'

Emily checked for a moment before sealing her letter with a wafer, her mind racing. 'I didn't realise you were well acquainted with him, Charles?' she remarked, in a voice which she hoped sounded merely conversational.

'Truth of the matter is I'm not, at least not very well. He was up at Oxford for a time when I was there with Sebastian and Simon Sutherland, but we were never what one might call friends, merely acquaintances only. Naturally I've seen nothing of him in recent years as I come up to town so rarely. But it just so happens that he was at my club last night, and we fell into talking. The next thing I know I'm inviting him to the party.' Charles appeared genuinely puzzled. 'Didn't see how I could do otherwise as his wife is closely connected to Hawkridge, though I cannot say that I care for Farrington over much.'

He raised his head to discover Emily staring fixedly at the wall behind him. 'Why, my dear girl, whatever is wrong? You appear as if you've seen a ghost.'

'No, not a ghost, Charles,' Emily assured him, hurriedly handing him the letter so that she did not delay his departure further. 'But I do suddenly feel as though someone has just walked over my grave.'

No sooner had Charles departed than Clegg returned to the library to inform her of the arrival of a second significant caller.

'You say you've shown Lady Farrington into the parlour? In that case you had better inform Lady Hester of her niece's arrival, while I entertain our visitor.'

Emily discovered Caroline already seated in one of the comfortable chairs, staring fixedly down at the empty hearth, appearing decidedly ill at ease. As this was only the second occasion she had put herself to the trouble of paying a visit to the house, this might well have been the case, but even so it did not account for the dispirited look in her eyes when she finally raised her head to see who had entered the room.

'Why, Emily!' Although the smile was slow in coming, there was no mistaking the warmth it contained. 'I informed the butler that there was absolutely no need to disturb you, and I was quite happy to await my aunt.'

'I wasn't doing anything important,' Emily assured her, slipping into the chair opposite. 'And I'm certain Lady Hester will be down shortly, now that she knows you're here. You do not need me to tell you how very fond she is of you.'

'I sincerely hope you're right,' she responded, with a decidedly wry smile this time, 'for I have come to ask if I may inflict my company upon her for a week or two. Courtney considers the spell in London has improved my looks and is convinced that a short stay in Bath will restore my health completely.'

So that was the excuse he was using to visit the West

Country, the cunning demon! It was an effort but somehow Emily managed to preserve her countenance. Clearly Sir Courtney wasn't above making use of family and friends when it suited his purposes. But Emily doubted that Caroline would stoop so low. Or indeed had ever been party to her husband's unlawful activities. She might have unwittingly aided him on occasions by passing on certain snippets of gossip, just as the loquacious Lady Hewley had undoubtedly obliged him by doing in recent weeks, but Emily didn't suppose for a moment that Caroline was in her husband's confidence. As Sebastian had intimated, the miscreant responsible for the death of Lady Elizabeth Sutherland wasn't the type to trust his secrets to a woman, not even his own wife.

'You'll forgive me for saying so Caroline, but the prospect of taking the waters doesn't seem to appeal to you overmuch.'

She shuddered. 'No, horrid stuff! But I'd far rather suffer that treatment than accompany Courtney on a visit to Lord and Lady Hewley. For some obscure reason he suddenly took it into his head to accept their invitation to stay at their country home which, I believe, is situated somewhere on the Somerset-Dorset border.' She sighed. 'I suppose I ought to feel thankful that he even considered offering me the choice of staying with my aunt.'

Lady Hester, who entered the room a moment later, didn't attempt to hide her delight at the prospect of having her niece to stay. Emily, on the other hand, wasn't infected by Lady Hester's enthusiasm. In fact, she was feeling decidedly uneasy over this latest turn of events. It would have been a different matter if Sir Giles Osborne had been in town, and she could have confided in him. With his vast experience Sir Giles would have been the ideal person to advise her and would have known exactly how to proceed. Emily was forced silently to acknowledge that she hadn't a clue. One thing was certain, though, sooner or later she was going to have to confide in someone, for it would be madness to suppose that she could bring about

Sir Courtney's downfall unaided. Yes, she reiterated silently, it would be exceedingly foolhardy to suppose that she could go ahead on her own, not to mention downright dangerous.

Sir Giles Osborne's continued absence from town only served to fuel Emily's misgivings and, on the day before she was due to leave the capital herself, she had almost made up her mind to confide in Sebastian, even though she was under no illusions that he would be annoyed with her for not having done so at the outset.

The ideal opportunity to unburden herself came early in the afternoon, when she received word that his lordship wished to see her and, taking courage in both hands, she marched resolutely into the library, only to discover his lordship looking gravely down at a letter in his hand.

'You've not received bad news, I trust?' she asked, momentarily forgetting her own troubles.

'Yes, and no,' he answered, tossing the letter on top of the papers on his desk. 'It's from Sir Giles Osborne. He's written to inform me that he expects to receive confirmation about a further boatload of contraband sailing from France within the next few days. Although he hasn't received details yet as to the precise location, he expects the shipment to be unloaded somewhere on the Hampshire coast. More importantly, he seems to suppose the person who has been accepting those stolen items of jewellery will be on board. The information he's received has always been accurate in the past, so there's every chance Lady Pilkington's ruby necklace will be changing hands.'

'Well, that's good news, surely?' she prompted, when he continued to look slightly down in the mouth.

'Yes, except…Sir Giles has also written to ask me to join him at his country home in order to be on hand should the exchange take place. Which means that I'll be unable to escort you to Dorsetshire, and might indeed miss the engagement party altogether.'

This was something that Emily had not expected, and it certainly gave her pause for thought. Her instinct was still to confide in Sebastian, and yet a niggling doubt manacled her tongue. Supposing she was wrong? Supposing a length of cord and not Sir Courtney Farrington's whip had been used to murder Lady Sutherland, leaving that diamond-shaped impression round her neck? Silently Emily was forced to own that she might be allowing her intense dislike of the Baronet to cloud her judgement. After all, she reflected, his engineering an invitation to Charles and Sarah's engagement party might stem from nothing more sinister than a desire not to be excluded from an exclusive country gathering as he'd be travelling in the area. If she was totally wrong about Caroline's husband, then it was imperative that Sebastian was on hand to witness the exchange of Lady Pilkington's necklace. Intercepting the courier would surely eventually lead to his uncovering the identity of the person behind the robberies?

His lordship, misinterpreting the reason behind her troubled look, sighed as he lowered himself into the chair opposite. 'I can understand your disappointment, Em. And I must confess that I'm not happy about the possibility of missing the engagement party, but…' He ran impatient fingers through his hair. 'I cannot refuse Osborne's request to be there. As I believe I mentioned to you before, he isn't really involved in my affair. He's far more important concerns of his own to worry about. It was good of him to offer to put me up at his Hampshire home, as my own, as you possibly know, is now leased.'

'Yes, I understand that. And of course you must go,' Emily said, before staring fixedly down at the hands in her lap. Her conscience suddenly began to smite her, and she couldn't resist suggesting, 'But just supposing the man you're after, Hawk, is among the guests at the engagement party?'

'Highly unlikely, I should imagine,' he didn't hesitate

espond. 'Those attending will be family, neighbours and close friends. You know yourself that Deverel doesn't come up to town very often.'

'True,' she agreed, casting him a furtive glance from beneath her lashes. 'But he happened to mention that he had invited one or two people during his recent stay.'

'Well, don't you worry your pretty little head over that. In he unlikely event of any jewellery going missing old Sir George Maynard will be on hand to deal with the situation.'

Emily gave a start. 'Good heavens! Of course…Sir George! I'd completely forgotten about him. He knows all about the robberies, doesn't he?'

'He does, yes,' Sebastian confirmed, frowning suspiciously. 'So remember what I've told you. You're not to become involved in the unlikely event that a robbery does take place, understand?'

Emily was able to hold his decidedly mistrustful gaze for all of five seconds before returning her attention to the hands resting in her lap. 'With the possible exception of my betrothal ring, those lovely earrings you gave me and my mother's pearls, I do not possess any item of jewellery sufficiently fine to tempt the blackguard you're after, unless you're prepared to let me don the Hawkridge diamonds for the occasion.'

'Assuredly not,' was his lordship's unequivocal response. 'Although,' he added, 'it's a timely reminder. I must ask Clegg before I leave tomorrow to ensure that they're returned safely to the bank.'

Emily didn't attempt to hide her astonishment. 'Do you mean to say that you haven't already done so, and they're still here in the house?'

Rising from his chair, Sebastian grasped her wrists, and drew her to her feet. 'No, it slipped my mind. But, my sweet wife, you were never in any danger. The servants have maintained strict vigil. I didn't suppose for a moment that a further attempt would be made to steal them, but there was just a faint chance.'

Experiencing a deal of admiration for the way she had taken his unexpected news, Sebastian gazed down at her tenderly. 'No one is more sorry than I am that I shall be unable to accompany you back to Dorset tomorrow, but be assured that if this business is completed in time, I won't fail to escort you to the engagement party. If not, then I'll be with you as soon as I can, so that we can make firm plans for our future.'

His determination not to delay their wedding ought to have brought untold joy; instead his words seemed to hang in the air, a tormenting reminder of her silent pledge to do all within her power to enable him to choose with whom he truly wished to spend the rest of his life, and a germ of an idea rapidly began to develop in her brain.

All the same Emily might well have taken time to consider carefully before embarking on such a drastic course of action if she hadn't happened to come upon the butler crossing the hall, when she emerged from the library a moment later, and the ideal opportunity to lay hands on the one object which might enable her to put her half-made plan into effect had not so conveniently presented itself.

Even though Sebastian had returned to his desk, and was now busily engaged in responding to certain letters he had received that day, Emily took the precaution of closing the library door quietly behind her, before bestowing a dazzling smile upon the loyal retainer. 'Clegg, his lordship has just informed me that he hasn't as yet arranged for the diamonds to be returned to the bank for safekeeping, and I was wondering whether you'd be kind enough to satisfy a purely feminine whim and bring them along to my bedchamber so that I might have just one last peek at them before I leave tomorrow?'

Evidently he did not consider the request in any way extraordinary, for he beamed down at her with all the indulgence of some doting uncle. 'It will be no trouble at all, miss. I'll bring the box along to your room directly.'

Clegg was as good as his word, and entered the bedchamber a few minutes later, carrying the velvet-covered box which he placed down on the dressing-table in front of her, before extracting the small key from his pocket and fitting it into the lock.

Only for a moment did Emily suffer a severe pang of conscience, which she succeeded in sweeping aside as deftly as she swept the bottle of scent off the corner of her dressing table. 'Oh, how clumsy of me!' she exclaimed, leaving the conscientious servant to retrieve the glass vessel, as she had known he would, before all its contents had seeped into the carpet.

'Thank you, Clegg,' she said, her fingers shaking only very slightly as she closed the lid of the velvet box, and turned the small key in the lock herself. 'You had better return this to the safe before my clumsiness causes more damage.'

Emily waited until she heard the click of the door, before drawing out the sparkling object which she had deftly secreted between the folds of her skirt. Well, she had done it now, and there was no turning back. Pray God she didn't come to regret this day's work!

Chapter Sixteen

'Well, Hawkridge, I've just received the news we've been waiting for. The landing will take place tonight. What is more, I also now know the exact location where the smuggled goods are to be brought ashore,' Sir Giles Osborne announced, returning to his library where he had left his guest alone a short time before to enjoy a glass of excellent burgundy. 'So we've time enough to fortify ourselves further before we set out for the coast.'

After replenishing their glasses Sir Giles resumed his seat by the hearth, and for a moment considered the gentleman whose company he had very much enjoyed during the past days. 'You'll forgive me for saying so, my boy, but you don't appear unduly excited at the prospect of at long last avenging the death of your friend. I know you're not so foolish as to suppose that you'll achieve your ambition this night. As you're fully aware it's unlikely the murderous rogue will risk exposure by handing over the booty himself. But the person he's entrusted to do so will eventually divulge all we need to know. I've experience enough to be certain of that.'

Sebastian did not doubt it either, and smiled grimly. There were aspects of the suave Baronet's work into which he would prefer not to delve too deeply. 'It was my choice to be here to witness the events tonight, even though I harboured no doubts whatsoever that I could have left everything entirely to you. And I still intend to be there, except…' He glanced up at the mantel-clock and sighed. 'It's just that I could have wished the exchange had taken place earlier in the week to enable me to attend Charles Deverel's engagement party this evening.'

'I'm sure your friend will appreciate the reason for your absence if you should ever choose to confide in him.'

'It isn't that,' Sebastian admitted, after tossing the contents of his glass down his throat with scant regard for its excellence. 'You will possibly consider this incredibly foolish, but I simply cannot rid myself of the uneasy feeling that something is wrong. My fiancée just didn't seem herself during her final week in London. And on the day of her departure…'

'It is true that I deal in facts, Hawkridge, but I do trust my instincts,' Sir Giles assured him. 'Might I suggest, though, that in this instance Miss Stapleton had understandably been feeling disappointed because you chose not to accompany her home?'

'No,' Sebastian answered with conviction. 'She isn't the type to take a pet over mere trifles. And yet she was damnably edgy about something on the morning she left London. What was worse she didn't seem able to look me in the eye.' Frowning heavily, he shook his head. 'Bad sign, that. The little minx always wore just such a furtive expression years ago when she was contemplating some devilment.'

'She's hardly a child now, Hawkridge,' Sir Giles pointed out, masterfully suppressing a chuckle.

'No, she isn't. Unfortunately, though, time has done little to temper her adventurous spirit,' he divulged, remembering with a further resurgence of unease the night she had borne him company in Kempton Wood. He shook his head, running an impatient hand through his slightly waving brown hair. 'I don't know, perhaps I'm just being—'

He broke off as the door opened, and was surprised when Sir Giles's butler informed him that he himself had a visitor, for only a select few knew of his precise whereabouts. His surprise quickly gave way to a sense of foreboding when he discovered the caller's identity.

'What's happened?' he demanded the instant his own major-domo, distinctly lacking his customary aplomb, was shown into the room.

Twisting his hat nervously, Clegg disclosed, 'The Hawk-ridge diamonds are missing, sir.'

When his master received the startling news in stony silence, the butler evidently thought it behooved him to explain a little further. 'I would have returned them to the bank on Monday, sir, as you instructed, had not James, the footman, contracted a severe chill. You were most particular that I shouldn't travel alone with them across town, so I waited until yesterday, when James was sufficiently recovered to accompany me. When I arrived at the bank, the clerk quite naturally wished to view the contents of the box before giving me a receipt, and when I unlocked the case only the bracelet was there.'

Pale and drawn, Clegg bore all the appearance of someone who had shouldered a heavy burden. 'Naturally, my lord, the first thing I did on my return to Berkeley Square was to instigate a thorough search of the house. When that proved fruitless, I felt you must be apprised at once, and set out first thing this morning by hired carriage.'

Sir Giles, studying his guest closely, could not help but admire the display of self-mastery. Apart from lines of deep thought etching his lordship's high forehead, he betrayed no signs whatsoever that he had just received such devastating news, and when finally he did speak, his voice was smooth and remarkably controlled.

'Only you and I have keys to the safe, Clegg,' his lordship reminded him. 'The last time I saw the diamonds was on the night of the break-in, when I felt the need to satisfy myself that they were indeed still in my possession. Since that night have you, for any reason, opened the safe?'

He took a moment to consider before divulging, 'Why, yes, sir, last week! Miss Stapleton asked to see the diamonds, so I took them along to her room.'

'And did you check the contents yourself before returning them to the safe?'

'No, sir, but surely…'

'It's all right, Clegg. I'm certain Sir Giles's servants will provide you with refreshments,' Sebastian said, before finally dismissing him with a nod of his head.

'It would seem, my dear friend, that your instincts have proved correct,' Sir Giles remarked, when the servant had departed and his lordship had turned his attention to the empty hearth, 'and your fiancée was indeed attempting to conceal something from you.'

'The fact that she took the necklace without my knowledge really doesn't concern me, Osborne,' Sebastian admitted, after a further moment's intense thought. 'The reason why she took it most certainly does trouble me, though. Since the night of our engagement party, she has betrayed no desire whatsoever to wear the jewels again, except in an attempt to draw out our quarry. So why should she have chosen to take them away with…' As his words faded so did most of his healthy colouring. 'Oh, my God!'

'What is it?' Sir Giles asked urgently, as his lordship unexpectedly rose from the chair and began to pace up and down, tension clearly visible in every contour of his muscular frame. 'What's wrong?'

'Damnable little idiot!' Sebastian cursed. 'She knows, Osborne… At least she's sufficiently sure in her own mind to risk taking the necklace in an attempt to trap him.' The fingers he ran through his hair this time were not quite steady. 'The day before she left town she as good as told me the man I'm after would be attending Deverel's engagement party. And like a fool I dismissed it out of hand.'

Sir Giles frowned at this. 'But why didn't she confide in you fully, Hawkridge? If she'd discovered something, why keep it to herself?'

His lordship shook his head, at a loss to understand this himself. 'I honestly cannot imagine. But I mean to find out.' He cast a further glance in the direction of the mantel-clock. 'I've several hours hard travelling ahead of me. As you heard, my butler travelled here by hired carriage, but I shan't avail myself of that. I'll make the journey in far less time on horse-back. Clegg can follow when he's refreshed himself and bring my belongings. Might I impose upon you still further, Osborne, by requesting a mount?'

'No imposition at all, my dear boy,' Sir Giles assured him. 'You may take the horse my elder son always rides whenever he pays a visit. The animal's up to your weight and will see you through the first stage of your journey, no trouble. You concern yourself with getting to Dorsetshire as swiftly as possible,' he added, accompanying Sebastian, who under-standably enough was not disposed to linger, out into the hall. 'You may safely leave the exchange at the coast to me.'

Emily took a final check of her overall appearance in the full-length mirror, before resuming her seat at the dressing-table in order to don the pair of diamond ear-drops which Se-bastian had bestowed upon her on the occasion of their engagement party, and surprised a look of mild disapproval on her maid's face. 'What is it, Skinner? Is something not quite to your liking?'

'You look lovely, miss, except…' Her dark eyes focused on the glinting gems now dangling from the shell-like ears. 'Are you sure your pearls wouldn't be more suitable?'

'Yes, they would,' Emily readily acknowledged. 'But I'm merely satisfying a whim, Skinner. Lord Hawkridge is unable to be with me tonight, and I wished to have something about me to remind me of him.'

The fact that Emily was sporting the beautiful sapphire-and-diamond engagement ring seemingly didn't occur to the conscientious maid who smiled benignly before going about the room collecting the soiled garments to take downstairs for laundering.

The instant the door had closed behind Skinner, Emily went over to the chest in the corner of the room to take out the two articles she had secreted there soon after her arrival back at her grandfather's home. Only for a moment did she hesitate before drawing out the loaded pistol and the small, drawstring purse. After all the soul-searching she had done after purloining the necklace, the anxiety she had suffered throughout the journey back to Dorsetshire, and the sleepless nights she had endured since her return, agonising over the safety of the necklace, not to mention the well-being of the other members of the household should an attempt be made to steal the diamonds, she wasn't going to lose her nerve now, at this the eleventh hour, she told herself, extracting the necklace and carefully securing it about her throat.

Thankfully, as things had turned out, Lady Luck had favoured her thus far. The journey from London had been blessedly uneventful, without so much as one of Sebastian's fine carriage horses casting a shoe; and although no attempt had been made to break in to her grandfather's property since her return to the house, Emily refused to be lulled into a false sense of security.

Sir Courtney might have believed her tale about the jewels being brought to Dorset by special messenger, and therefore had been prepared to bide his time before attempting to steal the necklace. She didn't doubt, though, that if he was the guilty party he would have planned to make his move that night, when he could be certain the jewels were in the house, and Emily was determined to avoid that eventuality at all costs if she could. There wasn't the remotest possibility that she could get the necklace safely locked away in her grandfather's bank until morning, therefore she had to find some way of persuading Sir Courtney to make an attempt at the party itself.

Of course any attempt on Sir Courtney's part to steal the necklace was far from a foregone conclusion. But it was as well to be prepared to act at a moment's notice and take every precaution, she reminded herself, swirling her lightweight cloak about her shoulders, and securing it about her neck, thereby cunningly concealing both necklace and pistol beneath the satin folds.

How fortunate it was that she wasn't having to attempt the escapade while still in town, where she would have had need of a chaperon, she reflected, discovering her grandfather awaiting her in the hall and quickly accompanying him outside to the waiting carriage. Lady Hester Dawlish might well have queried the necessity of donning a cloak on such a balmy evening, when a lightweight silk shawl would have proved quite adequate, whereas John Stapleton wouldn't concern himself over such trifles.

As she settled herself into the well-sprung carriage which Lord Hawkridge had insisted she make use of until his arrival in Dorsetshire, Emily smiled fondly across at her grandfather before something a little disturbing occurred to her, swiftly erasing the smile. 'You did mention that Sir George Maynard would be among the guests this evening, Grandpapa?'

Silver-grey brows drawing together in a suspicious frown gave her a timely reminder to remain on her guard. The vague and almost childlike mien he adopted for the most part disguised wonderfully well the shrewdness of a gentleman whose memory was remarkably acute on occasions, as his next words proved.

'You asked me that only yesterday, child. Why are you so keen for Sir George to be there?'

Emily hoped her careless shrug looked convincing. 'No reason really. It was just that I wouldn't like to think of you lacking the companionship of your particular friends this evening. And I did consider it odd that Sir George hasn't paid one call to the house since my return.'

'It wouldn't have mattered a jot if he had, you still wouldn't have seen him,' Mr Stapleton pointed out. 'You've spent most of the time in your room, pining over your fiancé's absence, I do not doubt.'

This wasn't altogether true. The reason Emily had spent so much time in her bedchamber was mainly because she had wished to keep a close guard on the diamonds, though she couldn't deny that she had missed Sebastian so very much, and had come perilously close on numerous occasions to dispatching Jonas Finn hotfoot into Hampshire with a letter confessing what she had done. She didn't doubt that his response would have been to come at once, angry and demanding an explanation. Undoubtedly he would then have taken matters into his own hands, have taken complete control. And that of course was precisely the reason why she had never put pen to paper. If her instincts had played her false, and Farrington turned out to be completely innocent, then all she was destined to face was Sebastian's anger and censure over taking the diamonds; if, on the other hand…

'Yes, Grandfather, I have missed him quite dreadfully,' she admitted, 'but I understand perfectly the reasons for his not being here. I dare say we'll see him before too many days have passed.'

'I'm certain we shall, my dear,' he agreed, reaching forward to pat her hand, and causing her a moment's acute alarm when his fingers came perilously close to the pistol concealed beneath the cloak. 'And who knows he might even surprise you by turning up tonight.'

Oh, Lord! I sincerely hope not, Emily silently prayed, appalled at the mere thought. She was prepared for a certain amount of criticism from friends and neighbours over decking herself out in fabulous gauds at a country party, but this would be as nothing compared to what she would be forced to endure if Hawkridge himself arrived to witness her appalling show of bad taste. She would be subjected to the most blistering tirade, or worse, and he might be just too angry to care who witnessed the encounter.

She refused to dwell on this horrendous possibility, and managed to turn her thoughts with very little effort onto something of far more import at the present time—namely, where she was going to conceal the pistol until the possible need for its use arose. Fortunately the ideal location was not long in occurring to her, and the instant they arrived at their destination she left her grandfather to join the long queue of guests, all patiently waiting their turn to greet the host and hostess, and made her way to the upper floor.

Having visited the Hall on numerous occasions in the past, Emily was no stranger to the layout of the house, and knew the precise location of each and every room. She had learned, when the newly engaged couple had found time to pay her a visit during the week, that Sarah, even with her vastly increased status, had chosen to remain in the bedchamber that she had used since first taking up residence at Deverel Hall until her marriage, when she would share Charles's apartments in the west wing.

After taking a moment to glance up and down the passageway to ensure that no one was lurking, Emily slipped quietly into the room which, reflecting the personality of its user, was both clean and tidy. Some detached part of her brain registered that there were rather more bottles adorning the dressing table than she remembered seeing before, but she didn't waste time in discovering what other changes had taken place as she scanned the room for a suitable hiding place, and her gaze quickly fell on the escritoire in the corner.

As it was highly unlikely that Sarah would take it into her

head to pen a letter during the party, Emily experienced no reluctance whatsoever in concealing the pistol beneath some papers in the top drawer; then, after laying her cloak over the back of the chair, delayed no longer in making her way back to the hall.

She was halfway down the stairs before her presence was first noted. Then all at once she seemed to become the focal point of all those queuing in the hall. Even her grandfather blinked several times at the lavish adornment about her slender neck, when at last she took her place beside him.

It was no more than she had expected, and Emily found it no difficult matter to return those prolonged stares of disapproval with a faintly mocking smile, though she might have wished that the normally tactful Lady Deverel, after greeting her as warmly as ever, had refrained from murmuring, 'Dear me, now that is a blunder,' because it induced both Charles and Sarah to exchange suspicious glances.

Consequently Emily was not in the least surprised when her friend came in search of her a short while later and made it impossible for her to refuse a brief tête-à-tête by finding someone willing to take her place at the card table. Not that Emily had any intention of attempting to avoid her friend, although she could not prevent a slight smile from curling her lips, when her elbow was taken in a surprisingly firm clasp and she was shepherded outside to a quiet spot on the terrace.

'Whose splendid notion was it to hold the party downstairs and not in the ballroom?' she asked, thereby neatly denying Sarah the opportunity to begin her inquisition. 'Yours, I do not doubt. What a clever girl you are to consider that in late June guests might welcome a stroll in the fresh air!'

She couldn't suppress a gurgle of mirth when grey eyes favoured her with an impatient glance. 'All right, dear, don't get on your high ropes. What is it you wish to say to me? I sincerely trust you're not going to take me roundly to task for my sheer bad taste in wearing this dazzling array of jewels?'

'I would never dream of doing such a thing,' Sarah assured her. 'But I should like to know what persuaded you to wear them, because unlike Lady Deverel, who seems to suppose that you might not realise that it is not the thing to wear diamonds in the country, I know better.'

'I had my reasons, dear,' Emily responded with a rueful half-smile, 'but for the present I should prefer to keep them to myself.' Not granting the opportunity for further questions, Emily slipped her arm through Sarah's and guided her back into the salon. 'I must not keep you from your other guests, but before you disappear perhaps you could tell me where our esteemed Justice of the Peace is skulking? I've seen neither hide nor hair of him since I arrived.'

'And you won't. He sent a note this morning with his apologies. Apparently he's taken to his bed, suffering from an annoying summer chill.'

'Oh, confound it!'

Needless to say, the startling reaction to Sir George Maynard's absence did little to lessen Sarah's suspicion that something was wrong. However, before she could enquire why his presence in particular was so important, Emily surprised her again by uttering a tiny sound somewhere between a squeal and a gasp as she stared across the room at the group of young gentlemen paying court to Drusilla Deverel.

'I'd forgotten Charles had mentioned that Michael might be here. You must excuse me, dear. I must speak with him. No doubt we'll talk later.'

Not granting Sarah the opportunity to detain her further, Emily withdrew her arm. She had little difficulty in detaching Lord Sutherland from the group of admirers, for he was as delighted by her presence as she had been by his.

'You're a sight for sore eyes, m'dear! Only arrived today and hardly know a soul here.'

She raised a mocking brow, as she cast a glance over her shoulder at Sarah's future sister-in-law. 'That, if I may say so doesn't appear to have placed a damper on your enjoyment of the evening.'

Michael didn't pretend to misunderstand. 'Devilish pretty girl, wouldn't you say?'

'Yes, very. But if you could manage to prise your thoughts away from the divine Drusilla for a few minutes, I should be very grateful.'

Obligingly he allowed her to lead him to two vacant chairs tucked away in one corner of the large salon, which had become increasingly crowded during the past hour. The trouble was, though, now she had managed to get him alone, Emily had no very clear idea of what to say or, more importantly, how much to reveal. Sir George Maynard's absence had come as a crushing blow and was something that she could not have foreseen. She had been relying on the local Justice of the Peace to aid her, if the need arose. That was out of the question now. One thing was certain, though, she must secure help of some sort.

'Are you, by any chance, staying here in the house, Michael?' she asked, after succeeding up to a point in marshalling her disordered thoughts. 'Then Charles must have told you that Hawk isn't to be here tonight,' she added, when she received a nod in response. 'He's at this moment trying to uncover the identity of the person who murdered your sister-in-law.'

She couldn't prevent a smile at the stunned expression. 'Yes, he has been endeavouring to do so since your brother's death,' she assured him.

'And Hawk might now know who's responsible?'

'He might, yes,' she answered taking a moment to study the pretty painted figures on her fan, before divulging, 'I, on the other hand, am almost certain that I do know. And it is my intention to trap him tonight.'

Lord Sutherland, if possible, looked more stunned than before. 'Do-do you mean that he's here?'

Emily drew her eyes away from the tall, elegantly attired gentleman who had just entered the room, and was being greeted by their hostess, and gazed into the startled young face of the man seated beside her.

'Yes, Michael. He's here.'

'But surely…?' His expression changed to one of puzzlement. 'Then why isn't Hawk here?'

'Because for reasons which I shall not go into I chose in the end to keep my suspicions to myself. But that isn't important now. We need proof, Michael. We must induce him to reveal himself.'

He glanced fleetingly at the necklace before raising troubled eyes to hers. 'emily, you don't mean you're going to let him steal the diamonds?'

'He'll not get his hands on the necklace, I promise you.' He couldn't fail to hear the determination in her voice. 'I sincerely hope that he'll make the attempt, though. And that is when I'm going to need your help.'

'Lord!' Michael clapped a hand over his eyes. 'Hawk will murder me for this!'

'Oh, no he won't,' Emily assured him, smiling ruefully. 'He'll be too busy murdering me to trouble himself about you. But I shall worry about that when the time comes.'

'What is it you want me to do?' he asked, smiling in spite of the fact that he was deeply concerned for her safety.

'That, I don't know yet,' she frankly admitted. 'A great deal will depend on the actions of our intended victim.' For the first time she betrayed her troubled state of mind by a deep frown. 'I want to avoid a scene here if I can. If by some miracle I do succeed in tricking him, and lure him away from the party, then be assured I'll get word to you.'

She rose to her feet. 'I assume you can rely on your groom to assist you?'

Michael nodded, as he rose too. 'Yes, he's a reliable fellow. He was my brother's servant before mine.'

'In that case I expect he'll wish to avenge his late master's death and be doubly willing to aid you. You can also enlist the help of Charles's groom. He's a reliable fellow too. But under no circumstances confide in Deverel himself. The fewer people involved in this the more chance there is of a successful outcome.'

She chose not to add that she feared that Charles, acting on Sebastian's behalf, would do everything within his power to prevent her from placing herself in danger. Michael, on the other hand, had been an inspired choice. He had his own axe to grind, and she strongly suspected that a desire to avenge his brother's death, not to mention the murder of his sister-in-law, was foremost in his mind at the moment.

'Come,' she said, placing the tips of her fingers on the sleeve of his beautifully tailored evening coat, 'let us dance. Then, afterwards, we must avoid each other as much as possible. I do not underestimate the villain we're after, Michael. If he suspects that we're plotting something, he'll not take the bait.'

Once again his young face betrayed clear evidence of unease. 'But surely if Hawk is on the trail of one of this blackguard's associates then there's no need for you—'

'There's no guarantee that he has been or will be successful in his endeavours, Michael,' she interrupted, determined not to lose his support. 'There's no guarantee that we shall be either, come to that. But if we let this opportunity slip away, there'll not be another.'

Thankfully he required no further persuasion and promptly escorted her on to the dance floor.

Chapter Seventeen

With no shortage of gentlemen requesting her as a partner, Emily spent much of the following hour dancing. To a certain extent this served her purpose admirably, for not only did it provide the opportunity to behave with a semblance of normality, but it also denied Sarah the chance to hold her in private conversation again, though she was frequently the recipient of her friend's suspicious, greyeyed scrutiny. Far less gratifying was that Sir Courtney Farrington, aside from acknowledging her presence with a slight inclination of his head, made not the least attempt to approach her on the few occasions she did find herself seated by the wall.

Having managed to keep pace with an energetic exponent of the lively country dance, Emily finally decided that a prolonged rest was most definitely required, and didn't hesitate to slip outside to the terrace, where she put her chicken-skin fan to immediate use. During the past week the weather had turned increasingly sultry, without so much as a suspicion of a breeze to take the edge off the rising temperatures and although the sun was too low in the sky now to punish the earth with its scorching rays, the atmosphere remained heavy begging for the rain which would freshen the air.

'If you were hoping to find it much cooler out here, Mis

Stapleton, I fear you are doomed to disappointment,' a smooth voice drawled directly behind her.

Only for an instant did Emily pause in her fanning to check the shudder of apprehension which threatened to ripple through her. Now was not the moment to falter, to succumb to a fit of nerves, she told herself, determined not to waste what might well turn out to be her one and only opportunity of achieving her objective.

'You are right, Sir Courtney.' Taking heart from the fact that her voice remained reassuringly steady, she turned at last to face the gentleman whom she had never seen less than impeccably turned out.

Even now, on this oppressive late June evening, when more than one gentleman guest had had recourse to a hand-kerchief in order to wipe beads of perspiration from a glowing brow, Sir Courtney Farrington appeared remarkably cool and composed, without so much as a golden hair on his head out of place, nor the merest hint of a wilt about his impeccably starched shirt points. It really was difficult to imagine that beneath that ice-cool reserve lurked the fiery, ungovernable temperament of a callous being quite capable of perpetrating the most despicable acts. Was she adroit enough to induce him to cast aside that ice-cool mantle and reveal his true nature? she wondered, somehow managing to coax her lips into a semblance of a smile.

'I can only be grateful that I'm no longer in town, sir. The heat there must be unbearable.'

'Yes, Hawkridge must be regretting his decision not to ac-company you.' He paused to take out his snuffbox. 'I believe someone did mention that he isn't here tonight.'

'Sadly not,' Emily concurred, her mind working furiously. He had come upon her quite unexpectedly, catching her breathless and fanning herself. Could she possibly use this to her advantage?

'Truth to tell, sir, I'm beginning to wish that I wasn't

either,' she added as a seed of an idea embedded itself firmly in her brain. 'I very much fear that I'm about to succumb to one of my annoying headaches. I'm very prone to them, especially at this season of the year,' she lied beautifully.

Instantly she was the recipient of a penetrating blue-eyed gaze. 'You do appear a little flushed, if I may say so, Miss Stapleton. But that might merely be the result of your recent exertions on the dance floor. Perhaps you will permit me to fetch you a glass of cool punch?'

'Please do not put yourself to the trouble, sir. It will not serve the purpose.' She hoped her sigh sounded convincing. 'I'm afraid the only thing to be done is to go home to my bed.'

'In that case, may I summon your carriage?'

Although not best pleased at the time, as it effectively denied her the chance to call upon the services of Jonas Finn and Sebastian's head groom should the need arise, Emily was now thankful that her grandfather had insisted on sending Lord Hawkridge's carriage back to the house, for it enabled her to say truthfully, 'In order not to add to the clutter of guests' carriages in Sir Charles's stable-yard, my grandfather instructed our coachman to collect us later, sir.'

'In that case, ma'am, permit me to put my own equipage at your disposal.'

She had been prepared for this and was ready with her reply. 'Do not think me ungrateful, but it wouldn't benefit me in the least to avail myself of your kind offer. My grandfather's house is but a short distance away, and will take me no more than half an hour on foot, if I cut through Kempton Wood.' She pointed with her fan so that he could be in no doubt as to the precise direction she would be taking. 'See, Sir Charles's shrubbery backs on to the wood. I can slip quietly away without anyone being the wiser and without causing a stir. Which I would much prefer, for I'm certain the walk would do me good.'

Only for a moment did Sir Courtney pause before making

use of the contents of his snuffbox. 'If you are determined to return home on foot, then you must permit me to escort you. It is unthinkable that you should go alone.'

Undeniably there had been a gleam of speculation in those cold eyes, but it quite failed to disguise the hint of wariness lurking there. If she appeared eager to accept his offer, might it not make him more suspicious?

'You are most kind, sir, but there is no need to trouble yourself. I've walked the distance many times without suffering ill fortune.' She waved her hand in a dismissive gesture. 'This is not London. There are no footpads lurking to attack the unwary. But if you wish to offer me assistance, you may do so by informing our esteemed hostess of my departure, who will in turn speak to my grandfather. I have no wish for him to cut his evening short on my account.'

For a moment it appeared as though he might argue further, but then he merely shrugged. 'If that is what you wish, Miss Stapleton.'

'It is indeed, sir.' Emily made to go back inside, then checked as she bethought herself of something else. 'I would be grateful if you would grant me a few minutes to slip quietly upstairs before informing Lady Deverel. She's a dear lady, but has a tendency to fuss. So I should prefer to make my escape before she discovers my intention to leave.'

Whether or not he believed her, or whether or not he would be tempted to try his luck and risk accosting her in the wood, was anyone's guess. He certainly made no attempt to escort her back into the salon, and yet she could almost feel those icy-blue orbs following her progress as she meandered her way past the happy, chattering guests.

Resisting the urge to glance over her shoulder to see if he had in fact decided to follow her out into the hall, Emily hurried up the stairs and along the passageway. Timing was all important. She must offer Sir Courtney the opportunity to follow her before Michael came in hot pursuit, and yet she must not delay too long before summoning her young protector, she decided, once again making use of the escritoire the instant she had reached Sarah's bedchamber.

After removing the pistol, she took out a sheet of paper, and was about to dash off a quick note to Michael when she clearly detected the click of the door, and swivelled round in the chair, her breath leaving her in a faint sigh when she discovered who in fact had followed her.

'What in the world are you doing here?' she demanded impatiently, before focusing her attention on the far more important task of writing her note.

'It might have slipped your memory, Emily, but this does happen to be my bedchamber. More to the point, what are you doing skulking in here?'

'Making free with your writing materials,' she answered, her amusement at her normally placid friend's waspish tone swiftly fading as a disturbing possibility occurred to her. 'Did anyone notice you following me up here…? Sir Courtney Farrington, for instance?'

As she had met him for the first time that evening, it took Sarah a moment or two to bring the gentleman to mind. 'I really couldn't say. What does it matter if he did?'

'Perhaps nothing…perhaps a great deal. But I've no time to go into that now.'

Hurriedly sanding down the short missive, Emily rose to her feet. 'I entrust this into your safe keeping,' she went on placing the letter into the hand Sarah automatically held out 'You are to ensure that Michael…Lord Sutherland receives it ten minutes after I've gone.'

Sarah could not have appeared more stunned. 'Gone…' Where are you going?'

'Home, dearest.' Emily watched a hurt look replace the astonishment in clear grey eyes. 'I would never leave your engagement party unless it was vital that I do so. I must right wrong, Sarah, and might never be granted the opportunity to do so again. I promise I shall explain everything, but I haven't the time now. I must walk back through Kempton Wood.'

Sarah's bitter disappointment was instantly forgotten. 'What, wearing those diamonds? You must be all about in your head!'

Emily managed a semblance of a rueful smile as she removed the necklace. 'My insanity has not yet progressed that far,' she assured her, placing the treasured adornment in Sarah's other hand, before reaching for her cloak and pistol, and hurrying over to the door. 'Remember, dearest, I'm relying on you to take care of the necklace, and see that Michael receives that note.'

Not granting Sarah the opportunity to delay her further, Emily slipped out of the room and, swirling the cloak about her shoulders, thereby once again neatly concealing the pistol beneath its folds, she hurried along the passageway towards the door leading to the back stairs, from where it was a simple matter to gain access to the mansion's side entrance. Thankfully she encountered none of the servants, who might have delayed her further, and was soon safely in the shrubbery where she was confident she would not be observed by anyone promenading in the formal gardens.

The fence which separated Charles's land from the wood proved no great obstacle, and there was still sufficient light, even though the evening was well advanced, to follow easily through the wood's main track. Yet everywhere seemed so still and quiet, with no hint of a breeze to rustle the leaves, and Emily was just beginning to fear that her woodland trek might prove a complete waste of time and energy, when she caught sight of that immaculately attired figure propped against the trunk of a substantial elm, just a short distance ahead.

'Why, Miss Stapleton, I'd almost given you up!' He waited until she was abreast of him before easing his back off the sturdy wooden support and sauntering towards her. 'You see, I couldn't reconcile it with my conscience to permit you to walk home alone.'

Exerting masterly self-control, Emily managed not to laugh in his face. 'You are all kind consideration, Sir Courtney,' she cooed, and was just silently congratulating herself on her own acting skills, when she detected the sound of a twig snapping and her self-confidence received a severe dent.

She could not take comfort in the hope that it just might be her young protector, ready to offer his aid should the need arise, for not enough time had elapsed for Michael to enlist the aid of his groom and follow. No, it was much more likely to be one of Sir Courtney's cronies, she swiftly decided, silently cursing herself for not considering the possibility that he would not attempt to purloin the necklace alone. She gained little comfort from the feel of the cold metal in her hand, for this would only offer her one shot. Her only hope now was that Sir Courtney would be cautious enough to delay his assault upon her until they were further away from Deverel land, where there was less chance of the assault being witnessed or overheard.

Seemingly he had considered this, for, much to her intense relief, he began to walk on, and she did not hesitate to keep step beside him. After all, it would not help her situation if he suspected that she was wary of him, or even remotely suspicious. It might help too if she could occupy his mind by making polite conversation.

'How long do you intend to stay in the area, sir?'

'Only until tomorrow, Miss Stapleton.' His smile was not pleasant. 'I shall have achieved what I came here to do by then.'

His words sent a chill down her spine. He sounded so supremely confident, but she dared not act yet. She had to give Michael time to reach her. 'Ahh, yes! If my memory serves me correctly you intend to stay with Lord and Lady Hewley.'

'Yes, but I do not envisage a long visit.' Now he sounded merely bored, which did not augur well for maintaining the conversation for any appreciable time. 'Hewley's company is a trifle tedious and his wife's attractions are limited.'

'If that is your opinion, I wonder you chose to accept the invitation in the first place,' Emily pointed out before she could stop herself.

Fortunately he seemed not to take exception to the thinly veiled sarcasm. 'It simply suited my purposes to do so, Miss Stapleton… Just as it suits my purpose to be with you now. And even though I find your company far more pleasurable than that of the majority of young women who have crossed my path in recent years, I believe I can dispense with it.'

Before she could avoid the contact, he reached out a hand to grasp her shoulder, forcing her to stop. 'I think we have ventured sufficiently far now.'

Considering she was under no illusions that her companion wouldn't think twice about putting a period to her existence, Emily was amazed that, apart from a strong sense of revulsion at his touch, she felt remarkably composed.

Easily shrugging off the long fingers, she turned to face him squarely, relieved at last to be able to dispense with the spurious display of polite amiability. 'I too shall be happy to dispense with your company, permanently,' she told him, mimicking quite beautifully the disdainful curl that she had glimpsed on Sebastian's lips whenever he had addressed the Baronet. 'Not so many will mourn your passing, least of all Lord Hawkridge who, incidentally, has worked tirelessly to bring you to justice since the death of his friend Lord Sutherland.'

His smug smile failed to disguise the faint glimmer of unease in his eyes. 'Clearly you are not ignorant of my past activities. Which, I am forced to own, surprises me somewhat. But I do not believe I'm in any danger of being linked with your—ah—unfortunate demise, my dear.'

'You are living in a fool's paradise, Farrington,' Emily took great delight in telling him. 'Unless I much mistake the matter a warrant for your arrest will be issued, if it has not been already, and the Runners will be hot on your trail. The means by which you have disposed of your ill-gotten gains has been—er—rumbled, as it were. Lord Hawkridge is at this present time in Hampshire, ready to intercept your courier who, I do not doubt, will be carrying Lady Pilkington's rubies. How long do you suppose it will be before your accomplice is persuaded to reveal your identity?'

The polished mantle Sir Courtney had donned to conceal his true character from the world at large was showing definite signs of wear. His mouth was now set in a cruel, thin line and his eyes glinted ominously beneath half-hooded lids as they focused on a spot somewhere beyond Emily's left shoulder.

'You heard that, Sloane?'

'Aye, sir. I heard, right enough.'

Out of the corner of her eye Emily saw Sir Courtney's loathsome henchman emerge through the undergrowth, with that cruel weapon of murder and torture held fast in one broad hand. She experienced a strong impulse to run, but curbed it. Hampered by petticoats, she wouldn't get far. No, her only chance, she silently acknowledged, was to delay their assault for as long as possible in the hope that Michael would soon be here.

She risked taking her eyes off Sir Courtney to cast his satellite a look of revulsion. 'I see your injury has all but healed now. I cannot tell you what satisfaction I derived from knowing I inflicted that upon you.'

'No, not yet!' Sir Courtney ordered, when Sloane, unfurling the whip, took a menacing step forward. 'You'll gain the satisfaction of taking your revenge soon enough. But first Miss Stapleton is going to satisfy my curiosity over something.' He regarded her intently. 'I'm intrigued to know, my dear, how came you to suspect me in the first place?'

It would have afforded Emily the utmost pleasure to deny him the satisfaction of knowing, but once again she was forced to suppress natural inclinations. Keeping him talking was the only sure way of buying herself more time.

Concealing her contempt was becoming increasingly difficult as she took a moment to look him over from head to foot.

'Your complete disregard for the feelings of others was your downfall, Farrington. And your desire to get your hands on the Hawkridge diamonds. You were not above making use of your wife to achieve your ends. No doubt you feared that without her you wouldn't be invited by Sebastian to attend his engagement party. And, who knows, perhaps you were right. But you really ought to have bided your time before forcing Caroline into Society, at least until the evidence of your debased practices had faded from her neck. I saw the mark, and swiftly discovered the means by which it had been inflicted.'

Once again Emily found her eyes drawn to the instrument of torture, the end of which now lay serpentine on the ground, like a venomous snake about to strike. 'The impression left about Lady Elizabeth Sutherland's neck was just too much of a coincidence.'

Just for a moment a hint of admiration flickered in the depths of his eyes, before disappearing beneath an almost maniacal gleam, as he too glanced briefly at the coil of leather at his henchman's feet. 'I became proficient in its use as a boy, when I practised regularly on my father's horses. Sloane too is a worthy exponent, as is my coachman, Parker. I cannot recall now which of us had the pleasure of squeezing the last breath out of Sutherland's wife and her pretty young maid.'

Emily felt sick to her stomach. He was utterly merciless and totally deranged. And she would be his next victim if help did not arrive soon. Dear God! Why was Michael not here? Farrington started talking again and she forced herself to listen.

'…And speaking of Parker, it is none other than my trusty coachman who is to travel to the coast with the rubies. The exchange does not take place until later tonight. Which will buy me some time, as I'm certain Hawkridge isn't aware of my identity quite yet.' He regarded her keenly. 'I'm almost certain that you didn't share your suspicions of my guilt with your fiancé, my dear, otherwise Hawkridge, cursed with a surfeit of nobility, would never have permitted you to place yourself in danger. I wonder too whether he knows that you have the diamonds?'

Emily had no intention of enlightening him, and after a moment he merely shrugged. 'Well, no matter. It is some justice, I suppose, to be able to deprive Hawkridge of his family's famous heirloom.' His expression grew noticeably harder. 'If it hadn't been for his infernal meddling, persuading my late father-in-law to change his will, I wouldn't have been forced to resort to robbery in order to support my lifestyle.'

'You did not need to resort to murder,' Emily countered, completely unmoved by the tale of woe. 'And your wife, at least, must be grateful to Sebastian. His interference, as you call it, undoubtedly saved her from an early grave.'

He appeared grimly amused. 'What a clever girl you are! And how well you know me, my dear. What a pity I cannot take you to comfort me during my enforced exile abroad. I shall, however, relieve you of the famous necklace. That will provide sufficient funds to support me for quite some time.'

He reached out an arm, clearly expecting her calmly to hand it over. Consequently Emily derived much pleasure from his look of astonished outrage when, a moment later, she pulled the tie on her cloak to display a throat naked of adornment.

'As you see I cannot oblige you, sir. But I am quite happy to present you with this,' and so saying she allowed the cloak to slip from her shoulders to reveal the pistol clasped in a hand that had remained remarkably steady.

Surprisingly, he appeared more concerned about the absence of jewels than the pistol levelled at his heart. 'Where is it!' he demanded through clenched teeth.

'I do not know, Sir Courtney,' she answered, incurably truthful. 'But I'm certain it is safe.'

'She might have the diamonds about her,' Sloane suggested, with a lascivious leer at the feminine curves concealed beneath the expensive silk trappings. 'Let's strip her to make sure.'

Sir Courtney shook his head, instantly vetoing the recommendation. 'I strongly suspect the diamonds are somewhere back at the house. And loath though I am to deny you your little pleasures, my trusty friend, our time would be better spent in attempting to locate their whereabouts, so let us not tarry. I doubt the chit can handle the pistol.'

His first assumption had been correct; his second could not have been more wrong, as he discovered to his cost when he made a foolish attempt to grasp the weapon.

'You murdering bitch!' Sloane roared after the deafening report had died away and he had watched his master, a fatal wound in his chest, drop to the ground like a stone.

Emily didn't waste a precious moment to listen to the string of invective which followed, but before she had run more than a few yards she heard the whip crack through the air, and felt the punishing sting as the lash ensnared her waist. The next moment she was on the ground, fighting for her very breath as Sloane slipped the leather coil about her neck, his expression every bit as maniacal as his late master's had been as he dropped to his knees, pulling ever tighter.

With the blood pounding in her ears, and her lungs feeling ready to burst, she was powerless to prevent the work-roughened fingers from hooking round the neckline of her gown, tearing the bodice down to her waist, and she could only pray that death would come before he carried out his evil intent. The hammering in her head intensified, culminating in a thunderous report. Then all at once she was conscious only of the heavy weight on top of her before sinking into oblivion.

Sebastian weaved his way between the carriages cluttering the driveway, before dismounting and placing his horse in the care of a stable-lad. No less weary than the gelding he had hired to cover the last leg of the journey, he made his way round to the Restoration mansion's front entrance. Dusty and dishevelled after the many hours spent in the saddle, he was in no fit state to be paying calls, least of all at a time when the master of the house was hosting a party. All the same the butler, who answered the summons a minute or two later, didn't hesitate to admit him, though he did tactfully suggest that his lordship might care to await Miss Stapleton in the library.

As he had no wish for his impromptu arrival to cause any undue stir, Sebastian was more than happy to oblige, and headed towards the book-lined room, blissfully unaware that from the head of the stairs a pair of troubled grey eyes was following his progress across the chequered hall.

After depositing hat, crop and gloves on an occasional table he helped himself to a glass of Charles's wine, and had only just begun to wash the dust from his throat when he detected the click of the door, and turned to see his friend's pretty fiancée regarding him rather quizzically from the aperture.

Striving to conceal his disappointment at not discovering Emily herself there, he came forward to take one slender hand briefly in his own, while apologising for his unexpected arrival and his appearing before her in such a dishevelled state.

Privately Sarah thought he looked wonderfully masculine in his riding garb, with his waving, brown hair in disarray tumbling over his forehead. As Emily herself had once remarked, his features were too sharply defined and rugged for him to be regarded as handsome by the vast majority of their sex. Even so, Sarah considered his easy grace and abundance of charm more than compensated for the slight prominence of an aquiline nose and a mouth that was fractionally too wide. Yes, she could well understand why Emily had always loved him so.

'Pray do not give it another thought, sir,' she told him, swiftly banishing the ludicrous notion which she had recently been harbouring that Emily was in any way enamoured of young Lord Sutherland. 'In truth I am very pleased to see you because—'

She broke off as Charles, and the young gentleman whom she had foolishly imagined had been vying for her friend's affections came striding into the room. 'Sebastian, how good it is to see you, old fellow! My butler just informed us of your arrival. He's still searching for Emily.'

'He'll not find her,' Sarah announced, thereby gaining everyone's attention.

Only Michael didn't appear surprised by the disclosure. 'Do you mean she's left already?'

If Sarah had once harboured some doubt as to the depths of Lord Hawkridge's regard for her friend, this was no longer the case. His face was suddenly ashen, and there was a momentary flicker of utter despair in his eyes, when she unhesitatingly handed him the note which Emily had penned and which contained just two lines: 'Follow me now into Kempton Wood. Miss Nichols will inform you of the precise direction to take.'

'What do you know about this?' Sebastian demanded, thrusting the brief missive into Michael's hand. 'Speak man!' he ordered, when Michael cast a wary glance in Charles and Sarah's direction. 'You're among friends. Why did Emily wish you to follow her?'

'She said she knew who was behind the robberies, and who was responsible for Elizabeth's death,' he disclosed softly, and then went on to relate, as far as he could remember, the gist of the conversation he had had with Emily earlier in the evening.

'Oh, my God!' Charles muttered. 'That was why she was wearing those wretched diamonds. She did so to lure him out.'

'But she wasn't wearing them when she left,' Sarah did not hesitate to assure them. 'She left the necklace in my care, and placed it in the safe.'

'I wish to heaven she had confided in me. Had I an inkling

of what she had meant to do, you may be sure I would have prevented her,' Charles announced, and surprised a glimmer of amusement in Sebastian's eyes.

'emily possibly suspected that you would, Charles, and turned to someone else she trusted, and one who, moreover had a vested interest.'

Resembling a schoolboy discovered indulging in some foolhardy prank, Michael hung his head. 'I'm sorry, Hawk I shouldn't have agreed.'

Sarah experienced a surge of sympathy and didn't hesitate to come to Lord Sutherland's defence. 'You are not to blame sir. The instant I saw the pistol, I realised that whatever she was planning to do was not without an element of risk to herself. I should have made more of an effort to stop her.'

Sebastian put an end to this catalogue of self-recrimina tions by raising his hand and saying, 'If anyone is to blame it is I. I should have been honest with her from the start, an should never have embroiled her in this business in the firs place. But that really doesn't help the present situation.' H turned back to Sarah. 'Did she say anything to you before sh left…anything that might give us a clue as to the identity o the man she suspected? Did she mention no one by name?'

'Only Lord Sutherland, and that I was to give him the not ten minutes after… No, wait a moment!' Sarah correcte memory stirring. 'She did mention someone—she asked m whether or not Sir Courtney Farrington had noticed me fo lowing her up the stairs.'

'Good gad!' Sebastian rounded on Charles, his expressio thunderous. 'Is that abomination here?'

If Charles had been in any doubt as to his friend's opinio of the suave Baronet, he certainly wasn't now. 'I don't qui know how he managed to persuade me to invite him…bu yes, he's here. I thought you knew. I feel sure I mentioned to Emily before I left town.'

'You possibly did,' Sebastian responded grimly, 'thou

why she felt the need to keep the information to herself if she did suspect him, and why she has gone to these lengths, when she knew full well I was on the point of unmasking the rogue, are questions she'll be made to answer in the fullness of time.'

'She did say something rather odd to me, my lord,' Sarah disclosed, thereby instantly regaining Sebastian's attention. 'When I asked her why she felt she must leave, she said that she had to right a wrong.'

His lordship's frown of consternation was proof enough that he was unable to enlighten her. He then turned to Michael, instructing him to return to the Salon to discover if Sir Courtney was about.

'You do suspect Farrington, then?' Charles asked the instant Lord Sutherland had departed to carry out the instruction.

'He's been my prime suspect from the very beginning,' Sebastian admitted, 'simply because the attack on Elizabeth Sutherland was so unnecessarily vicious—vengeful. He once asked for her hand, and she turned him down flat. It must have been a severe blow to his pride and, I suspect, he never forgave her. I judged all along that her murderer was someone who bore a grudge. And Farrington had never liked Simon either,' he disclosed, before once again turning to Sarah to discover precisely when Emily had left the house.

She glanced at the mantel-clock. 'Perhaps fifteen minutes ago.'

'In that case we'll waste no more time. Even if Farrington is still here, he might have arranged for one of his henchmen to accost Emily in the wood.' His lordship went striding over to the door, removing the pistol from his pocket as he did so. 'Charles, I might require your help. Arm yourself and Michael and then follow as soon as you can. Sarah, be good enough to return to the Salon now, and do your utmost to behave normally. If anyone should enquire into Charles's whereabouts then think up some suitable excuse for his absence. We must strive at all costs to keep what is happening here to ourselves.'

Confident that he could rely on them both, Sebastian did not wait for a response from either, and hurriedly left the house using the same door by which Emily had departed a short time before. His loose-fitting riding garb did not restrict movement and enabled him to reach the shrubbery swiftly and vault the boundary fence with ease.

Although outwardly composed, he was under no illusions as to the danger Emily was in. Nothing, however, could have prepared him for the sudden deafening report, and the sight which met his eyes as he rounded the bend in the track, and he spotted the figures on the ground just a few yards ahead. Without the least hesitation, or pausing to issue a warning, he withdrew the pistol from his pocket and fired in one swift and deadly accurate movement. The figure straddling Emily toppled forward, with the fatal lead shot embedded in his brain.

He wasted no time in hauling off the body of Hector Sloane and removing the restriction from about Emily's throat. For one agonising minute he was convinced it was too late, then blessedly he detected that pulsating throb, faint but reassuringly there. Even so, he was under no illusion that she had been badly hurt. Her throat, red raw, was bruised and swollen but apart from this injury he could discover no others, and could only thank God that he had arrived in time to save her from the violation which the late Lady Sutherland had suffered just prior to her death.

Reaching for her cloak, which lay on the ground just a few feet away, he covered her semi-nakedness, and gently cradled her in his arms. He continued to speak softly and was rewarded moments later by a slight movement beneath the eyelids, before they flickered open long enough for him to see recognition in the violet-blue depths.

'It is all right, my darling. You're safe now. I have you safe,' he managed to say in a voice throbbing with emotion.

She made a feeble attempt to raise her hand to her neck, and he knew instinctively what she was trying to convey.

know, my darling. The diamonds are safe, and so are you. Don't attempt to speak. Try to sleep now.'

It seemed with very little effort she obeyed, and Sebastian felt untold relief when her breathing became gradually less laboured, but even so he could not be completely easy until she had been thoroughly examined by a practitioner. The sound of running footsteps assured him that his most urgent concern would soon be put in hand, and he was able to focus his attention on the carnage surrounding him.

It wasn't too difficult to piece together what must have been the sequence of events. John Stapleton's pistol, lying close beside the body of Sir Courtney Farrington told its own tale. Emily had not hesitated to make use of the weapon, but then had been overpowered by the Baronet's accomplice, bent on revenge for his master's death. Thank God he had managed to arrive in time and had showed no mercy by delaying those few seconds in order to call out a warning. Had he done so the outcome might have been vastly different, and heart-rending for him.

Breathless and sweating profusely, his friends at last stood behind him, and it was left to Charles to ask the question foremost in their minds. 'Were…were you in time?'

'Yes, she's alive,' he hurriedly assured them.

'My God, Hawk!' Michael was appalled when he drew closer and saw the extent of her injury. 'Why, it's the same mark as was on Elizabeth's neck.'

'Yes, Michael. And made by that.' He gestured towards the whip which he had tossed several yards away. 'No doubt we'll discover everything in due course, but for now all that concerns me is Emily.'

He turned to Charles. 'I must get her back home. Whilst I'm gone, I'd like you and Michael to hide the bodies in the undergrowth. Was Farrington staying with you?'

He shook his head. 'No, at the village inn.'

'Good, that at least allows us to remove all evidence away

from here.' Sebastian rose to his feet, lifting Emily tenderly in his arms. 'First and foremost I do not want Emily's name linked with this. Also there's Farrington's widow to consider. For now say nothing. I'll return as soon as I can, and then we'll discuss what's best to be done.'

Chapter Eighteen

Emily retained few memories of what took place during the twenty-four hours following the attack. She vaguely recalled being carried back into the house by Sebastian, and being examined by the doctor shortly afterwards. She had some vague recollection too of waking and seeing Sebastian sitting beside the bed. When, however, the effects of the laudanum had finally worn off, Sebastian had not been there, only his letter, brief and to the point, advising her on how she must proceed.

These instructions were echoed by Sir George Maynard, looking far from well himself, who had paid a brief visit two days later. Although appalled that Farrington, a member of his own class, could have perpetrated such acts of violence, he was as one with Lord Hawkridge in the belief that nothing could be gained by revealing Sir Courtney's criminal behaviour to the world at large. Consequently, steps had been taken to make it appear as if Farrington and his groom had, in all probability, been set upon by the same persons, as yet unknown, who had been responsible for both the attack on Miss Stapleton and possibly the death of the young gentleman found in Kempton Wood just a few short months before.

It was a story which had been quickly spread abroad and

was now widely believed, for even her grandfather had not appeared in the least suspicious when he had discovered that one of the guests attending the party had been found murdered on the edge of Kempton Wood.

Only very few were privy to the truth, and Emily had been eager to discover precisely what had occurred after she had left the party. Unfortunately the doctor's insistence that she remain in bed for at least a week, and rest her voice as much as possible, and Skinner's determination to carry out his instructions to the letter, had resulted in all visitors, with the exception of Sir George Maynard, being denied admittance.

After suffering a surfeit of mollycoddling for five whole days without complaint, Emily managed to convince the doctor that she was well enough to receive visitors, and was impatiently awaiting the arrival of someone who had called daily to enquire after her, and who was eminently capable of satisfying her curiosity over all the events which had taken place the previous week.

Early in the afternoon her patience was rewarded when the eagerly awaited visitor came tripping lightly into the room, her cheerful smile dimming slightly at sight of the bandage about the slender neck, and the lack of colour in delicate cheeks.

'Are you sure you feel up to receiving visitors, Em?' she enquired, settling herself in the chair Skinner had placed in readiness for her visit by the side of the bed. 'You are a little pale, my dear.'

Dismissing this with a wave of her hand, Emily demanded in a voice that was still little more than a croaky whisper to know precisely what had taken place after she had left the party; and Sarah, having been forewarned not to encourage her friend to speak more than absolutely necessary, wisely decided to do most of the talking by giving a detailed account.

'After they had found you, Charles hurried back to the house to issue instructions that his carriage be made ready,

He then had a private word with your grandfather, and Mr Stapleton also travelled back here with you and Sebastian. After Lord Hawkridge had consulted with the doctor,' she continued, 'he returned to Deverel Hall in his own carriage, with Jonas Finn and his own head groom. The vast majority of our guests had left by that time, and no one, as far as we're aware, noticed Jonas driving Sir Courtney's carriage down the track which leads to the wood.

'The bodies of Sir Courtney and his companion were placed in the carriage and taken to the spot where we discovered that man some weeks ago. Lord Hawkridge followed in his own carriage and arranged things to make it appear as though Farrington had been attacked during his journey back to the inn in Kempton. He then went to consult with Sir George Maynard, revealing the happenings of the night, and it was agreed that the true facts ought to be suppressed.

'Surprisingly enough the vehicle was not discovered until the following morning by a carrier who informed the authorities at once. Sir George was then able to treat the incident as one of robbery and murder. We of course were instructed not to breathe a word to a living soul. No one—save ourselves, Charles, Michael, Lord Hawkridge and Sir George, that is—knows what really took place that night. Most people hereabouts are now aware that you were attacked on the same night, and believe the same people were responsible for Sir Courtney's murder.'

Emily did not need to ask who had been instrumental in concocting the fabricated tale, for she could guess, and could guess too where he was now. 'Sebastian is in Bath, I assume,' she murmured in a hollow tone which Sarah quite naturally attributed to the injury sustained to the throat.

'Yes, he was dreadfully weary, poor man. And little wonder after all the tasks he had taken upon himself to perform. Keeping a constant vigil over you that first night certainly didn't help, although, according to what Skinner told

me, he was intent on doing so. He hated leaving you, Em,'
Sarah assured her, noticing at last the wan expression. 'But
once he had been assured by the doctor that you were in no
danger, he felt he must travel to Bath to inform Lady Farrington personally of her husband's death. Whether he intended
to reveal the true facts to her, I'm not sure. But he did send
Michael into Hampshire to apprise a certain Sir Giles Osborne
of what had occurred.'

As Emily betrayed no surprise at learning this, she added,
'Evidently you are acquainted with the gentleman.'

Emily nodded, and then frowned at something that ought
to have occurred to her long before now. 'Hawk evidently discovered I had taken the necklace, and that was what brought
him hotfoot into Dorset on the night of the party.'

'Yes, dear. And he wasn't best pleased, I can tell you. He
couldn't understand why you hadn't confided in him. And
now that I know precisely what you've been involved in,
quite frankly, neither do I.'

'Hawk told you, did he, about the stolen items of jewellery and what he's been doing during these past few years?'

'Yes, dear,' Sarah confirmed. 'He also shamefacedly
admitted to the ruse he'd used to persuade you into an engagement. Which of course is quite irrelevant now. You love him
and you must know how much he cares for you. You've
always loved and trusted him, Em. So why on earth didn't you
tell him when you first suspected Farrington?'

Emily fell back against the mound of pillows, feeling
suddenly very weary. 'It was the only way I could think of to
right a wrong. And only time will tell if I have succeeded in
doing so too well.'

The following week a notice appeared in the newspaper
announcing Sir Courtney Farrington's demise. Several days
later Emily received a short letter from Sebastian, informing
her that he had accompanied his cousin and Lady Hester

Derbyshire, where he intended to remain with Caroline until after the funeral. Emily tried to convince herself that it was only natural that he should wish to support and comfort his cousin at such a time, but when her birthday, celebrated only by a small dinner-party, came and went without further communication from him, she gave up trying to delude herself that her worst fears had not been realised, and she ceased to wear the engagement ring, placing it for safe keeping carefully in a drawer.

Surprisingly enough the normally eagle-eyed Sarah did not remark upon the lack of adornment, but was the first to pass comment upon her friend's continued subdued state. Consequently Emily made a tremendous effort to free herself from the manacles of depression which had made her progressively more unsociable, and disinclined to leave the house, and to a certain extent she was moderately successful.

Before a further week had passed, she took to riding out with Jonas Finn each morning. As a result her physical condition at least improved. Her healthy bloom was quickly restored, and her voice, which had been worryingly slow to return to normal, at last lost its lingering husky timbre. Outwardly she appeared none the worse for her terrible ordeal, and friends and neighbours were not slow to remark upon how well she was looking. They were not to know that inwardly she suffered the agony of a broken heart which time alone might one day blessedly heal.

By the time an oppressive July had given way to a blisteringly hot August, Emily was sure that Sebastian would not leave it too much longer before he returned, and daily expected to receive the letter from him informing her of his intention to do so. In private moments she had battled with herself, torn between the strong urge to follow the inclinations of her heart and hold Sebastian to his promise to marry her, and the desire to do what was right by offering him his freedom. Her conscience, not without a supreme struggle, eventually won the battle over heartfelt desires, and she became increasingly confident that mentally she would be able to deal with the situation when it did arise in a dignified and courageous manner.

Nothing, however, could have prepared her for the encounter when it eventually did take place towards the end of August's first week. Calmly walking into the front parlour, quite unannounced, Sebastian caught her completely off guard. The book she had been reading fell from her hands to land on the floor at her feet, and she found herself saying, like some stammering halfwit, 'W-what in the w-world are you d-doing here?'

One expressive brow rose. 'Now that is a singularly foolish question, my girl. What in the world do you suppose I'm doing here?'

This was not quite the attitude she had expected him to adopt. There was not so much as a hint of contrition in his voice or a semblance of sadness in his expression. If anything he seemed slightly nettled. Taken aback, it was as much as she could do to stop her knees from buckling when he calmly pulled her to her feet and conducted a brief but thorough examination of her throat.

'Well, that appears to have healed nicely,' he remarked in a voice which contained neither sympathy nor gratification.

'Oh, y-yes,' she assured him, still puzzled over his manner.

'Left you with something of a nervous stammer, though, hasn't it?' His smile was distinctly unpleasant. 'Or is it perhaps that you feel somewhat apprehensive at my return?' Grasping her upper arms he shook her none too gently. 'And so you should be, my girl! What on earth possessed you to do such a damnably foolhardy thing? Come, out with it! I demand to know!'

That was all it required to free her from those last manacles of self-pity and regenerate her flagging spirits. 'How dare you adopt that attitude with me!' she snapped, easily shrugging

free from his clasp. 'Might I remind you that your guardianship ended almost three weeks ago.'

'Ha!' he scoffed. 'You don't suppose for a moment that that
would deter me from dealing with you as you deserve, do you?'

Incensed though she was at being treated in such a fashion,
Emily knew him well enough to be sure that he didn't make
a habit of issuing idle threats, and whisked herself round the
other side of the sofa, out of harm's way. He clearly derived
a degree of enjoyment out of the precautionary measure, for
although he did not laugh outright, there was a definite
glimmer of merriment in his eyes, and a noticeable softening
to the set of his mouth.

Swiftly deciding that it was in her own best interests not
to indulge in foolish, meaningless argument, which would
only prolong the agony, and allow him to tell her what he had
come all this way to say, she was about to suggest that they
sit down and talk things through sensibly, when a loud clatter
in the hall captured her attention.

'What in the name of heaven is going on out there do
you suppose?'

'I should imagine it's Jonas Finn and my groom bringing
in my trunk.'

'Your trunk?' she echoed, taken aback for a second time.
'But surely you don't propose to put up here?'

Once again those shapely, masculine brows came into play.
'Where the deuce do you suppose I'm going to put up…at the
inn in Kempton?'

Irritation was back in his voice, but she chose to ignore it. 'Do
you not think you'd be more comfortable staying elsewhere? I'm
certain Charles would be happy to put you up at the Hall.'

He regarded her in a mixture of surprise and exasperation.
'I shall be quite comfortable here, thank you. And you've no
need to fear for your virtue. I'm certain I can maintain sufficient control not to visit you in your bedchamber until after
the wedding.'

Just that one word echoed like so many tortuous hammer blows. 'No... There will be no wedding!'

It was out before Emily had time to consider what she was saying and, annoyed with herself, she made the mistake of turning her back on him. Sebastian was beside her before she knew what was happening. Grasping her arms far more roughly than before, he spun her round to face him squarely.

'What the devil do you mean there will be no wedding?' he demanded, his tone as harsh as the hold he retained on her. 'You jilted me before, virtually at the altar. You'll not do so again, my girl!'

No one could have mistaken the bitter hurt in his voice, and Emily raised her head to gaze up at him in dawning wonder. 'You still wish to marry me...? Truly?' she managed in a shaky whisper.

'Of course I wish to marry you!' He regarded her keenly, easily detecting the flicker of bewilderment and uncertainty in her eyes. 'I cannot imagine why you might suppose I should not.'

Seeing those soft lips tremble, Sebastian knew she was having the utmost difficulty in retaining her self-control, but even he, who knew her better than anyone else, was not prepared for the sudden eruption of emotion which swiftly followed.

Sweeping her up in his arms, Sebastian settled her on his knee in a chair, and made not the least attempt to check the heart-rending sobs. She was not a female easily moved to tears, and he strongly suspected that whatever it was that had brought her to this pretty pass had been distressing her for some considerable time, and she was better left to cry out her hurt.

When at last she grew more composed, he forced his handkerchief between her fingers, and waited patiently while the square of fine lawn was put to good use. 'That must rate as the most inexhaustible flow I've ever witnessed,' he teased gently, while repositioning her a little further away so that he could look down into a face ravaged by a severe bout of weeping. 'I think you had better explain what that was all about, don't you?'

From beneath wet lashes blue eyes glanced fleetingly up at him. 'I—I thought you would want to m-marry Caroline, now that she's free.'

In truth Sebastian had not been certain what to expect, but it certainly wasn't this admission, and he made no attempt to hide his astonishment. 'Marry Caroline…? What made you suppose that I'd ever contemplate doing such a thing?'

Her expression became guarded. 'Well, you wanted to once. I know you did.'

The idea that she was bamming him crossed his mind, but he quickly dismissed it. 'I'd like to know from where you gleaned that piece of utter nonsense. Certainly not from me. Or from anyone else who knows me either.'

This time she subjected him to a more prolonged look before lowering her eyes. 'But I overheard you talking with her.'

'When?' he demanded without hesitation.

'Years ago, a few weeks before Mama died. It was when you were trying to persuade Caroline not to marry Farring-ton. You said that there was someone else who loved her. And she said she knew, but that he couldn't marry her because he was pledged to someone else.'

After several moments of intense thought, Sebastian finally began to realise to what she was alluding, and sur-rised both Emily and himself by bursting into laughter. 'My darling girl, you could not have been more wrong! Caroline was referring to Tobias Trevenen, not me. When he and Caroline met years ago, he was already pledged to a neigh-bour's daughter and so could not offer for my cousin, even though he was deeply attached to her.'

This touched a chord of memory, and Emily regarded him in silence while she slowly came to terms with the very real possibility that she had been stupidly labouring under a mis-apprehension for a very long time. 'Oh,' she managed faintly.

'Oh, indeed,' he agreed, eyes narrowing as her cheeks developed the same hue as the blotches beneath her eyes. 'Would I be correct in assuming that your mistaken belief that I was in love with my cousin was the reason why you refused to marry me years ago?'

She had the grace to look shamefaced. 'Well, of course it was. How could I possibly marry you believing as I did that you were in love with someone else. And then more recently, when I believed you were in love with me, I was happy to marry you until…until I found out about Sir Courtney.'

'Ah, yes, Farrington!' He swooped down on this latest disclosure as swiftly as a hawk after its prey. 'In due time I expect you to tell me just why you began to suspect him. But for now I'll settle for knowing just why you chose to keep your suspicions to yourself.'

She appeared to find his crumpled, and rather damp neckcloth of immense interest. 'I wanted to tell you, and came close to doing so before I left London,' she admitted. 'But then I thought I could rely on Sir George Maynard's aid, and ended by enlisting Michael's.'

'And still I'm in the dark.'

Emily couldn't forbear a smile at this sarcasm. 'I did it for you, Hawk. I know how vicious gossip can be. If you had killed Farrington, or had a hand in his death, and then had wished to marry Caroline, there would have been talk. There would have been those quick to suggest that you had an ulterior motive for making Caroline a widow.'

Although touched by the admission, Sebastian had no reluctance in making his lingering annoyance plain, albeit in a milder tone than he might otherwise have adopted. 'If you ever do anything so foolish again, my girl, I'll have your liver and lights. The distress I suffered throughout the journey from Hampshire, agonising over whether I would arrive in time, not to mention the torment I experienced seeing that brute—'

Emily placed her fingers over his lips, gently silencing him. 'But you did arrive in time, and saved me. I knew it was you who shot Sloane, even before Sarah told me it was so.'

Lingering anger swiftly fading, Sebastian kissed her fingers before retaining them in his own. 'And then I had to leave you, praying that you'd understand.'

'I do now. Your love for Caroline is that of a brother.' His nod of confirmation wasn't at all necessary. 'How did she take it—the news about her husband?'

'She doesn't know the truth. Nothing could be gained by her knowing the extent of Farrington's iniquities. Then there's the child to consider. Why should little Alicia be made to suffer as a consequence of her father's despicable behaviour? She may favour him in looks, but blessedly has inherited her mother's nature.'

Emily nodded, in complete agreement, before asking what Caroline intended to do now.

'She will remain in Derbyshire until Farrington's cousin and heir takes up residence, and then she intends to live for a time with Lady Hester in Bath.'

Emily brightened as a thought occurred to her. 'Do you suppose she'll marry Mr Trevenen after a decent interval?'

'That is entirely between them. I did take it upon myself to write him a letter whilst I was in London, apprising him of recent events.'

'You've been to London? So that's what delayed your return?'

'And to Kent,' he informed her. 'I've dispatched my entire staff there to put the house in order. I had one or two loose ends to clear up too. I needed to see Sir Giles Osborne who, incidentally, was successful in intercepting Farrington's other villainous henchman.' He chose not to add that the miscreant had already received swift justice. 'Whilst I was in the capital I purchased our wedding bands, and acquired a special licence.'

He paused to place a lingering kiss on her lips. 'You see I had no intention of allowing you to change your mind…not this time.'

She smiled lovingly up at him. 'And I have no intention of changing my mind…this time.'

'Then you'll marry me, and soon?'

'Whenever you like,' she assured him the instant he had finished kissing her again.

'Then we'll say at the end of next week. Which will give me sufficient time to recover from all the travelling I've undertaken of late. And time for Budd to consider what food to prepare for the few guests we must invite. The rest of our family and friends must wait until the autumn, when we return to London and hold a large party to celebrate our union, because I fully intend to whisk you off to Kent and have you all to myself.'

The increased passion of his embraces gave Emily a fairly shrewd idea of what they would be doing throughout their stay in Kent. Even so her future husband contained sufficient control over himself to release her the instant the door opened.

'Why, Grandfather! Whatever brings you in here?' Emily asked, slipping off Sebastian's knee and surreptitiously attempting to straighten her attire.

'Devilish thing, but I can't recall,' he admitted, gazing absently about the room before fixing his myopic gaze on his lordship. 'Ah, so you are here, my boy! Seem to remember somebody telling me.'

'Grandfather,' Emily said shyly. 'We're to be married next week.'

'Capital notion, m'dear! Capital! Cannot understand for the life of me why you didn't marry the fellow years ago. Made for each other, you two. Thought so from the very first. You were born to be Hawk's lady.'

'And you do not object to the swiftness of the affair, sir?' Sebastian enquired.

'No, not at all, my boy. Best thing all round, if you ask me. Better to get the thing over and done with before she decides to shoot someone else.'

Sebastian's broad shoulders shook with suppressed laughter, but Emily could not have appeared more stunned. 'Grandfather, how on earth did you know that I shot…' Her words faded as she glimpsed that astute gleam which the mantle of vagueness failed to conceal.

'Because I discovered my pistol had been recently fired. Now I knew young Hawkridge here hadn't taken it from the house, and it wasn't likely to have been Budd or that new maid of yours, either.' He transferred his gaze to the highly amused gentleman holding his granddaughter's hand. 'I've warned her before that old Maynard doesn't like her going about shooting people, but she doesn't pay any attention to me. Best you take her off my hands now, my boy, and keep her out of mischief.'

Sebastian executed a neat bow. 'It will be my pleasure. Perhaps we can seal the bargain over a glass or two of port later, sir?'

'Capital notion! Come into the library.'

'Well!' Emily exclaimed in some exasperation the instant her grandfather had withdrawn. 'I've always maintained he notices far more than people realise.'

'I wouldn't be at all surprised,' his lordship agreed, once again holding her willingly captive in the circle of his arms. 'And I for one have always had the utmost respect for his intellect. As he so rightly remarked…we were destined to be together eventually, my Lady Hawk.'

* * * * *

HISTORICAL

*Powerful, engaging stories of romance,
adventure and faith set in the past—
when life was simpler and faith played
a major role in everyday lives.*

*See below for a sneak preview of
HIGH COUNTRY BRIDE
by Jillian Hart*

*Love Inspired Historical—
love and faith throughout the ages*

Silence remained between them, and she felt the rake of his gaze, taking her in from the top of her wind-blown hair where escaped tendrils snapped in the wind to the toe of her scuffed, patched shoes. She watched him fist up his big, work-roughened hands and expected the worst.

"You never told me, Miz Nelson. Where are you going to go?" His tone was flat, his jaw tensed as if he were still fighting his temper. His blue gaze shot past her to watch the children going about their picking up.

"I don't know." Her throat went dry. Her tongue felt thick as she answered. "When I find employment, I could wire a payment to you. Rent. Y-you aren't think-ing of bringing the sher-rif in?"

"You think I want *payment?*" He boomed like winter thunder. *"You think I want rent money?"*

"Frankly, I don't know what you want."

"I'll tell you what I don't want. I don't want—" His words cannoned in the silence as he paused, and a passing pair of geese overhead honked in flat-noted tones. He grimaced, and was impossible to know what he would say or do.

She trembled, not from fear of him, she truly didn't believe he would strike her, but from the unknown. Of being forced to take the frightening step off the only safe spot she'd known since she'd lost Pa's house.

When you were homeless, everything seemed so fragile, so easily off balance, for it was a big, unkind world for a woman alone with her children. She had no one to protect her.

No one to care. The truth was, she'd never had those things in her husband. How could she expect them from any stranger? Especially this man she hardly knew, who was harsh and cold and hardhearted.

And, worse, what if he brought in the law?

"You can't keep living out of a wagon," he said, still angry the cords still straining in his neck. "Animals have enough sense to keep their young cared for and safe."

Yes, it was as she'd thought. He intended to be as cruel about this as he could be. She spun on her heel, pulling up all her defenses, and was determined to let his upcoming hurtful words roll off her like rainwater on an oiled tarp. She grabbed the towel the children had neatly folded and tossed it into the laundry box in the back of the wagon.

"Miz Nelson. I'm talking to you."

"Yes, I know. If you expect me to stand there while you tongue lash me, you're mistaken. I have packing to get to." Her fingers were clumsy as she hefted the bucket of water she'd brought for washing—she wouldn't need that now—and heaved.

His hand clasped on the handle beside hers, and she could feel the life and power of him vibrate along the thin metal. "Give it to me."

Her fingers let go. She felt stunned as he walked away, easily carrying the bucket that had been so heavy to her, and quietly, methodically, put out the small cooking fire. He did not seem as ominous or as intimidating—somehow—as he stood in the shadows, bent to his task, although she couldn't say why that was. Perhaps it was because he wasn't acting the way she was used to men acting. She was quite used to doing all the work.

Jamie scurried over, juggling his wooden horses, to watch. Daisy hung back, eyes wide and still, taking in the mysterious goings-on.

He is different when he's near to them, she realized. *He didn't seem harsh, and there was no hint of anger—or, con-*

o think of it, any other emotion—as he shook out the empty
bucket, nodded once to the children and then retraced his path
o her.

"Let me guess." He dropped the bucket onto the tailgate, and
is anger appeared to be back. Cords strained in his neck and
aw as he growled at her. "If you leave here, you don't know
where you're going and you have no money to get there with?"

She nodded. "Yes, sir."

"Then get you and your kids into the wagon. I'll hitch up
our horses for you." His eyes were cold and yet they were
ot unfeeling as he fastened his gaze on hers. "I have an
mpty shanty out back of my house that no one's living in.
'ou can stay there for the night."

"What?" She stumbled back, and the solid wood of the
ailgate bit into the small of her back. "But—"

"There will be no argument," he bit out, interrupting her.
None at all. I buried a wife and son years ago, what was most
recious to me, and to see you and them neglected like this—
ith no one to care—" His jaw ground again and his eyes
ere no longer cold.

Joanna didn't think she'd ever seen anything sadder than
iden McKaslin as the sun went down on him.

* * * * *

Don't miss this deeply moving story,
HIGH COUNTRY BRIDE,
available July 2008
from the new Love Inspired Historical line.

Also look for SEASIDE CINDERELLA
by Anna Schmidt,
vhere a poor servant girl and a wealthy merchant prince
might somehow make a life together.

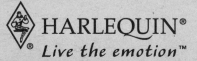

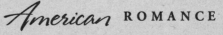
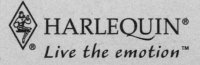

HARLEQUIN®
INTRIGUE®
BREATHTAKING ROMANTIC SUSPENSE

Shared dangers and passions lead to electrifying romance and heart-stopping suspense!

Every month, you'll meet six new heroes who are guaranteed to make your spine tingle and your pulse pound. With them you'll enter into the exciting world of Harlequin Intrigue— where your life is on the line and so is your heart!

THAT'S INTRIGUE— ROMANTIC SUSPENSE AT ITS BEST!

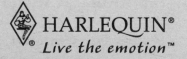

HARLEQUIN®
Live the emotion™

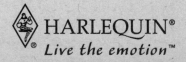

HARLEQUIN®
Presents®

The world's bestselling romance series...
The series that brings you your favorite authors,
month after month:

Helen Bianchin...Emma Darcy
Lynne Graham...Penny Jordan
Miranda Lee...Sandra Marton
Anne Mather...Carole Mortimer
Melanie Milburne...Michelle Reid

and many more talented authors!

Wealthy, powerful, gorgeous men...
Women who have feelings just like your own...
The stories you love, set in exotic, glamorous locations...

HARLEQUIN®
Presents®

Seduction and Passion Guaranteed!

HPDIR08

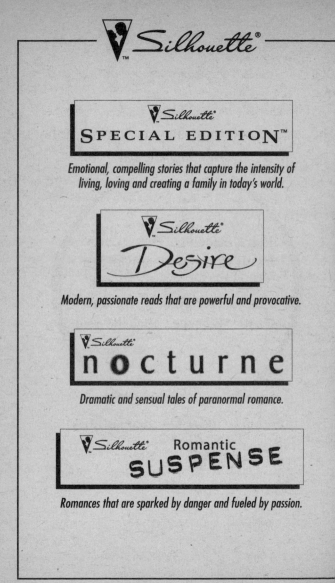

❦ *Silhouette*®

❦ *Silhouette*®
SPECIAL EDITION™

Emotional, compelling stories that capture the intensity of living, loving and creating a family in today's world.

❦ *Silhouette*®
Desire

Modern, passionate reads that are powerful and provocative.

❦ *Silhouette*®
nocturne

Dramatic and sensual tales of paranormal romance.

❦ *Silhouette*® Romantic
SUSPENSE

Romances that are sparked by danger and fueled by passion.